ABOUT THE AUTHORS

Amy McGavin is the pen name of a Scottish wife-and-husband writing team whose real names are . . . Amy and Gavin.

The couple's contemporary romance novels are set in the Highlands. Each story is crafted with humour and heart, with a wee bit of heat thrown in.

The pair live in Glasgow with their daughter and very lively cocker spaniel. When they're not writing, they enjoy exploring Scotland's breathtaking hills, glens, and beaches, then treating themselves to coffee and cake afterwards.

To keep up to date with all their publishing news, and gain access to exclusive bonus content, join their newsletter by visiting amymcgavin.com.

Newsletter

Captain of My Heart

AMY McGAVIN

GRUMPY GROUSE
PRESS

Captain of
My Heart

CHAPTER ONE

LACHLAN

The wipers screech across the glass, barely keeping up with the spray. I keep one hand steady on the wheel, the other braced against the console as another swell lifts us, drops us, makes the ferry groan.

"Passengers are asking how much longer, skipper," Kenneth's voice crackles through the intercom.

"Ten minutes." I nudge the *Calabrae* back on course as the wind shoves us sideways. "Maybe fifteen."

Should've known better than to trust Scottish weather. We left Corraig late, chasing what looked like a window. The skies had cleared, wind had eased. I either took the chance or cancelled the last sailing back to the mainland, and I'd no wish to spend the night moored at the island. The hundred or so passengers onboard wouldn't have thanked me for it either.

The hull judders, car alarms wail below, and my jaw tightens. Finn'll be pressed to the window, wondering where the hell I am. Promised him we'd build that fort tonight. Bloody stupid thing to say.

Then, through the murk, a glow. The harbour lights, blurred

but steady. At last. I ease back the throttle, the ferry shuddering once more before the engines settle into a steadier rhythm. My shoulders loosen, just a fraction.

"Easy now," I mutter, as much to myself as to her.

Almost there. Dry land. Finn's smile. Gus's wagging tail. Home.

◆ ◆ ◆

The front door is barely open before a golden retriever-shaped cannonball hurtles at me, paws thumping against my chest, tongue going for my face.

"Down, you daft beast!" I try to sound stern, but my hands find the sweet spot behind his ears, and Gus's whole body wiggles with delight.

"Da!" Finn barrels in right after the dog, grinning so wide I can see every one of his gappy teeth. "You're home! Can we build the fort now? You promised—"

"Whoa there, laddie." I slide Gus off me and ruffle my son's hair, dark brown like mine but with none of the grey creeping in at the temples. "Let me get through the door first, eh?"

My neighbour, Flora, comes into the hallway at her usual steady pace, a far cry from Gus and Finn's stampede. "The rain's fairly lashing down out there, Lachlan. You must've had a rough crossing."

"Aye, it was a bit lively, but we got in safe, that's what matters. Thanks so much for picking Finn up from after-school club. You're a lifesaver."

"Oh, hush." She smiles warmly, eyes crinkling. "I'm always happy to help, and it's good practice for when I've got Finn over the summer. He's eaten. We made a shepherd's pie, and there's plenty left over for you."

On cue my mouth waters. Long day, empty stomach.

"I helped mash the potatoes!" Finn chips in.

"Aye? Well done, mate." I hold my hand out for a high-five, and he slaps it with all his might. "You really are the best neighbour," I tell Flora. "Don't know what I'd do without you."

She shrugs into her coat, but there's something careful in the way she moves, protective almost, as if one arm is giving her bother.

"You all right there?" I ask.

"Fine, fine. Just a bit tired."

"Flora fell over Gus earlier," Finn blurts out. "He got all excited and knocked her right over."

"*Gus!*" At my tone the dog ducks his head, ears drooping. "What did you do?" He slinks off, tail between his legs. "I'm so sorry, Flora. Are you okay? Did he hurt you?"

"No harm done. I'm tougher than I look."

"It's her wrist, Da," Finn offers. "She's been rubbing at it."

"Och! Will you two stop fretting? I'm sure it's nothing. It'll be fine come the morning."

"Nope, you're going to get that checked out," I say. "I'll drive you to Raigmore."

"You'll do no such thing! You're only just back. Go eat your dinner and spend some time with your boy. It's an hour and twenty minutes to the hospital on a good day, and in weather like this? No, thank you. I'm staying put at home."

"At least let me—"

"I'm fine, Lachlan." She squeezes Finn's shoulder with her good hand. "Good night, love." And with that, she slips out into the rain before I can argue any further.

Finn stands frowning after her, lower lip stuck out in worry. "Is Flora really okay? Or was she just saying that?"

"Between you and me, lad, that woman is as stubborn as a Highland coo, and she likes to think she's as hardy as one too. We'll give her a wee visit tomorrow and see how she's doing then, but for now, tell me more about this shepherd's pie. I hear the potatoes were mashed by a master chef. A very *ticklish* master chef."

My hands shoot out, and Finn squeals, dodging away from me. "It's through here. C'mon!" He leads the charge through to the kitchen, Gus hot on his heels. He opens the fridge and pulls out a dish with both hands like he's unveiling buried treasure. "See, Da? Loads left."

One sniff of the food and Gus transforms into the picture of canine innocence. Suddenly he's sitting perfectly with big soulful eyes, his tail giving the tiniest hopeful swish.

I snort. "You honestly think you're getting some of this after knocking Flora off her feet? You're a chancer. Dream on, pal."

◆ ◆ ◆

I step back from our architectural disaster and try to find something positive to say.

"It's . . ."

"Amazing!" Finn bounces on his knees inside the lopsided structure, torch beam dancing across the blanket ceiling. "It's like a proper castle. Look, this bit's the throne room."

Amazing? Not the word I'd have used. The chairs are doing their best to hold up the throws, but the whole thing lists to one side like it's had a few too many whiskies. One corner has already

4

given up entirely, the blanket drooping down to brush Finn's head.

By the time I'd finished the washing-up, it was after eight, past Finn's usual bedtime on a school night. I tried suggesting we build the fort tomorrow instead, but his face crumpled in a way that punched a hole clean through my resolve. He doesn't ask for much, my boy. And after being late home again because of weather I admittedly couldn't control, I reckoned the least I could do was keep one bloody promise.

"Right then, Your Majesty," I say, grabbing his favourite book from the shelf, a Julia Donaldson tale about a hapless dragon. "Shall we have a story in your castle?"

I squeeze myself halfway into the fort—no small feat for someone my size—and Finn snuggles against my side and uses my arm as a pillow. Gus pokes his nose through the blanket doorway, decides there's not enough room for a golden retriever, and settles for lying guard outside with his chin on his paws.

Finn's eyelids are already heavy, and he soon lets out a jaw-cracking yawn. He tries to muffle it behind his hand, but it comes out anyway, all big and squeaky at the end. I barely get halfway through *Zog* when his breathing evens out, the torch slipping from his fingers to cast wild shadows on the walls. His mouth parts slightly, dark lashes resting against flushed cheeks.

Should move him to his bed. But I don't. Not yet. For a while I stay here in our wonky castle, listening to him breathe, his little body warm beside me.

Finally, I ease my arm out from under him and lift him carefully. He stirs, mumbles something about dragons, but doesn't wake. I tuck him into his bed, pull the duvet up to his chin, and press a kiss to his forehead.

"Night, wee man."

I head downstairs to the garage and flick on the light. The makeshift gym stares back at me—weights neatly racked, bench positioned just so, everything in its place. Most nights, after Finn's asleep, I work out here. I'd rather sweat out the day than sit on my arse watching telly.

Gus pads in behind me and settles on his old blanket in the corner. He knows the routine as well as I do. But tonight, exhaustion wins out over habit. "On second thoughts, pal, how about we make today a rest day, eh?"

Gus perks up, tail wagging like he's just won the lottery, because he knows what happens now. I head through to the kitchen, fish one of his dental sticks from the cupboard, and toss it to him. He snatches it out of the air and pads off to enjoy it in his favourite corner. I grab a cool beer from the fridge for myself and collapse into a chair at the kitchen table.

Checking my phone, I see there's a message in the Dadventurers chat, a group chat between me and two other single dads in the town.

STRUAN

Lachlan, thought I saw your ferry surfing a wave earlier. Radical, Cap'n 🐭 ⛵

Trust Struan to find the humour in a Force 8 gale.

LACHLAN

My arse hasn't unclenched yet. And I was late home, of course. Flora saved the day though

DOUGLAS

That woman's a saint

Huh, a quick reply from Douglas—that doesn't happen often. Struan's the clown, I'm the grump, and Douglas . . .

Douglas is the poor bastard with the "terror twins", as Struan and I call them behind his back. They're not *bad*, just . . . a little rumbustious. It's a miracle Douglas is upright.

STRUAN

More like a bloody angel. Don't know why she puts up with you

LACHLAN

Neither do I. And to thank her, my daft mutt bowled her clean off her feet

STRUAN

Classic Gus. She all right?

LACHLAN

Says she is. Reckon she hurt her wrist though. Hopefully it's nothing cause she's supposed to be looking after Finn over the summer

A little retirement income for her, a lifeline for me.

DOUGLAS

Ooft. If she's out, that's rough.

STRUAN

Aye. Easy fix, though. Just drop Finn off with Douglas's parents. They're already looking after two kids all summer. What's a third? 👼

DOUGLAS

Not happening. Sorry, Lachlan

They might be able to do an odd day here and there, but not six weeks

I'm already asking too much of them. My folks love me, just not THAT much

Struan only has his daughter at weekends, so he never has to worry about childcare. Probably explains why he's got more energy than me and Douglas combined.

LACHLAN

No way I'd expect your folks to take Finn too. Anyway, hopefully I'm stressing over nothing and Flora is fine

STRUAN

On the bright side, Lachlan, your life could be worse

You could've made this pile of shite

He sends a link to a news article. I tap it and squint at the headline: "Coming soon, the new app guaranteed to give your child nightmares!"

I skim the first few lines. It's about some AI storytelling thing that was supposed to let kids bring their imaginations to life. Apparently, though, the journalist testing it got it to tell a truly terrifying tale about monsters and gore.

DOUGLAS

Jesus. Now we've got to worry about shit like this too? As if bedtime wasn't traumatic enough already

LACHLAN

What pillock thought this was a good idea?

CHAPTER TWO

BLAIR

"Don't I know you from somewhere?"

My stomach drops. Glancing up from my phone, I force a smile. "Nope. Must be thinking of someone else."

The barista—a guy about my age with sleeve tattoos and gauged ears—squints at me like I'm a puzzle he's determined to solve. "Nah, I'm good with faces. You're definitely familiar. Anyway, what can I get you?"

"Vanilla latte with oat milk, please. Medium." I tap my phone against the reader, hoping the transaction will end this conversation. It doesn't.

"Seriously, it's gonna bug me all day. You work around here?"

I shake my head. "Nope. Guess I just have one of those faces."

A woman waiting at the pickup counter studies me then says, "Oh! Aren't you that girl from the article? About, you know, the creepy kids' app?"

Every muscle in my body tenses. The coffee shop suddenly feels too small, too warm, too full of people turning to stare at me.

"I don't know what you're talking about," I lie, but my voice comes out tight.

"I'm sure it was you," the woman insists. Then, to the barista, "It was all over the news. That AI thing that was supposed to tell bedtime stories but ended up giving kids nightmares instead?"

It never even launched. No kids were harmed. The only casualty was me.

The barista snaps his fingers. "That's it!" He shakes his head. "Man, what were you thinking?"

"Just the latte, please." I paste on another smile, like if I'm nice enough, this will end.

It doesn't.

"Touchy subject?" the barista asks.

The woman at the pickup counter waves a hand at me. "I'm telling you, it's her. I'm sure of it."

A guy at a nearby table glances over and whispers something to his friend, who looks over too.

There are low mumbles in the line behind me. The woman at the counter pulls out her phone. "Let me find that article again. I swear it's her."

Suddenly it's like I'm on trial and the coffee shop is the jury. That's when something inside me snaps.

"You don't have to find the article!" My voice cracks across the shop, louder than I intended. "Yes, it's me! Congratulations, mystery solved."

The woman forgets all about her phone and stares at me open-mouthed. The barista blinks. Some guy goes quiet mid-whisper. But I'm rolling now, and my words spill out faster than I can catch them.

"You think I wanted to work on that stupid app? You think that's why I went into children's publishing? No. I love books.

Books! Always have. But my boss, he had this shiny new idea, and he wouldn't shut up about how it was the future, how it'd look great on my résumé. So suddenly I'm sitting in meetings with a bunch of developers I've never met, pretending I know what the hell they're talking about. Me. A book editor. With zero tech background.

"But even if I wasn't an expert, I knew enough to know the damn thing wasn't ready. I begged my boss for more testing, more safeguards, but no! He wanted buzz, he wanted headlines, and so journalists got a pre-release version. One of them fed it some ridiculous gothic word salad, and *bam*! A tale Stephen King would've been proud of."

My hands are shaking, and even as the words fly out, a horrified part of me knows I should shut up. But I can't.

"Do the articles mention how the journalist set up the app to fail? Like, what kid asks for a story about 'encounters with nocturnal phantasmagorical manifestations'? But no, there's no mention of that, nor of my boss, who dreamed the whole thing up. Instead, my face has been plastered everywhere like I'm the Wicked Witch of Bedtime Stories."

The coffee shop is silent now. Even the espresso machine's hiss has given up.

"The app's been scrapped. I've been fired. And I'll never work in children's publishing again. Not such a great addition to my résumé after all. But my boss? Threw me under the bus and walked away clean. Left me the villain of the story."

A baby starts crying somewhere behind me, and the sound snaps me back to reality. I look around at the stunned faces staring at me. The barista, whose eyebrows look like they're about to make a break for freedom right off his forehead. The woman who recognised me, who's practically radiating regret, like she knows she lit the match that set me off. A businessman who pauses with his coffee halfway to his lips, as wide-eyed as if I'd just yelled, "Tax audit!"

Heat floods my cheeks. "I . . . I'm sorry. I shouldn't have . . . You know what, forget the latte."

I turn and hurry off, pushing through the door so fast I nearly collide with someone coming in. Muttering an apology, I stumble onto the sidewalk.

The harbour air is heavy and humid, salt and diesel tangling together with the smell of roasting nuts from a cart nearby. I grab onto a streetlight like it's a life raft, trying to catch my breath and wishing I could undo the last few minutes. *What the hell was that?* I don't explode at strangers. I'm the girl who says "excuse me" when someone elbows me in the ribs on the subway, who tips twenty percent even when the service is terrible. I don't have public meltdowns in coffee shops full of strangers.

Except apparently, I do now.

I just wanted a coffee, one small taste of normal. Should've known that was too much to ask.

A deep horn bellows in the distance. Across the water, the Staten Island Ferry glides toward Manhattan—the same ferry I used to take every morning to work, back when I had a job to go to. Beyond it, the skyline gleams like a postcard, all possibility and promise.

But I know better now. I know how quickly it can all fall apart.

My chest tightens. I can't keep doing this. Can't keep pretending I'm okay in a city where even a coffee run can turn into a public execution.

I need to get away from here. At least until this whole mess blows over and people find something else to gossip about.

◆ ◆ ◆

Twenty minutes later, I'm pulling into my parents' driveway, tyres crunching over the same cracked concrete I learned to rollerblade on. The pale blue clapboard house hasn't changed since I was a kid. White porch railings, Mom's overgrown hydrangeas spilling over them, the gnome by the steps standing guard.

I moved back in with my parents after my ex and I crashed and burned. Just a temporary arrangement, of course, or so I assured them. That was seven months ago.

Yeah. Living the dream, right?

When I step inside, the cool blast of air conditioning hits me, carrying with it the smell of fresh-baked cookies and a hint of lemon cleaner.

"Blair? That you?" Mom calls from the kitchen.

"Yeah." I close the door behind me and lean against it, suddenly drained.

"You okay?" She pokes her head out, apron dusted with flour, bangs sticking to her forehead.

"Fine," I say automatically, then pause. "Actually, you know what? Not fine. Really, really not fine."

"Oh, sweetheart. Hold on, let me get this apron off so I can hug you properly. Come through here." She ushers me into the kitchen, where snickerdoodles cool on a rack. She tugs off her apron and gathers me close, holding on like she can squeeze the not-fine right out of me. "What happened?"

"Well—"

"Oh, hi, Blair." Dad appears in the doorway, reading glasses perched on his nose, probably fresh from cross-checking some cousin twice removed in his family tree. He's always elbow-deep in an obsession, and right now it's genealogy. "Everything okay?"

I tell them about the barista who wouldn't drop it, the woman who recognised me, my spectacular meltdown in front of an entire coffee shop. "And I left without even collecting my coffee," I finish.

"Well, that I can fix," Mom says. "One coffee coming right up. And a cookie."

"And if you can set up a meeting with your old boss," Dad says, "I'll fix something else. By introducing his jaw to my fist." He flexes his hand.

"Dad!" I scoff. Violence isn't in his vocabulary, unless you count shouting at the Maple Leafs from our couch. Dad's Canadian. Mom too. Me as well, technically, though we moved to New York when I was six months old.

A few minutes later we're all at the kitchen table, each with coffee and a cookie. Mom leans in a little, offering a small, encouraging smile as if to say she's right here if I need her. Dad peers at me over the rim of his mug, glasses sliding down his nose.

"I think . . . I need to get away for a while," I admit, twisting one of my rings around and around my finger. "New York is just too much right now. I need to go somewhere no one's heard of the app, or of me."

Mom rests her hand on top of mine. She and Dad exchange a look, but neither speaks. Not yet. They're giving me space.

"Before, I'd have gone to Toronto. Stayed with Granny and filled up on clootie dumpling and reruns of *Bake Off* until the world made sense again. But . . ." My throat tightens. "That's not an option anymore."

Mom's face softens. "I know, sweetheart. I miss her too."

I take a gulp of coffee. In less than a year, a breakup, a funeral, and a pink slip. My very own hat trick of heartbreaks. From years of editing children's books, I know how often writers build things around threes. Trust me, it's a lot less charming when you're the one starring in the story.

"You know," Dad says in his I'm-about-to-announce-something voice, "your grandmother was sixteen when she moved to Canada from Scotland. I don't only dig into my own ancestors, you know."

Mom turns to him. "Really, Michael? Our only child admits she feels she has to leave New York, and your response is a genealogy fun fact? Honestly, *sometimes* . . ." She throws her hands at the ceiling in frustration.

"Wait a second," I deadpan. "Dad, are you telling me Granny was Scottish? Oh my God, that explains so much! Like her accent . . . and the clootie dumpling . . . and the fact I called her 'Granny' instead of 'Grandma'."

Dad chuckles. "Sarcasm is the lowest form of wit, Blair."

"But the highest form of intelligence," I shoot back, finishing the Oscar Wilde quote.

"Maybe," he says, lips twitching. "But there *was* a point to me bringing up your grandmother's birthplace. The Brits have this thing called an ancestry visa. If one of your grandparents was born in the UK, you can get a visa that lets you live and work there. For years, if you wish."

I blink at him. "Why do you even know that?"

"Because your father's head is stuffed with useless trivia," Mom says, casting him a fond look. "Well, most of it is useless, but this time it might actually help. Blair, if you feel like you need to get away for a while, what about Scotland?"

Scotland. I turn the idea over in my mind. Land of Granny's birth. Of rolling hills, ancient castles, and people who probably couldn't care less about an AI storytelling app.

"Maybe. Maybe a few months in another country is exactly what I need." Even as I say it, the idea grows on me. I'd wanted to get away from New York, but why not leave the US altogether? Hell, why not put an entire ocean between me and my very public firing?

"Yeah." My voice is steadier now. "Mom, Dad . . . I'm going to Scotland."

CHAPTER THREE

BLAIR

I stumble off the plane at Glasgow Airport feeling like I've been put through a blender. My hair's doing something that defies both gravity and any known style, my mouth tastes like I've been chewing on airplane upholstery, and my sweater is more wrinkled than a scrotum.

But hey, I'm in Scotland. The home of Scotch and shortbread, and hopefully a place where nobody's heard of a certain disastrous AI app.

The rental car counter is staffed by a cheerful woman with an accent so thick I only catch about half of what she says. She hands over keys to what she assures me is a "lovely wee motor"—I catch that bit—though when I find it in the parking lot, it looks more like a sardine can with wheels.

"Right," I mutter, walking around to what should be the driver's side but isn't. "This is fine. Totally fine. People do this every day."

The steering wheel is on the wrong side. The gearshift is in the wrong place. Even the dashboard is back to front. But I adjust the seat and mirrors, and grip the wheel.

"Okay, Blair, you've got this. It's just driving. On the opposite side of the road, with none of the controls where they're supposed to be. But you'll be fine."

I inch out of the parking space, nearly clipping a post, and somehow make it onto what I think is the correct side of the road. A truck thunders past, and I grip the wheel tighter. In New York, driving meant stop-and-go traffic, honking horns, and the occasional creative gesture from fellow motorists. Never thought I'd miss that chaos, but when I come to my first traffic circle, I realise New York driving wasn't so bad after all.

Somehow I get through it in one piece, and the GPS in its crisp British accent tells me it's a four-and-a-half-hour drive to Ardmara, the small Highland town where my grandmother grew up. I've booked a hotel room there for a few nights. Seemed as good a place as any to start my Scottish adventure.

The first stretch is highway—grey asphalt and steady traffic through urban sprawl. I start to think I'm getting the hang of this. Then something magical happens. The landscape opens into wide valleys and rolling hills so green they almost hurt my eyes.

I turn off the main road onto a much narrower one, edged with stone walls determined to scrape my mirrors off. At a gas station in literally the middle of nowhere, I'm rung up by a guy with a beard that could house small wildlife. He insists on giving me directions in an accent I pretend to understand. I nod enthusiastically, praying the GPS has this because I definitely don't.

Back on the road, the landscape gets even wilder. Mountains loom ahead, their peaks shrouded in mist. I catch glimpses of lochs—actual lochs!—silver-grey under the shifting clouds. Sheep dot the hillsides, completely unbothered by my little rental car puttering past.

Then the road crests a hill, and there it is: the coast, with water that stretches to the horizon, dotted with islands that look like they've been scattered by some giant's careless hand.

And nestled against the water, like something from a fairy tale, is Ardmara.

The town hugs the shoreline in a gentle crescent, its buildings stepping down toward the harbour in tiers. From up here, I can see that the houses along the waterfront are painted in soft pastels—pale yellow, mint green, dusty pink, lavender blue. As if the town decided it needed a bit of extra cheer to compete with the moody Scottish sky.

A white ferry cuts through the dark water, heading straight for the port with a trail of foam in its wake. Even from this distance, I can make out tiny figures on its deck.

"Okay, Granny," I murmur. "Let's see what your hometown is all about."

The road winds down and into Ardmara. Soon I'm driving along the waterfront, the town wrapping around me like a warm hug.

I find the Harbour Inn easily enough—it's right there in the name, after all—a three-storey building painted a cheerful yellow with window boxes overflowing with petunias. The woman at the front desk has silver hair in a neat bun and the kind of smile that should be bottled and sold as a cure for jet lag.

"Welcome to Ardmara, dear," she says, handing over an actual metal key, not some plastic card. "First time in Scotland?"

"First time in Europe," I admit. "Your town is beautiful."

"Och, we think so. Your room's just up the stairs, second door on the left. Lovely view of the harbour. I have it down that it's three nights you're staying with us, yes?"

"That's the plan, but I might stay longer. I'm sort of playing it by ear."

"Well, I'd be glad to extend your stay if that's what you decide to do. Though with the school holidays coming up, it does get busy. You've timed it well, anyway. Weather's been a bit iffy lately, but it's due to brighten up from tomorrow."

My room is small but spotless, with a tartan bedspread that screams, "Yes, you're in Scotland." Outside the window, fishing boats bob in the water. The ferry I saw from the hill is now tied up, and cars pour from its belly, clattering down the ramp.

One quick shower and a change of clothes later, I head back downstairs. "Can you point a jet-lagged American toward a good coffee?" I ask the receptionist.

"Oh, the Lighthouse Café does a lovely cup, and their shortbread is the best on the west coast. It's on the pier. You can't miss it."

Outside, the air is sharp with salt and seaweed, and cleaner than I'm used to in New York. A seagull eyes me from a streetlight, head cocked as if hoping I'll produce a sandwich from thin air. When I don't, it loses interest.

The Lighthouse Café sits at the base of an old lighthouse, its windows looking straight out over the harbour mouth. Inside it's a cosy little place with mismatched tables and chairs and the kind of atmosphere that makes you want to settle in with a good book. The woman behind the counter greets me with the same easy warmth as the hotel receptionist, and—blessedly—no spark of recognition. No curious probing about my spectacular career implosion. Just a smile, a latte, and a slab of shortbread I order on the receptionist's recommendation.

I sink into a corner chair to enjoy it. The shortbread is buttery perfection, crumbling on my tongue with just the right amount of sweetness, while the coffee nudges me a little closer to human.

After I'm done, I pull a black-and-white photo from my bag.

Mom found it when we cleared out Granny's house. It shows Granny as a young girl, no more than eight or nine, beaming at the camera from in front of a whitewashed stone cottage with an arched doorway and climbing roses. It's the house Granny grew up in. I've no clue where it is, but how hard can it be to track down one cottage in a town this size? Besides, who doesn't love a little treasure hunt?

I leave the café and soon discover finding Granny's cottage could be harder than I expected. Ardmara is no Manhattan, where everything's numbered and runs in logical lines. No, this place was designed by someone who likes surprises. The streets curve and twist without warning, and every time I think I'm getting my bearings, the road I'm on decides to become a different road entirely, or splits into two paths that both look equally promising and equally likely to lead me in circles. I don't really mind, though, because every person I pass offers a smile or a nod, like they're genuinely happy I'm here. Of course, I *could* stop and show people the photo, ask for directions, but that would spoil the fun. I want to solve this myself.

Before long I'm somehow back at the waterfront, passing a bakery piping out the smell of fresh bread, only for it to be instantly upstaged by the fishmonger next door. A little further on, there's a window overflowing with tweed caps and tartan scarves, plus a bulletin board advertising everything from ceilidhs to craft fairs.

I'm half-distracted by all the window boxes and painted storefronts when I spot a small building with ARDMARA LIBRARY painted in neat letters above the door.

Books used to be my world. My passion, my career, my whole identity. Manuscripts, deadlines, endless tracked changes, back-and-forth emails with authors. Now books are just a reminder of everything I've lost. I should walk past, keep looking for Granny's house, focus on the reason I'm here.

But my feet have other ideas. Before I can talk myself out of it, I'm pushing through the library door.

It's small and cosy, with shelves that reach the ceiling and a bay window fitted with a cushioned bench. What stops me in my tracks, though, is the children's section.

A colourful mural of sea creatures spills across the wall, and on a display table, picture books are fanned out just so. Before I can stop myself, I'm gravitating toward the table. *Just a quick look*, I tell myself.

Right in the centre of the display is a Katie Morag book, *Katie Morag and the Two Grandmothers*. Because of course it is. I pick it up almost without thinking, my thumb tracing the familiar cover art, the feisty red-haired girl on her windswept island, perched on a bench between her fancy mainland grandma in pearls and her practical island granny in rain boots.

God, I haven't seen one of these books in years. I flip it open, and there's Katie in her tartan skirt, washing a sheep in a bubble bath. A couple of pages later, she's rolling its wool into curls under a hairdryer. The illustrations are just as charming as I remember, full of character and life, with that slightly chaotic energy that makes them so appealing to kids—and that once upon a time, curled on my granny's couch in Toronto, was irresistible to me.

My throat tightens. Granny read these to me every summer when I stayed with her while Mom and Dad worked back in New York. We'd spend entire afternoons on the couch, me tucked under her arm, working our way through Katie's adventures. Granny loved that Katie was Scottish like her, and I loved that

Katie was brave and got into scrapes and always figured her way out of them.

Those summers with Granny weren't just visits, they were the foundation of everything I became. While other kids were at day camps or glued to screens, I was discovering that stories can transport you anywhere, that books can be friends, that reading is magic. It's because of those long lazy afternoons with Granny that I fell in love with children's literature in the first place. That I chose a creative path instead of following my parents into accounting or healthcare administration.

A career I worked so hard for. A career that's now behind me.

I close the book and set it back, blinking hard.

"Can I help you with anything?"

I turn to find a woman about my age watching me with kind eyes. She's a little shorter than me, with long, frizzy dark-blonde hair pulled back in a ponytail and a soft, curvy figure in a baggy moss-green cardigan.

"Oh, I'm not local," I say. "I'm not here to check anything out or anything. Just . . . having a look around."

She laughs, a genuinely warm sound. "Aye, I could tell you weren't local. I've lived in Ardmara my whole life—I know every face in this town. I'm Ellie. Technically, I'm just the library assistant, but since the actual librarian is based at a hub forty miles away, I pretty much run the place."

"Nice to meet you. I'm Blair, and as I'm sure the accent already told you, I'm American."

"And a fan of children's books?"

"Yes. I actually worked in children's publishing in New York . . . until recently. You know what? I just flew three thousand miles across the Atlantic to escape that world, only to wander straight into a library. Ironic, huh?"

"I get that. People give up smoking more easily than books."

I decide I like this woman. The laugh, the cute cardigan, the no-nonsense wisdom. It all puts me at ease.

We drift into easy conversation, about the library, about Ardmara, about my first impressions of Scotland. Inevitably, Granny comes up. I tell Ellie about my reason for visiting and how I'm hoping to find the house she grew up in. I did want to track it down on my own, but jet lag is once again creeping in and the town's winding streets have me hopelessly turned around. What the hell. I reach into my bag and pull out the photo.

"Actually, I don't suppose you could help me? I only have this old photo to go on."

I hand her the black-and-white picture. She studies it for a moment, then her face lights up. "Oh, that's Douglas Fraser's house! It's on Braeview Drive, just past the turn-off for the old kirk ruins. You can't miss it. It's still got those climbing roses, though they're a bit more established now."

She gives me detailed directions, drawing a little map on a scrap of paper when I look confused about which fork in the road she means. Quaint, but probably more useful here than Google Maps.

"Thanks so much," I say, tucking the photo and map back into my bag. "I really appreciate it."

"No bother at all." She pauses. "So, you don't know anyone in Ardmara, and you're travelling by yourself?"

When I nod, she brightens. "Well, if you fancy some company later, you're welcome to come round to mine for dinner. Nothing fancy, mind. Probably just pasta and whatever vegetables are threatening to go off in my fridge. But it might be better than sitting in a hotel room on your own, eh?"

I blink at her, genuinely surprised by this small act of kindness. In New York, librarians are lovely, but they don't typically invite random tourists home for dinner.

"I . . . thank you. That would be lovely. Though I should warn you, I might not be the best company. It's been a long day, and I'm mostly running on caffeine and shortbread at this point."

"Och, I'll take my chances. Worst-case scenario, you faceplant in the food and I get a funny story to tell."

Ellie sketches me a second map, this one leading to her house, and tells me to come by about six. And just like that, I've made a Scottish friend.

◆ ◆ ◆

Following Ellie's hand-drawn map, I wind my way through Ardmara's maze of streets, past more cheerful nods from locals and a tabby cat that judges me from a garden wall. Cats, it seems, are the same in any country.

The town is almost offensively picturesque. Every corner I turn reveals another postcard-worthy view of stone cottages with colourful doors or glimpses of the harbour through narrow gaps between buildings.

Braeview Drive turns out to be a quiet residential street that climbs gently away from the town centre. The houses here are older and weathered by years of salt air and storms. About halfway up the hill, I stop dead in my tracks. This is unmistakably the house from the photograph.

The whitewashed stone walls gleam in the sunlight. Just as Ellie said, the roses are more established now, climbing high across the front wall in a cascade of pink blooms. But the arched doorway is exactly the same, and even the little window to the left of the door has the same deep-set frame.

I pull out the photo and hold it up, comparing. Yep, this is it. This is where Granny played as a child, where she learned to speak with that soft Scottish lilt that never fully left her, even after seventy years in Canada.

Standing here, I can almost see her, a gap-toothed little girl with braids and mud on her knees, probably getting into the same kind of scrapes as Katie Morag. Maybe she climbed that rose trellis, or hid behind those stone walls during games of hide-and-seek.

For the first time since I stepped off the plane, I'm sure I've done the right thing. This trip, this crazy impulse to flee to Scotland, it was exactly what I needed. Granny would have loved knowing I came here, that I found her childhood home.

I glance around the quiet street. A few houses along, an elderly man tends his garden, and he gives me a friendly wave when he catches me looking. Everyone here really is so welcoming. Surely Douglas—that was the name Ellie said, right?—wouldn't mind if I knocked and explained the connection. Maybe he'd even invite me in for tea, let me see what the inside looks like now.

What's the worst that could happen? He says no, and I politely leave.

Go on, Blair. Do it.

So I walk up the short path and knock on the wooden door. The sound echoes, but no footsteps follow. I wait a moment then knock again. Nothing.

He must be out. Oh well.

I step back and pull out my phone to take a picture of the house, trying to frame the shot just like the old photo of Granny. At least I'll have this to show Mom and Dad.

But as I'm sliding my phone back into my pocket, I can't

resist one more look. Just a quick peek through the front window—not to spy or anything, just to imagine what it might have looked like when Granny lived here. I cup my hands against the glass and lean in, trying to see past the reflection.

The living room beyond carries the clutter of real life. A sagging couch faces the fireplace, flanked by a jumble of toys that haven't made it back into their box, while a lopsided Lego tower sits proudly on the coffee table. Not a show home by any stretch, but it's got a comfortable, lived-in feel. I try to picture it years ago when Granny was young, maybe with different furniture and—

"Oi! Get away from there."

I jerk back from the window and spin around to find a man striding up the path toward me. He's tall and broad-shouldered, dark hair falling into eyes that aren't the least bit friendly. There's a rough, outdoorsy edge to him, like he spends his days under open skies, not hunched over a laptop in a Starbucks. If he didn't look like he'd happily toss me into the harbour, I might even call him handsome. At his side, a golden retriever wags and prances at the end of its leash, radiating a joy its owner clearly doesn't share.

"I'm so sorry, I—"

"Ah. American. That explains that," he mutters, just loud enough for me to hear. Then, louder: "You do realise people actually live their lives in this town, right? We're not just tourist attractions to be gawked at. How would you like it if I pressed my face against your living room window?"

My cheeks blaze. "Oh my God, I . . . I really am sorry. Is this your house?"

"No, it's my mate's, and I'm sure he wouldn't appreciate someone peering in at him, or at his kids. The man deserves a bit of privacy."

The golden retriever chooses this moment to strain forward,

tongue lolling out, desperate to reach me with what's clearly an agenda of face-licking and slobbery affection. I instinctively retreat a step, which only makes the dog more determined until his owner gives him a firm tug back.

"I wasn't—this was—my grandmother—" I'm flustered and tired, and the words don't come out right.

The man shakes his head, and I catch a flash of green eyes that would be gorgeous if they weren't filled with disdain. "Oh, brilliant. Another American over here tracing her roots." He actually does an eyeroll.

That does it. "Excuse me?"

He goes on glaring at me.

And here I'd been thinking everyone in this adorable little town was friendly and welcoming. Apparently, I've found the one guy who missed that memo. The one person who thinks being a complete ass to strangers is acceptable behaviour.

The really annoying part? Though he's not said much, his accent is criminally hot. Low, rough, and distinctly Scottish in a way that does inconvenient things to my pulse. Which only makes me more irritated with him, and with myself.

"You know what?" I snap. "Forget it."

I brush past him and stalk away as fast as my legs will carry me, my face burning.

So much for Highland hospitality.

CHAPTER FOUR

LACHLAN

The moment I step into Ardmara Leisure Centre, the chlorine tang from the pool hits my nose. Add in the faint aroma of sweaty trainers and a greasy waft from the café, and it's hardly inviting. But the worst is yet to come.

I head for the soft play, better known to the dads of Ardmara as "the Pit". Partly because of the massive ball pit in one corner, but mainly because spending time there is, well, the pits. As soon as I push open the door, the noise smacks into me—squeals, crashes, the thrum of kids high on sugar.

Most folk would turn around and flee, but I'm not most folk. I'm a single dad on a Saturday afternoon.

At our usual table, Struan and Douglas are nursing cups of what the leisure centre optimistically calls coffee. I make my way towards them, crossing a floor with that special stickiness only a thousand spilled juice cartons can produce.

"Da!"

The shout comes from somewhere in the maze of tunnels and slides, and I scan the chaos until Finn's dark head pops up behind one of those foam block things. He waves both hands at me, grinning wide.

Sticky floors, migraine-inducing noise, the fact I'd rather be anywhere else—doesn't matter. The kid still manages to drag a smile out of me. I give him a wave, and he disappears back into the chaos.

I drop into the empty chair opposite Struan and Douglas. "Thanks, lads. Appreciate you keeping an eye on Finn while I walked Gus."

Douglas scratches at his ginger beard, stifling a yawn. He looks knackered, as usual. "Easy job. He's no bother, unlike my pair." Right on cue, a wild shriek erupts behind him, and Douglas groans. "Sounds like one of mine. If I don't turn round, maybe I can pretend I didn't hear it."

Struan grins, his tawny curls pulled into a man bun that's as effortlessly casual as he is. Unlike Douglas and me, who are permanently one coffee away from collapse, Struan's got this laid-back vibe that makes single parenting seem like a hobby, not a never-ending battle. "You've tried that one before. Hate to break it to you, mate, but it never works out."

Before Douglas can reply, Isla trots over, her curly ponytail bouncing. She's a smaller, tidier version of her dad, and she fixes Struan with a look far too sensible for her seven years. "Daddy, the twins are having a ball war, and I don't think they're supposed to."

Well, that's denial off the table. We all glance towards the pit, where Rosie and Logan—miniature versions of Douglas with the same flaming hair—are pelting balls at each other, as well as at any poor kid who stumbles too close, while laughing their heads off. A couple of younger children watch on from a cautious distance, wide-eyed. Their mothers, meanwhile, pin us with the look that says, "Are you going to step in or what?"

Finn hovers at the edge of the pit, eyes lit up at the sight of the twins' carnage.

"Oi, Finn," I warn. "Don't even think about it."

He grins sheepishly and ducks back into the tunnels.

Douglas sighs and raises his voice. "Logan! Rosie! The balls are for sitting in, not throwing. Pack it in." Then, to Isla: "Thanks for telling us, Isla."

She nods and skips back into the fray.

Douglas catches my eye and jerks his chin at Struan. "All right for some, eh? One kid, he's only got her at weekends, and she's *sane*. How the hell is that fair?"

"Tell me about it," I say, standing. Not that I'd trade Finn for anything. "Right, I'll grab a coffee and some juices for the kids. You two for more caffeine?"

A few minutes later I'm back with a tray. The four kids barrel over, flushed and sweaty, down their cartons in seconds, then tear straight back into the mayhem.

"Meant to say, Douglas, I caught some American lass peering into your front window when I was walking Gus. Face right up against the glass. No sense of boundaries, some of these tourists."

Douglas barely reacts. I suppose when you're raising twin tornadoes, a window-peeper probably doesn't even register on your list of daily trials. Struan, though, perks up, eyes lighting with interest. "An American lass, you say? Was she fit?"

"Didn't notice."

"Which means yes," Struan says with a grin.

I shoot him a look. "Which means I was too busy fuming at her complete lack of manners to notice anything else."

"Ah, come on, Lachlan. You're not blind. Tall? Short? Blonde? Brunette? Give us something to work with here."

Despite myself, my mind drifts back to the encounter. She was tall—probably up to my nose—with straight blonde hair grazing her shoulders, and pale blue eyes that went wide when I told her to back off. Looked all guilty until she snapped right back at me. Had slim curves in all the right places, that one. And these long legs that—

Christ. I shake my head, annoyed with myself for even thinking about it.

"Why does it matter?"

"Because some of us still remember what it's like to appreciate the finer things in life," Struan says with a waggle of his eyebrows. "Besides, it's tourist season. Fresh faces, new possibilities . . ."

I shake my head. Trust Struan to try to turn a privacy invasion into a hook-up opportunity. He sees them everywhere. Douglas and I just see laundry piles and empty lunch boxes.

"Anyway," Struan says, leaning back, "don't you have bigger things to worry about than nosy tourists? Like who's going to watch Finn when the summer holidays start next week?"

I grimace. "Don't remind me. Three more days of school, then he's off for six bloody weeks."

Turns out Flora did hurt herself when she tripped over Gus. Fractured her wrist, in fact. No way she can look after a six-year-old all summer.

"I've tried everything. Clubs are full, childminders too. Thought I had a university student lined up—home from Edinburgh for the summer—but she's taken a job in France instead. Can't really blame her. But with most folk in town run off their feet for tourist season, nobody's sitting around waiting to be my last-minute saviour."

Struan drums his fingers on the table. "So advertise for a nanny. Stick a note in shop windows, post on the community Facebook. Offer them the granny flat. Someone passing through will bite."

The so-called granny flat isn't really a flat at all, just a wee self-contained unit behind my house. It's been sitting empty since I moved in, gathering dust.

"Aye, brilliant," I say with a snort. "Invite a stranger to live in my back garden."

Douglas shrugs. "Better than no childcare at all."

I huff out a breath. Much as I hate to admit it, they're right. What choice do I have?

CHAPTER FIVE

BLAIR

It's been two days since I arrived in Ardmara, and I'm starting to feel almost human again. The jet lag has finally loosened its grip, and I've settled into something that could generously be called a routine. Wake up. Coffee at the Lighthouse Café. Wander around town with no particular destination. Try not to think about my spectacular career implosion.

I'm not entirely succeeding on that last part.

I'm back at my corner table in the café, the same spot I claimed on my first day, nursing my second latte of the morning. My phone sits on the scratched wooden surface in front of me, browser open to a job search site I have no business looking at.

Picture-book editor, acquisitions manager, content coordinator . . . each listing a tiny knife twist. I'd give anything to have my old life back, but I've torched every bridge. My reputation is in ashes. And still I keep looking, even though there's a beautiful view to be admired out the window.

It's like picking at a scab. You know it'll only make things worse, but your fingers have other ideas.

My phone buzzes with a text from Ellie.

ELLIE

> Fancy a walk along the waterfront later? The weather's supposed to be gorgeous.

A smile tugs at my lips. Dinner at Ellie's on Saturday night was exactly what I needed—good food, easy conversation, and someone who didn't know or care about my professional disasters. She cooked a huge pot of penne, just like she'd promised, and we spent hours talking about books, local folklore, and her life in Ardmara. It felt like the kind of evening I used to have back before work deadlines defined my entire life.

BLAIR

> Sounds perfect. I'll message you later?

ELLIE

> Brilliant! x

The little "x" at the end makes me grin. I'd forgotten how naturally affectionate people can be when they're not constantly stressed about subway delays and rent prices.

I close the chat and go back to the job site before catching myself.

God, Blair. You flew three thousand miles to get away from this crap. Stop torturing yourself!

I put down my phone with more force than necessary, earning a curious look from the woman at the next table.

"Sorry," I mutter, then down the rest of my latte. I stand and head to the counter to drop off my mug, the kind of small-town courtesy I'm still getting used to. In New York, you leave your dishes and someone else deals with them. Here, it feels rude not to help.

As I'm about to leave, something on the community bulletin

board catches my eye. A plain white sheet, taped dead centre, standing out amid the colourful flyers all around it.

NANNY WANTED
Caring for a 6-year-old boy over the summer holidays. Weekdays, 8 to 4. Live-in accommodation available. Must be good with dogs. References required. Immediate start.

A phone number is printed at the bottom in the same no-nonsense black text, along with a request to text, not call. Slightly unusual, but maybe whoever it is can't always get to the phone.

A nanny? The idea shouldn't interest me, but it does. Maybe it's the promise of "live-in accommodation"—a lot better for my bank account than bleeding money on hotel bills. Or maybe it's that I'm someone who needs a bit of focus, or else I spiral into doomscrolling job boards for a career that's already gone up in flames.

And then there's Granny. All those summers in Toronto, she was basically my nanny. There'd be a kind of symmetry in me coming here and looking after a kid, the way she once looked after me.

Of course, there are catches. "Must be good with dogs"? Yeah, I'm more of an admire-from-a-distance person. And "references required"? Let's just say my glowing professional ones went up in smoke with the rest of my career.

I sigh. Well, that rules that out then.

Except . . . does it? I mean, I *did* work in children's publishing. I like kids. And back in high school, I babysat for pizza money. Maybe that counts for something.

I'm already in Scotland on a whim. What's one more impulsive life decision?

Before I can overthink it, I punch the number into my phone. I hesitate briefly, wondering if this is madness, then fire off a quick text to ask if the position is still available.

◆ ◆ ◆

The address leads me to the very edge of town, where the road simply stops and open country takes over. I park beside a low stone wall and step out.

Wow.

The house sits alone on a gentle rise, a solid stone cottage with slate-grey roof tiles and white-painted window frames that gleam in the late-afternoon sun. It's beautiful, but what really catches my breath is the view. From here, I can see across the water to what must be the island the ferry travels to—dark against the horizon, with smaller rocky outcrops scattered around it like stepping stones. The sea shifts with colour, silver-grey where clouds throw shadows and deep blue where the sunlight breaks through. Far off, the white wake of a boat slices across the surface.

Holy crap, this is gorgeous. If I got this job, I'd wake up to this every morning.

Behind the main house sits a smaller building, and I wonder if that's the "live-in accommodation" mentioned in the ad. It's basically a tiny house in its own right, with a view that would cost a fortune back home.

I could definitely see myself here for a month or two. Making breakfast in that little place, watching the ferry come and go, learning to appreciate the slower pace of life. It would be like stepping into a different world from the one I left behind in New York.

Okay, Blair. Time to make a good first impression.

I fix my curtain bangs, which the sea breeze has already started rearranging, and check my reflection in the car window. Presentable enough. I've gone for casual but responsible—dark jeans, a soft blue sweater, and my most comfortable boots. The kind of outfit that says "trustworthy with children", or so I hope.

Earlier, I shot Ellie a message, pushing back our walk. We can chat by the harbour later. For now, I have to talk someone into trusting me with their kid. And their dog.

I walk up the path to the front door—painted red, the only splash of colour against the grey stone—and take a deep breath. This is it. My chance at a fresh start, at something completely different from the disaster I left behind.

I ring the doorbell and wait, mentally rehearsing my opening lines. *Smile*, I tell myself. *Be warm but professional, emphasise your experience with children's books and how that translates to under-standing kids.*

The door swings open, and my smile freezes on my face.

Standing in the doorway is the grumpy man who confronted me outside Granny's old house. The one who accused me of invading his friend's privacy and made snide comments about Americans tracing their roots.

"You again?" So, he's recognised me too. "What, are you here to peer in *my* windows now?" Then realisation dawns in his green eyes, the same ones I found irritatingly attractive during our last encounter. "Christ. You're not Blair, are you?"

He doesn't need me to answer him. My face says it all. Yes, I *am* the woman he's been texting about the nanny position.

"You've got to be kidding me," he mutters.

"I—" My brain has apparently decided to go on strike because no other words follow. I don't know what to say. I wasn't expecting the nanny ad to lead me to this man, the only person in Ardmara who's allergic to friendliness.

Before I can form a coherent response, a golden blur barrels past his legs. The dog from the other day—tail thrashing, tongue lolling—launches at me like I'm his long-lost best friend. He plants his paws on my chest, stretching up to lick my face.

"Oh! Uh, hi there, boy." I give his head a tentative pat, trying not to flinch. "You're very . . . enthusiastic."

The man watches with barely concealed scepticism. "Gus, down." The dog drops back to all fours, tail still thumping.

"Good dog," I say weakly, giving him another pet. "I love dogs. Absolutely love them."

Judging by the look on the man's face, he doesn't buy it. Can't blame him.

This is a disaster. I should leave. And yet for some reason my feet stay put, as if I can still salvage this train wreck.

"So . . ." I say. "You're Lack-lan?"

"*Lachlan*," he corrects, pronouncing it with that throat-clearing sound Scots use in *loch*. I give it another go and end up sounding like I'm choking on a cracker. He rolls his eyes. Of course he does.

Right. I'm normally an optimistic person—or at least I was before a certain AI app turned my world upside down—but even I know when to cut my losses. It's time to go. This was a bad idea.

"Sorry," I say, stepping back. "This obviously isn't going to work, so I'll get out of your hair." I spin on my heel and walk off.

There's a pause, a reluctant exhale, then Lachlan calls, "Wait!"

I turn back. He looks like he's wrestling with himself.

"I'm sorry. That was uncalled for. I'm knackered, not an arsehole. Well, not always." He scrubs a hand through his dark-brown hair. "Seeing as you came all the way here, why don't you at least come in, have a coffee, and hear a bit more about the position?"

I fold my arms. "Is there any point when you're clearly not going to give it to me?"

"Aye, well . . . who knows? I've not exactly been flooded with applications."

Under my breath I mutter, "Why does that not surprise me?"

He chooses not to hear that and steps back, giving a little jerk of his head toward the kitchen. "At least have a coffee."

I hover. My gut says *bad idea*. Everything about him radiates prickly energy. But I wanted this job before I knew I'd be working for him, didn't I? And if the role is to look after his kid while he's off at work, how much contact would I really have with him anyway?

Before I can decide what to do, a boy edges into view, peering around the doorway. Same dark hair as his father, but with wide brown eyes and an adorable gap-toothed smile that just about knocks the wind out of me. "Are you the new nanny?" he asks.

Lachlan coughs. "Well, we'll see about that. I was just asking Blair if she'd like to come in and chat about it some more."

Oh God. There's no way I can bolt now. Not with the kid watching me. His dad may be all storm clouds and scowls, but the boy beams like it's always summer inside. I can't say no.

So I force a smile, nod, and step on in. The dog—Gus, was it?—bounds inside too, tail wagging in welcome.

Lachlan leads me through to the kitchen. The space is spotless. Countertops gleaming, not a crumb or coffee ring in sight, not even a rogue Lego or bit of kibble on the floor. It's the polar opposite of what I glimpsed through the window of Granny's old house the other day. That place was all scattered toys and delightful domestic mayhem. Here, everything is neat almost to the point of being sterile.

The only pop of colour comes from a cork board on the wall, covered in children's drawings: neon-bright dinosaurs, stick figures with enormous grins, a rainbow that tips drunkenly to one side. Otherwise, the kitchen is muted greys and careful order.

"Take a seat," Lachlan says, gesturing to the oak table. "How do you take your coffee?"

"Milk, no sugar. Thanks."

As he busies himself at the counter, the golden retriever flops onto a bed in the corner, and the boy slides into the chair beside me, legs swinging, eyes bright with curiosity.

"Oi," Lachlan says without turning around. Classic parental superpower: eyes in the back of the head. "This bit isn't for you, Finn. It's grown-up business. Go play for a bit."

"But I'm *really* good at asking questions," Finn protests.

I can't help but smile. Honestly? I'd rather be interviewed by the kid.

"Off you go," Lachlan says, not unkindly but firm.

Finn drops to the floor with a quiet, "Fine." He shoots me a quick grin before hurrying off.

Lachlan sets a mug in front of me, puts down another for himself, and takes the opposite chair, folding his broad arms across his chest. Interview stance: defensive, expression neutral, all business.

He doesn't waste time with pleasantries. "Right, then. What sort of childcare experience do you have?"

"Well, I worked in children's publishing for years," I say, aiming for breezy confidence. "Thinking deeply about what kids want, what they respond to, what engages them . . ."

His expression doesn't change. At all. I plough on.

41

"And I babysat through high school. Board games, bedtime routines, the works." Ten years ago, but it still counts, right?

Lachlan takes a slow sip of coffee, like he's giving my answer time to marinate. "If you used to work in publishing, what are you doing applying to mind a bairn? Seems a bit of a step sideways."

I shrug, keeping it light. "Needed a break. Figured it was time to remind myself there's more to life than the inside of a Manhattan office."

His expression doesn't shift, but at least he doesn't press. He does, however, say, "References?"

"From my babysitting days?" I laugh a little too brightly. "I could track down one of the families, if you really want. Their kid's probably in college now, but hey, nobody died on my watch."

One dark eyebrow lifts, unimpressed. I'm definitely not winning him over with my sparkling wit.

"I've also become friends with Ellie Macpherson," I try. "She'd vouch for me."

The name doesn't seem to register. Strange. I thought this was a small town where everyone knows everyone else. "She works at the library?" I add.

He gives a small grunt. Approval? Disapproval? Impossible to tell.

"Look," I say, leaning forward. "I'm reliable. Flexible. Good with mess. And I give really excellent hugs."

Nothing. Not even the twitch of a lip.

"Hugs aren't part of the job description," he says flatly. "And I'm not a fan of mess."

I glance around the pristine kitchen. *You don't say.*

We talk through the basics: hours, duties, expectations. He

asks me a few more questions, and I notice he glances down at his phone before each one, like he's working through an interrogation script he wrote in advance, point by point. When we get on to transport, I mention I've got a rental car, so I'd be able to take Finn on day trips or shopping or whatever.

"And you do know we drive on the left here?" Lachlan says. "Because a lot of tourists seem to forget that partway through their visit. I swear, the number of times—"

"Oh my God, you drive on the *left*?" I interrupt. "How did I drive up four and a half hours from Glasgow without realising that?"

For a split second, genuine alarm flickers across his face before he realises I'm just pulling his leg. He doesn't seem to find it funny.

Okay, new tack. "Can I ask about Finn?" I venture. "What's he like?"

For the first time since I walked in, something shifts in Lachlan's posture. He relaxes slightly. And when he speaks, his tone is softer, a little warmer. "He's a good lad. Smart. Curious. Big imagination."

Ah. So there's the human being hiding under all that gruffness.

"And . . . his mom?" I ask gently.

The warmth vanishes. "Not on the scene." The finality in his tone makes it clear that topic is off-limits.

Well, I can't say I'm surprised. Living with this level of grumpiness would wear any woman down. Can't blame her for bailing.

Before I can think of a safer follow-up question, his phone buzzes. He glances at the screen and frowns. "Sorry, I need to take this. Give me a few minutes." He steps out the back door and into the yard, phone already at his ear.

I'm left alone with my coffee and the muted sound of his voice through the glass. A moment later, small footsteps pad into the kitchen and Finn settles back into the chair beside me, a stuffed dragon under one arm. "So, are you going to be my nanny?"

I grin at his directness. "I don't know yet. What do you think? Am I nanny material?"

He studies me with comical seriousness, chin tilted, eyes narrowed. Then he nods. "You seem nice. And you're not scary-looking. I think you'd be good."

Nailed it.

"Any tips for getting your dad to smile?" I whisper.

Finn considers this. "Maybe tell him something about boats? He likes boats. He's a ferry captain, you know."

"Boats, huh?" I file that away. "Good to know. Now, what do *you* like?" I glance at his toy. "Dragons?"

He nods enthusiastically. "My favourite film is *How to Train Your Dragon*. Have you seen it?"

"Seen all the movies. Read all the books."

His mouth drops open. "*All* of them?"

"Every single one. Isn't Astrid just the best?"

He looks aghast. "What? No, Hiccup and Toothless are the best. Astrid is all right for a girl, I *suppose*."

It turns out knowing *How to Train Your Dragon* is the only cue Finn needs to unleash a torrent of dragon facts upon me, complete with swooping hand gestures and sound effects. I listen, nodding seriously as he explains the difference between a Deadly Nadder and a Monstrous Nightmare, or tells me about how he's been practising his dragon-training skills on Gus.

44

Talking with this kid is a *lot* easier than talking with his dad. All I have to do is throw in a comment here or there, then I can sip at my coffee as he chatters away. Best interview I've ever had, hands down.

After a little while, a flicker of movement catches my eye, and I glance toward the back door to find Lachlan standing there, phone call apparently finished. He's watching us, expression unreadable. How long has he been listening?

He steps back into the kitchen. "What did I say about grown-up business?" he asks Finn, but his tone is more resigned than annoyed.

"Sorry," Finn mumbles, though he shoots me a smile that suggests he's not sorry at all. "Blair knows *all* about dragons, Da."

"Does she now?" Lachlan's eyes flick to me—still impossible to read—then back to his son. "Off you go. Blair and I have to finish up here."

Finn disappears down the hallway, and the kitchen is suddenly a whole lot quieter. As Lachlan sinks back into his chair, I remember Finn's advice. Boats. Right, worth a shot.

"You know, I come from Staten Island," I say. "I used to take the ferry every day for work. Finn mentioned you're a ferry captain?"

"Aye," Lachlan says. And that's it. He doesn't go off on some passionate monologue about boats the way his son did about dragons. He confirms his occupation and says no more. Shuts the conversation down. So much for my attempt at small talk. That sank fast.

I shift awkwardly. "Anyway . . ."

"That was my neighbour on the phone," he says. "Flora. She usually helps with Finn, but she's injured her wrist." He studies me for a moment. "Flora knows everyone, so I asked her about

Ellie at the library. She had her number, so after I finished talking to Flora, I gave Ellie a call."

My stomach drops. I *did* offer him Ellie's name as a reference, but I hadn't expected him to check up on me so quickly, literally while the interview is still ongoing.

"She had nice things to say about you."

Relief washes over me. "Oh. That's good."

He nods once then fixes me with that steady green stare. "Look, I'll be straight with you. You're the only person who's applied. It's two days till the summer holidays, and I'm out of options. Finn's usually shy with folk he doesn't know, but he wasn't with you. He was blabbing away to you about dragons like you've been pals for years, and I reckon that's as good a sign as any."

He pauses, then adds, "So, if I've not scared you off, how about a trial? You can do Wednesday to Friday, then we'll see where we're at come the weekend. What do you think?"

I can't stop the smile tugging at my mouth. After weeks of humiliation, it's just nice to be offered a job, even one I never imagined doing before this morning.

"Wednesday it is, then," I say. "I won't let you down."

I catch sight of Finn peeking around the doorway, still clutching that dragon. He gives me a thumbs-up and a grin that could light the whole room.

CHAPTER SIX

BLAIR

I pull up outside Lachlan's house at seven forty-five the next morning, my hotel room key already returned and my suitcase stuffed in the trunk of the rental car. I climb out, and the morning air hits me like a slap of pure Scottish freshness, all crisp and clean like the world's been powerwashed overnight. Everything glistens with leftover raindrops—the stone walls, the slate roof tiles, even the pebbles crunching underfoot. It's the kind of morning that makes you want to take deep, cleansing breaths and declare yourself ready for a fresh start.

Which is exactly what I'm doing. Right? This is my fresh start. My new adventure. Not me running away from my problems to play nanny for a grumpy Scotsman and his adorable kid.

Definitely the fresh start thing.

Taking a deep breath of that impossibly clean air, I head to the front door and knock. After a moment, it swings open.

"Morning," Lachlan says.

Oh, for crying out loud. He's in a ferry captain's uniform: navy trousers, crisp white shirt with actual epaulettes. Gone is the rumpled, scowling man from yesterday's interview. In his place stands someone who looks like he stepped off the cover of *Nautical Monthly* or whatever magazine features unfairly attractive sea captains.

The uniform transforms him completely. The tailored fit emphasises his broad shoulders, the white shirt makes his green eyes even more striking, and there's an authority to him now that does inconvenient things to my pulse. He looks competent. Professional. Commanding.

This is a problem. A big problem. I'm supposed to be working for this man, not ogling him like some lovesick teenager.

"You all right?" he asks, and I realise I've been staring like he's a particularly fascinating museum exhibit.

"Fine! Yes. Good morning." I give myself a mental slap. *Get it together, Blair.* "You look very . . . official."

"It's called a uniform," he says drily.

Before I can embarrass myself any further, Finn appears at his father's elbow. He's also in uniform, a neat little school outfit with a tiny blazer and tie that makes him look approximately seventeen times more adorable than he did yesterday. And he was adorable yesterday.

"Blair!" He beams at me. "It's my last day of school before the holidays. I'm *so* excited!"

He bounces from foot to foot, and I can't help grinning back. Growing up in New York, our strictest dress-code rule was no crop tops. Otherwise, it was a free-for-all. The formality of British school uniforms is both charming and slightly surreal—little kids dressed for board meetings.

"That *is* exciting," I say. "Ready for summer adventures?"

"Yes! We're going to have a lot of fun, right?"

"*So* much fun."

"All right." Lachlan pulls a key from his pocket and holds it out to me. "You've got today to get settled. The granny flat is around the back, just follow the path through the garden."

Granny flat? Is that what they call it here? It sounds like somewhere you'd store elderly relatives rather than house a temporary nanny.

"Oh, and here's a key to the main house too." He produces another key. "I do have one task for you today. Give Gus his lunch at half twelve and take him for a walk. His bowl and lead are on the kitchen work surface. Flora usually does it, but with her wrist . . ."

"Of course. No problem." I nod confidently, like I'm totally prepared to handle an enthusiastic golden retriever and definitely know what "half twelve" means. Is that twelve thirty? Or eleven thirty? Or something else? I should probably ask, but admitting I don't understand basic time references seems like a poor start to my employment.

Gus himself chooses this moment to make his entrance, tail already wagging like he's powered by pure joy. He pushes past Lachlan's legs to greet me, and I give him a pat on the head.

"Is that you finished your breakfast, Gus?" Finn asks, crouching to ruffle his ears.

"Normally, Gus would be first to the door," Lachlan observes. "But food wins over guests. Every time." He checks his watch—an actual watch, not his phone, because of course he's the kind of practical, masculine guy who still wears a watch—and frowns. "Right, we need to go. Finn, grab your bag."

Finn hurries back into the house, leaving me alone with his father for a moment. The silence stretches, tipping into awkward.

"I hope the granny flat is okay," Lachlan says finally. "It's been a while since it's been used."

Something in his tone makes me pause. "Oh. Okay. How long is 'a while'?"

"A few years."

A few years? "Right. I'm sure it'll be fine."

Famous last words, Blair. Famous last words.

Finn reappears with his backpack, and Lachlan gives Gus a scratch behind the ears before shooing him inside and locking the front door. As they walk down to their car, Finn gives me an enthusiastic wave, like I'm already part of the family.

"See you later, Blair! I can't wait for tomorrow!"

I wave back, smiling at his excitement. At least one of us is confident this is going to work out.

After they drive away, I stand in the sudden quiet for a moment, keys in my palm, doubt creeping in. What the hell am I doing? Twenty-four hours ago I was a tourist. Now I'm about to move into the backyard of a man who I suspect believes tourists are a minor plague upon Scotland.

This is either the most spontaneous, adventurous thing I've ever done, or the most spectacularly stupid. Guess time will tell.

I follow the gravel path around the side of the house and through the backyard to the "granny flat". The small building mirrors the main house's architecture—same grey stone, same slate roof, just scaled down. Its front door is even painted the same red as the main house's. It's charming, at least from the outside.

I slide the key into the lock, turn it, and push open the door.

Oh.

The smell hits me first, a musty, stale dampness, like air that's been trapped for years. Dust motes swirl in the sunlight. Cobwebs decorate the corners like unwelcome party streamers.

My heart sinks a little as I step inside and survey my home for, potentially, the next six weeks.

It's a studio layout, with the bedroom, sitting area, and kitchenette all sharing one main room. A small table and two chairs sit by the window. The sea view is spectacular, though currently filtered through glass that hasn't seen a cleaning cloth in a long time. There's also a tiny shower room with a toilet and sink.

Okay. Less cottagecore dream, more meh than magical. But sure.

I throw the windows wide and let in the fresh sea breeze.

Right. I wanted a focus, didn't I? Something to distract me from wallowing in my career implosion. Well, cleaning this place from top to bottom will definitely keep me busy.

Under the kitchen sink, I find a pair of gloves and some basic cleaning supplies. I dig my phone out of my pocket and fire up some music.

"Okay, Blair." I roll up my sleeves, remove my rings—all five of them—and pull on the gloves. "You wanted an adventure. Time to make this place livable."

As Taylor Swift starts singing about shaking it off—how appropriate—I grab a cloth and get to work. Not the peaceful morning of settling in I'd imagined, but hey. At least it's keeping my hands busy and stopping me from doomscrolling job boards.

◆ ◆ ◆

At half past twelve—and yes, I did text Ellie to confirm that "half twelve" means "half past twelve" and not some mysterious Scottish time concept—I take a break. My back aches, and I'm pretty sure I've inhaled enough dust to qualify as a human vacuum cleaner, but the place is starting to look, and smell, like somewhere a person might actually want to sleep.

I pull off the gloves, wash my hands, and head to the main house. Gus is waiting for me just inside the door, golden body wriggling with excitement. He springs up on his hind legs, front paws thudding into my ribs, tongue going straight for my face.

"Ugh! Seriously?" Grimacing, I twist my head away, but he still gets me square on the cheek.

Just great. Oh well, after a morning of dust and cobwebs, what's a little dog slobber, right?

I push him down gently, and he sits, panting, tongue lolling.

"Okay, Gus. It's confession time. During my interview yesterday, I might've oversold my love of dogs. Truth is, I don't have much experience with your kind. But if you're nice to me, I'll be nice to you. Deal?"

He barks once, tail thumping the floor, and I decide that counts as a yes.

We head through to the kitchen, which is just as spotless and gleaming as it was yesterday—the polar opposite of the cobwebbed annex I've been battling all morning. Honestly, it's hard to believe the same man owns both spaces. Credit where it's due, though. Keeping a place this pristine while living with a six-year-old *and* a golden retriever? Pretty damn impressive.

I spot Gus's lunch bowl and leash on the counter—sorry, "work surface"—just where Lachlan said they'd be. But there's something else waiting beside them. A roll of poop bags.

Oh God.

When I talked myself into this whole nanny gig—fresh start, roof over my head, something to occupy me—I somehow conveniently forgot about the less glamorous realities of dog ownership. Like the fact that dogs poop. And apparently, I'm expected to deal with it.

Gus, oblivious to my mini meltdown, dances in place. He clearly knows what time it is, and he can't fathom why I'm taking so long to serve him.

I take the bowl and set it down on the floor. "Here you go, boy. Luncht—" He dives in before I can even finish the word, vacuuming up kibble like it's his last meal on earth. Twenty seconds later, the bowl is spotless and he's looking up at me expectantly.

"Wow, boy. Did you even chew any of that? Well, it's walk time now, I guess."

I pocket a few of the dreaded poop bags, clip his leash to his collar, and head for the front door.

You've got this, Blair. Picking up poop can't be that *bad.*

I've barely locked the door behind me when Gus explodes forward like he's been shot from a cannon, nearly yanking my arm from its socket. The leash goes taut, and the next thing I know, I'm being dragged down the hill toward the beach.

"Whoa! Gus! Slow down!" I stumble, trying to dig my heels in, almost tripping over my own feet, and just barely avoiding faceplanting. It's not until we hit the pebble beach that I manage to rein him in. Panting, I glance back at the descent I just took way faster than my legs ever agreed to. "Jesus!"

Considering how commanding and authoritative Lachlan looked in his uniform this morning, you'd think he could've at least trained his dog not to murder the nanny.

Once I'm reasonably sure my shoulder is still attached, I let Gus lead me along the beach. He's in his element. Me? Not so much. Just as I'm starting to get the hang of things—leaning back against Gus's enthusiasm, finding my balance on the shifting stones—he comes to an abrupt stop and assumes "the position".

Oh, great. Here we go.

Sure enough, Gus does his business while I look away, giving him some privacy. Not that he's bothered about modesty. When he's done, he comes over to me and wags his tail proudly, like we've achieved something great together.

I eye the fresh pile with deep suspicion. This is *not* how I pictured my Scottish adventure. I'd imagined misty castles, dramatic cliffs, maybe even a kilt sighting or two. Not . . . this.

Still, a job's a job. Wrinkling my nose, I pull a bag from the roll, crouch down, and scoop it up. Trying my best not to gag, I attempt to wrestle the bag into a knot.

"Hello there! Lovely afternoon, eh?"

I nearly jump out of my skin. Whipping around, I see a cheerful old man in a flat cap strolling by, smile wide and friendly.

"Oh! Um . . ." My eyes dart to the bag dangling from my fingers. ". . . yes. Lovely day."

He tips his cap and continues on, whistling, while I stand frozen, clutching a bag of dog poop and wondering how, exactly, my life came to this.

◆ ◆ ◆

By evening, the granny flat is unrecognisable. Even the musty smell is gone, replaced by the warm, garlicky scent of the chicken stir-fry sizzling on the ancient stovetop. Now, sitting on the windowsill and lording it over the view like he owns the place, is a cheerful little potted plant I picked up from a local store. I've already christened him Gerald.

I'm stirring the stir-fry when there's a knock at the door.

Wiping my hands on a dish towel, I open it to find Lachlan standing outside, holding a sheet of neatly typed paper.

"Oh! Hi." I take a step back. "Um, come on in. I can put the kettle on. I've been shopping—got teabags! How British of me, right?"

He shakes his head, staying firmly planted on the threshold. "No, I won't stay. Just wanted to have a quick chat." His gaze slips over my shoulder, eyebrows lifting in surprise. "Oh, wow. You've done a good job with the place." His gaze lands on Gerald. "And you got a plant."

"That's Gerald," I explain. "He seemed lonely at the store."

I thought Lachlan might think it was cute I named the plant. Should've known better. He looks at me like I've grown another head. "Oh. Right. *Anyway* . . . how did the walk with Gus go at lunch?"

Straight onto business. Typical.

"Great! No problems at all," I say breezily, while my shoulder twinges at the memory of being dragged down that hill. For half a second, I consider telling Lachlan his dog is basically nuts, but I catch myself. Not even started my first proper day on the job yet. Probably best not to complain about his beloved pet.

"Good. Right." He holds out the paper. "I wanted to give you this. It's a routine for Finn. It's fairly fixed—he likes it that way."

I take the sheet and scan it. My eyes widen as I read aloud: "Eight: breakfast. Two slices of toast, cut diagonally, with jam. Strawberry, not raspberry. Eight fifteen: brush teeth for exactly two minutes." I look up at him. "*Exactly* two minutes?"

"He has a timer," Lachlan says matter-of-factly.

Right, because what kid doesn't have a toothbrush timer?

I keep reading. "Nine: outdoor play, weather permitting. If

55

raining, indoor activities: Lego or books. No screens before eleven."

Is this guy *trying* to model himself on Captain von Trapp?

"It's just to help you get started," Lachlan says, though his demeanour suggests this routine is about as flexible as reinforced concrete. "Finn thrives on structure."

"Of course." I put the paper down on the table. "Thank you. This is very . . . thorough."

"My phone number is there too, in case you need it. Anyway, I'll leave you in peace." He turns to go, then stops. "Oh, actually, one last thing. My neighbour, Flora, might pop over tomorrow, just to check how you're getting on."

Perfect. An inspection. On my first day.

"That's lovely," I say. "I look forward to meeting her."

"Right. Well, I'll see you in the morning, then. Night."

And with that, he's gone, striding back toward the main house.

I close the door then take another look at the routine sheet. I wonder if Lachlan gave Flora a copy too. Maybe she'll show up tomorrow with a clipboard and a red pen. God forbid I give Finn his toast in rectangles.

"Oh, Gerald," I say, glancing over at my potted plant. "What have I got myself into?"

CHAPTER SEVEN

BLAIR

I leave the granny flat, nerves buzzing despite the sunshine. Through the kitchen window of the main house I catch a glimpse of Lachlan moving around in his ferry captain uniform. Once again those crisp white epaulettes do inconvenient things to my pulse, but I shove the feeling aside.

Focus, Blair. First day. Don't screw it up.

Ten steps and I'm at the back door. The world's most convenient job—with the world's grumpiest boss.

I knock, and it opens almost immediately.

"Morning." Lachlan checks his watch and gives a curt nod. "Right on time."

"Wouldn't want to mess up the schedule on day one," I say with a smile. He doesn't return it, but there's no scowl either, so I'm going to call that progress.

Gus bounds into the kitchen. I know what to expect now, so I'm ready for him when he jumps up. "Uh-uh! No licking." I push him back to the floor. "But yes, it's good to see you too."

I shoot Lachlan a glance, hoping he noticed my excellent dog wrangling, but he gives me nothing.

Next Finn bounces in. "Blair! It's the holidays. No more school!"

I hold up both hands like I'm fending off a tidal wave of enthusiasm. "Wow, someone's wired this morning! What did you have, three cups of coffee?"

Finn laughs. "I don't drink coffee!"

I widen my eyes and give a theatrical little gasp. "You don't? Then all this energy is natural? Oh boy, I'm in trouble."

Maybe I'm imagining it, but I *think* Lachlan's lips twitch, just a little. A smile from Captain Grumpypants? Because of something *I* said? That is a good start to the day.

Of course, it's gone almost as soon as it appears. Lachlan pulls Finn in for a quick hug and ruffles his hair, then he bends to give Gus a scratch. "I've already fed this one," he tells me. "If he gives you the puppy eyes, ignore him. He's chancing it."

"Understood."

Lachlan straightens to his full height and nods at me, a gesture that somehow manages to convey "don't screw this up" and "good luck" in equal measure. "Right, I'm off. Any problems, you've got my number. Otherwise, I'll see you at four."

Without another word, he heads for the front door. It clicks shut behind him, and just like that, I'm in charge of a small boy and a large dog. For eight hours.

"Well, then." Shaking off any doubt, I clap my hands together. "Breakfast time!"

Gus perks up, tail going into overdrive, and I give him a pat. "Not you, boy. You already had yours, remember?"

I prepare Finn's breakfast as Lachlan described. Two slices of toast, cut diagonally—not a rectangle in sight—served with strawberry jam. I set the plate down on the kitchen table, and Finn digs in. I hover by the table as he chews, the quiet stretching.

Shouldn't I be, I don't know, engaging him? That's what good nannies do, right? But suddenly I have no idea what to say to a six-year-old boy.

Oh God. Why has my mind gone blank?

I'm about to launch into some inane chatter about the weather when he saves me from myself. "Where are you from?" he asks.

Thank you! That's something I can talk about.

"New York. Do you know where that is?"

He nods seriously. "Aye. It's where Spider-Man lives."

I can't help but smile.

"Don't worry, I know Spider-Man's not real," Finn adds. "But I've seen New York in the films. That's where the Statue of Liberty is, right?"

"You got it. I used to take a ferry to Manhattan every day for work, and every morning I'd see the Statue of Liberty on the way."

We chat a bit more about New York, which Finn thinks looks "really busy" but "like a lot of fun". He says he's never been anywhere like that before. When he finishes his last bite, I send him to brush his teeth, and exactly two minutes later, he's back again.

"All done!" he says. "What's next?"

"Well, the next item on your dad's schedule isn't until nine, which makes this free time, I guess. What do you want to do?"

"Want to see my room?"

"Sure."

Finn leads the way to the bottom of the stairs, where he points at my Converse sneakers. "No shoes on the upstairs carpets."

"Oh, of course." His father has him well trained. I kick them off then follow him up to his bedroom, which unlike the rest of the house explodes with colour. The walls are papered with drawings: vibrant dinosaurs, rainbow dragons, stick-figure scenes, and what appears to be a very ambitious attempt at painting the view from his window. It's chaotic and joyful and absolutely perfect.

At least Lachlan hasn't imposed his bland, neutral taste on his son's space.

"This is amazing. Did you do all of these?"

Finn nods proudly and launches into enthusiastic explanations of each piece. He's just pointing at a yellow cloud with four legs and telling me, "And that's Gus, of course," when Gus himself lumbers into the room, one of my shoes dangling from his mouth. He comes over to me, tail swishing as if to say, "Look what I found!"

"Um . . . thanks, Gus. Can you, uh, put it back now?"

He just looks at me, shoe still clamped in his jaws.

"Gus *is* allowed in your room, right?"

"Of course. He's part of the family. And I *think* it's fine for your shoe to be in my room, as long as it's not on your foot."

That logic seems watertight to me.

We spend the next bit looking through Finn's books and building a small Lego spaceship, with Gus supervising from his spot on the rug (still guarding my shoe). Finn peppers me with the kind of questions that make perfect sense in a six-year-old's head but would sound mad coming from anyone else.

"What's your favourite dinosaur?" he asks, carefully attaching a Lego wing.

"Hmm. Probably a Triceratops. They look friendly but could definitely handle themselves in a fight."

He nods approvingly. "Good choice. If you could live on any planet, which would you pick?"

"Well, not Venus. Too hot. Maybe one of Jupiter's moons? What about you?"

"Saturn. The rings would be like having a giant playground in the sky."

I'm just contemplating this delightfully weird reasoning when I catch sight of his clock. "Uh-oh, how did that happen? We're two minutes late for 'outdoor play, weather permitting'. And weather is definitely permitting—it's gorgeous out there."

I stand, brushing stray Legos off my jeans. "So, Finn, any playgrounds around here?"

"Aye. Down by the seafront, near the Lighthouse Café."

"Oh, I know that place. They do very good coffee."

"And top hats!"

I frown at this. Top hats? Yesterday Finn *had* looked adorable in his school uniform, but surely a six-year-old in a top hat is a bit much, even for British people?

"You like to wear . . . top hats?"

Finn dissolves into giggles. "They're not actual hats. It's a marshmallow with chocolate on the bottom and a Smartie on top." He licks his lips. "They're so good."

"Oh. Well, the schedule doesn't say anything about a morning treat . . . but it also doesn't say anything about *not* having a morning treat. And it *is* the first day of your summer vacation. Got to celebrate a little, am I right?"

"Aye!" Finn grins.

I wink at him, then look down at Gus, who's finally abandoned my shoe in favour of following our conversation with the intense focus of someone hoping the word "walk" might come up.

"You coming too, Gus?"

He gives a happy woof that I'm pretty sure means "absolutely yes, and can we go right now, please?"

◆ ◆ ◆

Fifteen minutes later, we're down by the pier, and I've got a to-go latte as well as a top hat of my own. Because why not?

The marshmallow is soft and sweet, the chocolate base is rich, and the Smartie on top—which, it turns out, is nothing like the tart American candy I expected but more like a tiny M&M—adds the perfect crunch.

"Mmm, that was ridiculously good," I say to Finn, who demolished his in record time.

"Told you. Oh!" He bounces on his toes. "Look! There's the ferry. My da is captaining that."

I follow his pointing finger to a vessel in the distance, cutting through the dark water, gliding toward town, white wake trailing behind it. Squinting, I can just about make out tiny figures moving on the deck.

"Wow. He must really know what he's doing to steer something that size."

Finn nods. "He goes to Corraig and back twice every day. That's the island way out there. The ferry is called the *Calabrae*, and he says she's a good ship."

There's something sweet about the way he talks about his father's work, like being a ferry captain is the coolest job in the world.

We make our way toward the playground, and nearly everyone we pass offers a "Good morning" or stops to give Gus a pat, which he accepts like visiting royalty. An elderly woman with one of those wheeled shopping bags tells me what a "bonny wee laddie" Finn is, while a man out walking his dog asks if Gus is behaving himself.

God, this place really is ridiculously friendly. In Manhattan, smiling at strangers earns you weird looks. Here, it seems rude not to.

We're almost at the playground when Finn suddenly takes off running. "Logan! Rosie!" he shouts, waving both arms above his head.

Two kids about his age are perched on the jungle gym— twins, by the look of them, both with the most spectacular red hair. The girl waves back enthusiastically while the boy slides down the fire pole to meet Finn.

Within seconds, all three are deep in animated conversation, and I'm left standing there with Gus, feeling a little redundant.

"You must be Finn's nanny."

I turn to find an older couple on a nearby bench, both smiling warmly at me. The woman's red hair is streaked with silver, while the man has a neat beard and weathered features.

"That's me," I say, walking over with Gus. "Well, I'm on a three-day trial. Assuming it goes okay, I'll be Finn's nanny for the summer. I'm Blair."

"Donald," the man says, standing to shake my hand. "And this is my wife, Roslyn."

"Lovely to meet you both."

"We're the twins' grandparents," Roslyn explains, nodding toward the redheaded duo now engaged in what appears to be a very serious game of tag with Finn. "We're looking after them this summer. And as much as we love them both, they're *full* of energy. It's going to be a long six weeks."

Donald chuckles. "We're hoping they tire themselves out at the park."

"Finn's dad, Lachlan, is friends with our son, Douglas," Roslyn adds.

"Oh!" I perk up. "Is that the Douglas who lives on Braeview Drive, in the house with the beautiful climbing roses?"

"Aye, have you met him?"

"Well, no, actually, but . . ." I explain about the photograph, about Granny growing up in that very house, about my quest to find it on my first day in town.

They don't remember Granny—which makes sense, given she was older and left when she was sixteen—but that doesn't stop them from being fascinated by the connection. Soon we're deep in conversation about old Ardmara, about how the town has changed over the decades, about the families who've come and gone.

The sun warms my shoulders as I listen to their stories while watching Finn tear around the playground with his friends. Gus has settled at my feet, panting contentedly in the shade.

I'm getting paid for this. To sit in the sunshine, chat about my granny, and watch a happy kid play with his friends.

Despite my earlier doubts about working for Captain Grumpypants, this might actually be a pretty sweet job.

◆ ◆ ◆

Back at the house, I set Finn's lunch in front of him at the kitchen table. It's a bowl of tomato soup and a cheese sandwich, cut diagonally because apparently even sandwiches have rules in this house.

"Careful not to spill on your pants," I say, settling into the chair across from him with my own food.

Finn, who's just taken a sip of water, chokes on it, nearly

64

spraying it across the table. "Why would I spill on my *pants*?" he gasps between giggles.

I blink at him. "Um, because you're six, and statistically six-year-olds are a high-risk group for lunchtime disasters?"

He shakes his head, his grin so wide it shows every gap in his smile. "But . . . that'd mean spilling on my *underwear*."

"Your what now?"

"My pants." He pats his legs for emphasis. "These are trousers. Pants go under."

"Oh. Right." I give him a sheepish smile. "Cultural translation issue. Don't spill on your trousers. Or your pants, for that matter."

Finn dissolves into fresh giggles, and I can't help but laugh too. Note to self: add British clothing terminology to my rapidly growing list of things I need to figure out.

We're still working our way through lunch—Finn happily dunking his sandwich in his soup while I try not to cringe at the soggy mess—when there's a knock at the front door. Gus goes into full alert mode, bounding toward the sound with a woof.

"Who's there, boy?" Finn jumps from his seat and follows after him.

Ah. Could this be the neighbour, Flora? And if so, what's she going to think about the fact we're behind schedule? Because Finn and I should really be onto "quiet time: reading or drawing" by now.

I follow Finn down the hallway to the front door and open it up to find an older woman—seventies, maybe—with silver hair pinned in a neat bun, kind eyes behind wire-rimmed glasses, and her left arm tucked into a sling.

"Hello, dear," she says to Finn while patting Gus with her good hand.

"Flora! Blair told me not to spill on my pants." He cracks up again. "That's really funny, right?"

Flora's eyes crinkle with amusement. "Oh my, that is funny. Though I suppose Blair's not wrong—spilling soup on your pants would be quite the catastrophe."

So this is Flora. No clipboard, no stopwatch, just warmth. Thank God.

"Hi. I'm Blair, the new nanny. Well, trial nanny. We'll see how it goes." I step back to let her in.

"Lovely to meet you, dear." She comes into the hallway and reaches into a small bag, pulling out a pack of colouring pencils. "I brought these for you, Finn. Thought you might like a few new colours for your drawings."

"Brilliant!" Finn takes them reverently. "Thank you, Flora. Look, Blair, there's even a gold one."

"Wow, that's really special." To Flora I say, "Please, come through to the kitchen. I'm afraid we're still eating. We're a bit behind schedule . . ."

Flora waves away my apology. "Finn seems to be getting on just fine: he's laughing and having a ball. I don't think the schedule being a wee bit off is likely to cause him any issues." She leans in conspiratorially. "Between you and me, Lachlan can plan things in a little too much detail sometimes."

"You have no idea how glad I am to hear that."

"Oh, aye. Don't get me wrong, structure is good for bairns, but there's such a thing as being too rigid about it."

In the kitchen I gesture toward an empty chair at the table. "Can I get you a tea? Or coffee?"

"Oh, really, I don't want to impose. I just wanted to pop in and give Finn his pencils."

"Please," I insist. "We'd love your company. Wouldn't we, Finn?"

He nods eagerly.

"Well, in that case, a tea would be lovely, thanks."

A few minutes later we're all seated at the table, Flora now with a steaming mug in front of her.

"So you were supposed to look after Finn over his summer vacation?" I ask before taking another spoonful of soup. I've already apologised for eating in front of Flora, but she insisted I eat away.

"Aye, that was the plan. I'm retired now but I spent thirty-odd years at Ardmara Primary School. Never had children of my own, so I've always loved spending time with the wee ones."

Gus nudges at Flora with his nose, tail wagging, hopeful for some more attention.

"Oh, you're being nice to me now, are you?" Flora says, scratching behind his ears. "After you gave me this injury, you daft dog?"

"Wait, *Gus* gave you your injury?"

"Aye, that he did. In all his excitement to get out for his walk, he knocked me clean off my feet. Down I went, right onto my wrist."

I stare at the golden retriever, who's now sitting prettily beside Flora's chair, looking like a poster dog for good behaviour. Yesterday he nearly dislocated my shoulder dragging me down the hill to the beach. Might've been nice if Lachlan had warned me Gus literally put Finn's last caregiver out of action.

We chat easily over tea, Flora asking about my impressions of Ardmara and sharing stories about the town's quirks. She's got the kind of gentle humour that comes from years of managing kids, and I can see why Finn adores her.

When she finishes her tea, she stands to go. "Right, I should leave you two to get on with your day."

"There's no rush," I say. "Stay as long as you like."

"That's very kind, but I don't want to get in the way of you two having fun. Besides, I've got some errands to run."

After I see her out, I turn to find Gus sitting in the hallway, tail thumping against the floor.

"So *you* hurt Flora's wrist?" I put my hands on my hips. "And what do you have to say for yourself?"

Gus just pants back at me, tongue lolling out. But Finn says, "I feel bad about Flora getting hurt. Also, she's *really* good at baking. She used to bring me biscuits and shortbread and things, but now she can't because of her wrist."

"Well, I know it's not in your dad's plan for the day, but how about we do a little baking for Flora? We could make cookies and take them over to her house?"

Finn's face lights up. "Really? We can do that?"

"Why not? It's a nice thing to do for someone who's been so kind to you."

Not exactly "quiet time: reading or drawing", but surely even Captain Grumpypants can't object to us doing something nice for his neighbour. Right?

◆ ◆ ◆

An hour and a half later, the cookies have cooled, been packaged up, and delivered to Flora along with a drawing Finn made of Gus looking appropriately sheepish, holding a sign that says "SORRY" in wobbly letters.

Now we're back in Finn's colourful bedroom for story time, a good bit later than Lachlan's schedule dictated, but I'm choosing to focus on Flora's reassurance that being a "wee bit off" won't cause any disasters.

Finn has selected *The Gruffalo* from his bookshelf, and we settle into the cosy corner of his room, on a beanbag big enough for both of us, with Gus curling up at our feet. I crack open the familiar picture book, clear my throat dramatically, and begin.

I start off in my normal voice, but when the fox talks, I drop my tone to a sly, wheedling whisper. Finn giggles so I lean into it. For the mouse, I go tiny and squeaky; for the owl, high and hooty; and for the snake, I add a ridiculous hissing lisp. By the time I get to the Gruffalo himself—complete with a growly monster voice that makes Gus lift his head in alarm—Finn is cracking up, clutching his sides and giggling so hard he can barely catch his breath.

I'm not sure this is the "quiet time" Lachlan had in mind, but honestly? I haven't had this much fun in months. There's something pure and joyful about sharing a story like this. No marketing meetings, no target demographics, no worrying about whether it'll perform well in the marketplace. Just the simple magic of words and voices and a kid who thinks you're the funniest person alive.

It reminds me of those long summer afternoons with Granny in Toronto, curled up on her couch while she read to me in different voices. She used to make the Three Bears sound like a gruff Scottish family, and her Little Red Riding Hood had a very posh English accent. I'd beg her to read the same stories over and over because I loved the way she brought them to life.

Maybe that's what Finn and I will do this summer. Maybe we'll build our own tradition of stories and silly voices.

When we finish the book, Finn smiles contentedly. "I really like that story."

"I could tell. Have you read all the stories on your bookshelf?"

He nods. "Loads of times. Da reads to me every night, but he doesn't do the voices like you do. He just reads them normally."

Of course he does. I can't imagine Captain Grumpypants doing a squeaky mouse voice.

"It's nice to read a story you already know you're going to love," I say, "but it's also nice to read something new. How about tomorrow we swing by the library, see my friend Ellie, and borrow some new books for you to read? Sound good?"

Finn's eyes light up. "Aye!" Then: "I didn't know you had a friend in Ardmara."

"Well, I do. Two friends, actually."

"Who?"

"Ellie—and you, of course."

The smile that spreads across Finn's face could power the entire town.

CHAPTER EIGHT

LACHLAN

I push through the front door, shrugging off the day's tension, braced for the usual chaos of boy and dog hurtling towards me like I've been gone a year instead of a day.

Nothing.

"Hello?" I call, tossing my keys onto the hall table. The clatter sounds too loud in the silence. No thunder of paws on the floorboards, no shout of "Da!" Strange. Gus never misses my homecoming. The daft beast has an internal clock set to four on the dot.

I wander through to the kitchen and stop short.

Christ.

Dishes piled in the sink. Flour dusted across the work surface. What looks like cookie dough welded to the side of my mixer.

Baking? That sure as hell wasn't on today's schedule. A tea towel lies crumpled on the floor, and something sticky is smeared across the table.

I run a hand through my hair, jaw tightening. Really? I don't want to come home after eight hours of running a ferry to find my kitchen looking like a bomb has gone off.

Muffled voices drift down from upstairs—Blair's, mostly, doing some sort of theatrical performance by the sound of it. I follow the noise up to Finn's room, where his door stands ajar.

Through the gap, I can see them settled in the corner on his beanbag. Blair's got *Zog* open across her lap, and she's putting on quite the show. Big booming lines for Madame Dragon, squeaky ones for the pupils, even a croaky growl when Zog takes a tumble. Finn's in stitches, actual tears on his cheeks.

And there's Gus, the traitor, lying on his back with his legs in the air while Finn rubs his belly. The dog's in absolute heaven, a happy grumble rumbling through the room. Well, that explains why he didn't come running when I got home.

I find myself leaning against the doorframe, oddly transfixed. I've read that book to Finn a hundred times, but never like this. I just . . . read it. Normal voice, normal pace. Gets the job done, and Finn enjoys it well enough. But watching him now, gasping for breath, it's clear this is something different.

Then Blair glances towards the door and spots me, and just like that, the magic stops.

"Oh! Hi." She closes the book, a little flustered. "We were just—"

"Finishing up," I say, stepping into the room. My voice comes out sharper than I intended, but the kitchen downstairs is still fresh in my mind. "Finn, how was your day?"

"Brilliant!" He bounces on the beanbag. "We went to the park and I saw Logan and Rosie, and we got top hats from the Lighthouse Café, and Blair does the best voices ever, and—"

"Sounds like you had quite the adventure." I look pointedly at Blair. "Though I noticed the kitchen isn't quite how I left it."

Her face falls. "Oh God, yes, I'm so sorry. I-I'll go do the dishes right now."

The apology is immediate and genuine, but I'm already wound up. I'm probably overreacting but I can't seem to stop myself. "No, you won't, because I'm only paying you until four. Besides, when I get home, I want to be able to relax in my own house with just me and my son and my dog."

Something flashes in Blair's eyes, and for a second I think she's going to give me both barrels. Her mouth opens and I brace myself.

But then she swallows whatever she was about to say and nods stiffly. "Of course. I'll make sure to keep things tidier tomorrow. That is, assuming I haven't already lost the job?"

"No," I confirm. "But you're still very much on trial."

Gus finally gets up and pads over to me, nudging at my leg with his nose. I ignore him for now. Not the time for behind-the-ear scratches and a chat about his day.

"Right. Well," Blair says, standing and smoothing down her jeans. "I'll see you tomorrow morning, then."

She gives Finn a quick smile then slips past me and down the stairs. The back door clicks shut behind her.

The silence stretches. Finn scowls at me.

"Finn—" I start, but he scrambles off the beanbag and digs through his toy box like a lad on a mission. Then he turns to me, wielding a bright orange Nerf gun, and—

Thwack.

The foam dart nails me square in the chest then bounces off to land at my feet.

"You were mean to Blair!"

Christ. A minute ago he was laughing his head off, completely content. Now he's firing projectiles at me like I'm the enemy.

"Look, Finn, I'm paying her to keep an eye on you, not to make a big mess I have to tidy up when I get home."

"But . . . but . . ." His lower lip juts out in that stubborn way that means he's really upset.

This isn't how things usually go between us. Finn and I get along. We're a team. But here he is, glaring at me like I've committed some unforgivable sin.

Right. Time to reset.

I drop into a crouch and hold my arms out wide, wiggling my fingers menacingly. "Oh no . . . I think I feel the tickle monster coming . . ."

Finn's scowl wavers. "Da, no . . ."

"Aye! The tickle monster is here, and he's looking for little boys who fire darts at their fathers!"

I lunge forwards, and Finn shrieks with laughter, dodging around his bed. "No! Not the tickle monster!"

"There's no escape!" I chase him around the room, Gus bouncing alongside us, barking excitedly and trying to join in the game. When I finally catch Finn, I scoop him up and tickle his ribs until he's giggling so hard he can barely breathe.

"Okay, okay!" he gasps. "I surrender!"

I set him down, and he's grinning again, the earlier tension forgotten. That's more like it.

"Right then," I say, ruffling his hair. "We'd better start thinking about dinner. But first, we've got some tidying up to do downstairs. Why were you two baking anyway?"

"We made cookies for Flora," Finn explains, following me down the stairs. "Because she can't bake anymore with her hurt wrist, and I felt bad about that. We made some for you too, for after dinner. And maybe *I* can have one after dinner?"

Something twists in my chest. They made cookies for Flora.

And for me. Shit, that was a nice thing to do, and yet I tore into Blair. Was I too harsh on her?

Maybe. Okay, yes. But then the whole point of hiring help is to make my life easier, not harder. I can't come home every day to a load of dishes to do.

I fill up the basin while Finn chatters away about his day. He talks while I wash dishes and he dries them. He talks while I prep the salmon and he scrubs the potatoes. He talks while we eat. Even with his mouth full of potato—which I'd normally tell him off for—he won't stop going on about Blair.

"And she knows all about *How to Train Your Dragon*. All the films and all the books. And she said we can go to the library tomorrow to get some new stories, and—"

"Slow down there, lad. Chew your food."

But he barely pauses for breath. "She's really funny too. She told me not to spill my soup on my pants, but she meant trousers, and we both laughed at that. And—and I really like her smile, Da."

I nearly choke on a forkful of salmon. Christ, isn't he a bit young to be noticing things like that?

But then I think about Blair's smile—how it lights her whole face, how those pale blue eyes crinkle at the corners—and I have to admit he's got a point.

"Aye, Finn," I say carefully. "She does have a nice smile."

Too nice, probably. And those long legs in her jeans, and the way she moves with that easy American confidence . . .

I shake my head. Where the hell did that come from?

After dinner we try the cookies. Sweet, chewy . . . annoyingly good, really. Which only twists the knife about how I spoke to Blair earlier.

Even through bath time and the bedtime routine, Finn

doesn't stop talking about her. He's full of plans for tomorrow: the library visit, art time, maybe another trip to the park. One day together, and apparently they're best friends.

Christ. If this is what ignoring the schedule looks like, maybe it's not as important as I thought.

When I finally get him settled in bed with *The Gruffalo*, he's still at it.

"Blair knows loads about books because she used to work with them. And she said—"

"Finn." I hold up the book. "Story time now. We can talk more about Blair tomorrow."

He nods but fidgets against his pillow. "Da? Can you do the voices like Blair does?"

The question hits me in the chest, just like that Nerf dart earlier. I've been reading to this boy every night for years. And now, after one day with that American lass, apparently I'm not good enough anymore.

"Don't you like the way I normally read them?" I say, probably more defensively than I should.

"I do, but Blair makes them sound so funny. The snake goes like this." He attempts a hissing voice then bursts into giggles.

I force a smile and open the book. "Right, then. Let's just read the story, shall we?"

But even as I start reading, my mind drifts. One day. She's been here one bloody day, and already Finn's looking at me like I'm a boring parent who doesn't know how to make story time fun.

When I close the book, Finn goes back to chattering about what he and Blair are going to do tomorrow, and I have to cut him off.

"If you want to do all these fun things with Blair without

76

getting grumpy, you'll need your sleep. Time to stop talking and shut your eyes."

◆ ◆ ◆

I pace around the kitchen for ten minutes after putting Finn to bed, replaying the whole bloody mess in my head. The way Blair's face fell when I snapped at her. Finn shooting me with his Nerf gun . . .

Christ, I was an arse. She did something thoughtful, something that made my son happy, and I tore into her for making a mess. The right thing to do would be to apologise. Not my strong suit, but there it is.

Before I can talk myself out of it, I'm out the back door and walking the path to the granny flat. Light glows in the window. Right. Here goes nothing. I knock, maybe harder than necessary, but only because my nerves are getting the better of me.

"Just a second!" Blair's voice is muffled through the door, then I hear footsteps.

The door opens, and Christ alive, I should have thought this through better.

She's in her pyjamas: thin cotton shorts riding high on long legs and a top that clings to every curve and hollow, leaving nothing to the imagination. Her nipples are tight against the fabric, clear as day, and for a second I'm frozen. All higher brain functions go offline while my body reacts like I'm eighteen again.

Eyes up. Eyes up! For God's sake, man, look at her bloody face!

But her face throws me too, because she's gazing at me with a mixture of surprise and wariness, nothing like the easy warmth she showed Finn earlier. I've well and truly wiped that away.

"Lachlan." She crosses her arms over her chest, probably

trying for modesty, though all it does is draw my attention back to what she's trying to hide. My throat goes dry. I force myself to look anywhere but there, scrambling to remember why I came out here in the first place.

"Didn't think I'd be getting any visitors. You made it clear after four o'clock it's just you, your son, and your dog."

I nod dumbly, fighting the urge to stare at my boots like an awkward teenager. "Aye, well . . ." I swallow and focus determinedly on a spot just over her left shoulder. "Look, I just wanted to say . . . sorry. I was a bit off with you earlier."

"No, you were crystal clear. You don't want to come home to dishes, and I told you, it won't happen again."

"Aye, but . . ." I tap my knuckles against the doorframe. "I could have been a bit more polite about it."

"Yeah, you could have."

I catch a whiff of something floral—her shampoo, maybe. *No, Lachlan, stop getting distracted.*

"Aye, well, that's all I wanted to say. Oh, and thank you. Finn had a good time today. Hasn't shut up about you all night."

A ghost of a smile crosses her lips, there and gone so quickly I almost miss it.

"And that was a nice thing you did," I continue, the words coming easier now. "Dropping in baking for Flora. Thanks for that. And obviously, if you go to the shops to buy anything, like ingredients for baking, I'll cover all that. You just tell me how much I owe you."

"Understood. Well, if that's everything . . . good night, captain." A hint of mischief curling her lips, she eases the door shut, like she's having the last word. Which, of course, she is.

CHAPTER NINE

LACHLAN

The windscreen wipers battle the rain as I pull into our driveway. Another grey Scottish Saturday, the kind that makes you grateful for a warm house and nowhere to be. We've just been at the Pit—soft play with Struan, Douglas, and their bairns, our usual weekend ritual—and my ears are still ringing from the noise. A quiet afternoon at home will do me just fine.

"Right then, lad," I say, switching off the engine. "What's it to be? We could stick on a film, maybe build that Lego castle you've been on about, or—"

"Can we ask Blair to join us?"

I blink, caught off-guard. Not the answer I was expecting. "Blair doesn't work weekends, remember? She gets her own time."

Finn unbuckles his seat belt but doesn't move to get out of the car. Instead, he turns those big brown eyes on me. "But she's probably lonely in the granny flat all by herself. And it's raining, so she can't even go for walks or anything."

Blair's second and third day with Finn went well, so she's

officially his nanny for the summer. But that doesn't mean I want her encroaching on our weekend time.

"Blair's a grown-up, Finn. She can take care of herself. Besides, I was looking forward to some time with just my boy." I ruffle his hair. "Come on, let's get inside. You'll have to run—you don't want to get soaked."

We make a dash for the front door, and once we're inside, I shake the water from my jacket while Finn kicks off his muddy trainers. Gus dances around us, thrilled to have his people home again.

"So," I say, hanging my jacket on the hook by the door, "what's it to be? A film? Lego?"

"Hmm . . ." Apparently, neither of those options are grabbing his interest. "Maybe we could build another fort?" he suggests finally, though his tone is flat and there's none of the usual spark in his eyes.

"Aye, brilliant idea," I say with more enthusiasm than he's giving me. "We could make it even bigger than the last one. Enough room for you, me, *and* Gus this time."

"And Blair?"

There it is again. I bite back my irritation and crouch down to his level. "Look, son, Blair's with you Monday to Friday. Weekends are when she gets a break, and when you and I get our time together. Just the two of us, like always."

His brow furrows, like he's trying to puzzle something out that doesn't make sense. "Are you saying she only likes being with me because it's her job?"

Christ. How do you explain to a six-year-old that the world is complicated, that people can care about you and still need to be paid to spend time with you?

"It's not that simple, lad. Blair does get paid to look after you, aye, but that doesn't mean she doesn't enjoy it. But even people who like their jobs need time off. And I like spending time with you too, you know. You're my favourite person in the whole world."

Finn considers this, chewing on his lower lip the way he does when he's thinking hard. "Okay," he says finally. "Can we still make the fort?"

"Absolutely."

We build this one in the living room for extra space, but even as we gather supplies—blankets from the cupboard, cushions from the sofa, chairs from the kitchen—I can tell his heart isn't in it. He goes through the motions, helping me drape the blankets and arrange the cushions, but there's no excitement in it. No joy.

Twenty minutes later we've got a decent fort set up. Not bad, if I do say so myself. Gus has already claimed a corner as his own, circling twice before settling down with a contented huff.

"Right then," I say, crawling inside and patting the space beside me. "What happens in here now we've finished it?"

But Finn doesn't follow me in. He sits cross-legged outside the entrance, picking at a loose thread on one of the cushions.

"Finn? You coming in?"

"I think I'll just go to my room," he says quietly.

My heart sinks. "What? But we just built this. Don't you want to—"

"I'm just tired." He stands. "Maybe later."

And with that, he trudges upstairs, leaving me sitting alone in our blanket fort like a proper fool. Even Gus looks at me with something that might be pity.

Sighing, I crawl out of the fort, haul myself up, then head through to the kitchen. I flick the kettle on, and while it rumbles away, I grab myself a mug, toss in a teabag, and get the milk ready. I'll give him a bit of time before I go up and see how he's doing.

I carry my tea through to the living room, but I've only taken a few sips when the front door creaks open and a voice calls, bright but hesitant, "Hello? Lachlan?"

Frowning, I set the mug aside and get to my feet. Gus is first into the hall and I follow him to find Blair, rain-spattered and smiling faintly, with Finn at her side, his hair damp, his shoes leaving wee puddles on the mat.

What the—? When did he even leave the house? I didn't hear a thing. Must've been when the kettle was boiling. The cheeky wee bugger actually sneaked out to see her.

"Sorry to interrupt," Blair says, patting a very happy Gus, "but Finn turned up at my door."

"Finn!" I run a hand down my face. "You can't just wander off without telling me. And you definitely can't bother Blair when she's not working."

"But I'm not bothering her! Blair said she *does* like spending time with me." He says it with pride, like he's just cracked the case of the century.

"Of course I do." Blair crouches to Finn's level and ruffles his damp hair. "You're a cool dude." She glances up at me. "I told Finn that, yes, I do get paid to look after him, but some people are just lucky enough to get paid to spend time with their favourite people."

Finn beams, delighted.

Didn't I say near enough the same thing twenty minutes ago? Yet somehow when *she* says it, he gets it.

"Right, well, thanks for clearing that up," I say. "But we should let you get back to—"

"Can Blair come in?" Finn interrupts. "Blair, we built a fort and it's the biggest one ever. You could be the princess!"

"Finn, no, Blair's got her own things to do. We can't—"

"Honestly, I don't mind." Blair stands and brushes raindrops off her jacket. "I was just reading, and it's pretty nasty out there anyway."

"See, Da? She wants to come in."

I find myself caught between my son's pleading eyes and Blair's amused smile. The smart thing would be to stick to my guns, maintain the boundaries. But Finn looks so hopeful and Blair seems genuinely happy to be here, and I'm starting to feel like a right bastard for trying to keep them apart.

"I suppose . . ." I say. "If you're sure you don't mind."

"I'm sure." Blair shrugs out of her damp jacket, and I take it and hang it on the hook next to mine.

"Right," I say. "Er . . . can I get you a tea? Coffee?"

"Oh, that would be—"

"Come on!" Finn grabs Blair's hand and pulls her towards the living room. "Come see the castle!"

And just like that, any hope of normal adult conversation is gone. Blair lets herself be dragged away, laughing at Finn's enthusiasm, and I follow behind like a spare part in my own house.

"Wow," Blair says after taking in the fort. "This is incredible, Finn. It's like a real medieval castle."

"It is, isn't it?" When Gus pads back into the fort, Finn adds, "Gus is the guard dog. Every castle needs one."

"So what happens in this castle?" Blair asks, settling on the floor.

"Well, we could play knights and dragons." Finn's eyes light up with the spark that was missing earlier. "I'll be the knight, you can be the princess, and Da can be the dragon. But not a nice one like Zog, Da. A scary one. Okay?"

Playing make-believe with my son? Fine. Normal. Expected, even. But with an audience? With *her* watching me crawl around on the floor making dragon noises? The thought makes my skin crawl.

"I don't know, lad. Maybe—"

"Oh, come on," Blair says, grinning up at me. "Don't tell me the big scary ferry captain is afraid of a little role-playing."

There's a challenge in her voice, and something about it makes my jaw clench. "I'm not afraid of anything."

"Prove it."

Finn claps his hands together. "This is going to be brilliant." He points to the fort. "Get in, Blair! The princess is trapped in the tower, and the dragon is guarding her, and I have to rescue her."

Blair plays along immediately and crawls into the fort, then peers out at us. "Oh no!" she cries in an exaggerated damsel-in-distress voice. "I'm trapped! Normally, I'd karate-kick the dragon myself, but I'm a little under the weather, so . . . rescue required."

Finn giggles and brandishes an imaginary sword. "Don't worry, Princess Blair! Sir Finn is here to save you."

Both of them look at me expectantly. Christ. This is ridiculous. I'm a grown man. I don't do this sort of thing in front of people.

But Finn's face is so hopeful, and Blair's watching me with that amused smile, and before I know what I'm doing, I'm dropping into a crouch and letting out a tentative growl.

"That's it, Da. But scarier!"

Right. No point half-arsing it. I take a deep breath and properly roar, loud enough to make Gus jump and Blair's eyes go wide with surprise.

"The dragon guards the princess!" I bellow in my best monster voice. "No one may pass."

Finn shrieks with delight and charges forwards with his imaginary sword. "I challenge you, dragon!"

And suddenly I'm chasing my son around the living room, roaring and stomping, while he squeals and dodges and Blair cheers him on from the fort. It's completely mad, but Finn is laughing so hard he can barely stay upright, and despite myself I'm starting to enjoy it.

"The knight is quick," I roar, lunging for Finn and missing deliberately. "But the dragon is quicker."

"Run, Sir Finn!" Blair calls out. "He's gaining on you."

Ten minutes later, we're all breathless and laughing. Finn has "defeated" the dragon (me lying dramatically on the floor, tongue lolling out), rescued the princess, and saved the kingdom. Blair is clapping and cheering, and Finn looks like he might burst with pride.

"That was amazing, Da," he says, throwing himself down next to me. "You're the best dragon ever."

I sit up and run a hand through my hair. "Aye, well, don't tell the other dragons. They'll get jealous. Anyway, as fun as that was, I reckon it's time for Blair to head back to the flat. She's probably got things to do, and we need to start thinking about din—"

"No!" Finn jumps up, his face falling. "She can't go yet."

"Finn—"

"Can Blair stay for dinner?" he asks, those big brown eyes doing their thing. "Please?"

Blair laughs awkwardly and holds up her hands. "Oh wow, that's really sweet of you, but I should—"

"*Please?*" Finn turns to her now, and I can see her resolve wavering. "It's silly for you to go eat by yourself when we're eating here. We should all eat together."

Christ. Can't argue with that logic, but . . .

I look at Blair, hoping she'll decline and save me from this awkwardness. Instead she watches me with raised eyebrows, waiting for *my* response.

"Fine," I mutter. "Blair can stay if she wants."

Finn whirls back to Blair, practically bouncing on the spot as he waits for her answer.

"In that case," she says, "I accept."

Well, shit. How has this happened? This is supposed to be our space—me, my boy, and the dog. No one else. And yet here she is, slotting herself in like she belongs.

I'm pretty sure she knows exactly how uncomfortable this makes me. Maybe that's why she's staying—payback for all my grumpiness.

If so, well played, Blair. Well played.

◆ ◆ ◆

In the kitchen Blair asks, "So, what's on the menu?"

"It's a Saturday, so . . . spaghetti bolognese," Finn says.

"You have that every Saturday?"

Finn nods solemnly. "Aye. Sundays are roast chicken, Mondays are chilli con carne, Tuesdays are baked potatoes . . ."

"Really?" Blair turns to me, genuinely surprised. "And you never change it up?"

I pull the mince from the fridge and set it on the work surface. "Makes shopping simple. I know what I'm cooking, and I know we're eating well."

"Sure, but . . ." She tilts her head, studying me. "Don't you ever want to mix things up a bit? Try something new?"

I shrug, already reaching for the onions. "Not really."

But as I begin to chop them, I catch Finn leaning towards Blair, cupping his hand around his mouth. "I do," he says in what he probably thinks is a subtle whisper. "I'm *so* bored of chilli."

The little traitor even rolls his eyes. Isn't he a bit young to be giving me attitude about my perfectly sensible approach to family nutrition?

"Right," I say. "Finn, you can help me with the bolognese. Blair, if you want to make yourself useful, the cutlery is in that drawer there."

Soon Finn is on his usual stool beside me, stirring the onions and garlic while I add the mince to the pan. Blair moves around the kitchen setting the table, and I try not to notice how naturally she navigates the space, opening the cupboard to grab plates like she's been here for months, not days. She didn't need me to point out the cutlery drawer. Gus does circuits between us, sniffing at Blair's heels before trotting back to check for dropped food.

"Can you put my place next to yours?" Finn asks Blair.

Really? He normally sits next to me. But I'm thirty-one, not six—I'm not about to sulk about my pal choosing another seat. Not much anyway. I add the tinned tomatoes to the pan.

Once the sauce has been bubbling for a bit, I dip the wooden spoon in for a taste. Needs a bit more seasoning but it's getting there.

"Here," I say, offering Finn the spoon. "What do you think?"

He tastes it seriously, considering. "Mmm. Good, but maybe a wee bit more salt?"

"Aye, I think you're right." I add a pinch more and give it another stir.

"Let Blair have the next taste," Finn suggests.

Letting Finn taste off the spoon is one thing. Letting her? Feels . . . different. Too bloody intimate. I jab the spoon back into the pan, staring at the sauce like it's the most fascinating thing I've ever seen.

"Da?" Finn prompts.

Nope, not happening. I taste another spoonful and nod with finality. "There you go. Perfect."

Finn frowns. "Blair, Da's being weird and won't give you his spoon, but here—" He rummages in the drawer, comes up with another, and hands it to her. "You can use this one."

Blair steps closer, amusement tugging at her lips. She takes the spoon, tastes the sauce, and I definitely don't watch the way her mouth closes around it. Definitely not. If my face feels hot, it's just the steam from the pan. That's all.

"Mmm, that's really good," she says. "Perfect amount of salt."

The spaghetti is ready a few minutes later, and I plate up: three for us and one for Flora, with another plate on top of hers to keep it warm.

I glance out the window. Looks like there's a break in the rain, so I tell Finn to get his shoes on then hand him Flora's portion. "Right, wee man. Can you take this round to Flora for me?"

"Aye, Da." He takes it carefully in both hands, and I hold the back door open for him.

"Don't run," I warn. "You'll spill it everywhere."

I close the door again behind him, leaving Blair and me alone in the kitchen. The silence stretches, filled only by the sound of Gus's hopeful panting and the tick of the wall clock.

"That was nice of you," Blair says finally.

"What was?"

"Looking out for your neighbour like that. Even grumpy ferry captains have their soft spots, apparently."

I raise an eyebrow at that, but she smiles innocently.

"Flora's been very good to us over the years. It's the least I can do."

"Still, it's sweet. Very . . . community-minded."

"Hmm." I turn to the hob and busy myself wiping it down.

A minute later the back door bursts open and Finn crashes back in, cheeks flushed, obviously having run the whole way back.

"Flora says thank you and that it smells brilliant," he announces, kicking his shoes off. "Can we eat now? I'm starving."

We settle around the kitchen table and tuck in.

"Wow, this is really good," Blair says after her first bite. "You two are a great team."

Finn beams proudly.

"It's just bolognese," I mutter, twirling spaghetti around my fork.

"Still, it's delicious." She nods toward the window. "And what a view to eat it with. I bet you never get tired of looking out at the water."

I glance out at the grey sea, choppy with whitecaps. "It's all right."

Christ, I sound like a right misery. But something about having her here, in our space, at our table, has me on edge. This is where Finn and I have our best conversations, where he tells me about his day, where we make our plans. It's ours.

Finn, thankfully, seems oblivious to the tension. He's already got sauce around his mouth and is slurping up long strands of spaghetti, not a care in the world.

"Finn," I warn. "Manners."

"But it's more fun this way." He demonstrates by sucking up an especially long piece, which snaps back and flicks sauce onto his chin. Blair laughs, the sound warm and easy.

Finn isn't the only one playing up. Gus positions himself by Blair's chair, chin resting on her thigh, angling for scraps.

"Gus, no begging," I say.

"It's okay." Blair reaches down to give him a pat. "He's not bothering me."

"Trust me, he's shameless. Don't encourage him."

"All right. Sorry, Gus. This princess isn't sharing with the castle guard dog. But Finn, why don't we tell your dad about our adventure at the library on Thursday?"

And just like that, Finn's off. Between mouthfuls, he gives an animated account of their trip to see Blair's friend Ellie, how they picked out new books, how Blair helped him find a series about Vikings he's now obsessed with.

He doesn't stop there, though. He tells me all about the other stuff they've got up to these past few days, with Blair chiming in now and then, reminding him of things he's left out, like their failed attempts to teach Gus new tricks, or the hot chocolates they sipped down at the harbour. Soon the two of them are talking over each other in their excitement, swapping memories and nudging each other's laughter along until it's like I'm eavesdropping on a secret world they've built together.

And as awkward as it feels having Blair in our space, I've got to admit I enjoy these glimpses into my boy's days. Aye, I heard bits and pieces the last few evenings from Finn, but Blair has this way of telling stories that makes me feel like I was there, experiencing it all alongside them. She remembers the little details, and finds humour and wonder in ordinary moments.

It's a gift, really. Her ease with words, her ability to bring stories to life. No wonder she used to work with books.

Plus, she's clearly already had a positive impact on Finn. There's something about him tonight—more confidence, more chatter, more of everything. And aye, I get it. A pretty American lass giving him her undivided attention day after day? That'd put any boy in a good mood.

I've not exactly been great at welcoming Blair, but maybe I could start by being less of a monosyllabic bastard. Ease off, just a little.

"Sounds like you two have crammed a lot into three days," I say. "And Vikings, eh? Did you know they made themselves at home on these shores for a few hundred years?"

Blair's eyes brighten. "*Really?* I wonder if any of their descendants are still around. Anyone in this town grumpy, gruff, and fond of travelling by boat?"

Finn snorts with laughter, nearly choking on his spaghetti. "That's you, Da!"

I shake my head, but damned if a reluctant smile doesn't tug at my mouth.

The laughter dies down, and for a minute we're all busy with our plates. Then Finn, out of nowhere, looks at Blair and says, "Do you have a boyfriend?"

Wow, where did *that* come from?

Blair chuckles. "Uh, no. No boyfriend."

"Why not?" Finn probes.

"Finn," I say. "That's not something you ask."

"Oh." He shrugs and gives Blair an apologetic smile. "Sorry."

"No need to apologise." Blair gives him a smile back, the same one Finn told me the other day he likes. Warm, bright, too bloody easy to look at.

And damn if I'm not more interested than I should be in Blair's declaration that she doesn't have a boyfriend. Unhelpfully, an image flashes through my mind—Wednesday night, Blair at the door of the granny flat, those skimpy pyjamas clinging to her body, the outline of her nipples clear through the thin fabric. My pulse quickens, and a flush of heat crawls up my neck.

Christ, Lachlan. She's the nanny. You're her employer. What the hell is wrong with you?

I focus on my plate, twirling my spaghetti like it's the most fascinating thing in the world. Finn's chatter fills the silence, but I'm only half listening, too busy telling myself off for letting my head go where it bloody shouldn't.

After we're all done, I waste no time collecting our dishes and dumping them by the sink. "All right, lad. How about you and me watch a bit of telly before we start the bedtime routine, eh?"

Finn nods enthusiastically. "Can Blair stay too? And can she do my story tonight? She's so good at it."

His words land like a kick in the gut. Bedtime is *our* thing. My one constant with my boy, no matter what else the day throws at us. And now he wants her instead?

But before I can say anything, Blair steps in. "Oh, I'd better get going, but I've had the best time with you today, Finn. Besides, we both heard your dad's dragon impression earlier. He can do voices when he wants to. So tonight, when you're snuggled up in bed for a story, you tell him, 'Da, you have to do the voices, for *all* the characters.' Okay?"

Finn giggles and glances my way. "Will you do the voices, Da?"

Well, shite. I don't know whether to feel grateful to Blair for excusing herself, or annoyed at this sneaky wee move. How's a father meant to keep his son's respect when he's squeaking like a mouse or shrieking like a frightened princess?

Still, Finn's so tickled by the idea that all I can do is say, "Aye, fine. I'll give it a shot."

Finn is delighted. I shoot Blair an unamused look. She smiles right back at me, fluttering her eyelashes with mock innocence.

Bloody woman.

CHAPTER TEN

BLAIR

I'm back in the granny flat, changed into my pyjamas—soft cotton shorts and a matching top—and still a little bemused by how well today turned out. Who knew an afternoon of forts and dragon battles with a six-year-old could leave me grinning hours later? And his grumpy father actually joined in. That part still makes me shake my head.

At the little table by the window, I sit with a candle flickering beside me, its warm vanilla scent filling the air. It's just for vibes, not visibility. The sun takes forever to set here.

Pen in hand, notebook on the table, I'm mulling over possible story ideas. There's something about this place—the wild Scottish coastline, the tightknit community, the slower pace of life—that's got my creative juices flowing. I've always wanted to write my own stories. Back in New York, between manuscript deadlines and acquisition meetings, there was never time, but I told myself I'd get to it someday. When things slowed down. Well, I have time now, but none of the ideas I've come up with so far feel right. None of them make me think, *Yes, this is the story I need to tell*.

I tap my pen against the paper, frustrated. It turns out

wanting to write and having something worth writing about are two very different things.

A knock at the door interrupts my war with the blank page. I stand and open it to find Lachlan on my doorstep, hands shoved deep in his pockets.

"Oh! Hi." Heat creeps up my neck as I realise this is the second time he's seen me in my pyjamas, and they're only one step up from underwear.

I cross my arms over my chest. Doesn't stop him sneaking a glance at my boobs before quickly looking away, his jaw tight.

Great. Just what I needed to make this interaction even more awkward.

"Sorry to bother you," he says, his gaze now fixed somewhere over my shoulder. "But I wanted to apologise. About today, I mean. Making you work on what was supposed to be your day off. I know you didn't sign up for Saturday duties, so I'll be paying you extra. Overtime rates, since it was the weekend."

I shake my head. "Absolutely not."

"Blair—"

"I went along voluntarily, I enjoyed myself, and you treated me to a tasty dinner. I don't expect payment for that."

He meets my eye and studies me, like he's trying to figure out if I'm being serious or just polite. Whatever he sees in my expression must convince him because he nods slowly.

"All right. Well, thank you. For today. Finn had a brilliant time, and I . . . ." He trails off then clears his throat. "I should let you get back to whatever you were doing."

He's already turning to leave when I hear myself say, "Do you want to come in for a hot drink?"

He hesitates. "I don't want to intrude."

"It's not intruding if it's an invitation. If I had something stronger, I'd offer that, but I've no drinks cabinet yet."

I fully expect him to turn me down. Instead he says, "I've got whisky and beer in the house. I could fetch us something?"

"Full disclosure," I say, wincing, "I'm not a big fan of Scotch."

His mouth twitches, almost amused. "What kind of blasphemy is that? You're in Scotland, lass."

Lass? I kinda like that.

"I know. But it just tastes like . . . I don't know, liquid campfire? Mind you, it's been a while since I tried it, so . . . okay. I'll give it another shot."

"Right answer. I'll be back in a minute."

While he's gone, I take the opportunity to pull on a baggy hoodie, eliminating the risk of any further boob-related distractions.

He returns with a bottle of Scotch and two glasses, which he sets on the table. "Let's see if we can convert you." He pours two measures, hands me one, and we settle at the table, facing each other. "This is a proper Highland single malt. None of that blended rubbish. Try it."

I take a tentative sip and immediately start coughing. "Oh God, that's—" I wheeze, eyes watering. "That's terrible."

Lachlan laughs—a real laugh, warm and unguarded. "Don't gulp it. Let it sit on your tongue. Like this." He demonstrates, taking a small sip and holding it in his mouth before swallowing.

I try again. This time I manage not to choke, though I still make a face. "It's marginally less terrible?"

"Progress," he says drily. "Give it time. It's an acquired taste."

"Like you?" The words slip out before I can stop them. "I mean—sorry, that came out wrong."

But he doesn't look offended. If anything, he looks intrigued. "An acquired taste, am I?"

"Well, you have to admit, you weren't exactly welcoming when we first met."

"That's fair. I'm not great with new people."

"You don't say."

A sly grin tugs at his mouth. Sitting this close, I can't help but notice details I've missed before: a touch of silver at his temples, ginger threads in his beard, the lines etched between his brows from years of scowling at the world.

"Not like you, of course," he says. "You seem like the sort who can make friends with anyone. Humans, plants . . ." His gaze shifts to the windowsill. "Gerald, wasn't it?"

"Hey, don't mock Gerald. He was lonely at the shop, practically begging me with his little leaves. I rescued him."

Smirking, Lachlan takes in the rest of the granny flat: the flickering vanilla candle, the cheerful throw draped across the bed, the postcards I've been collecting on my wanderings with Finn. "You've made this place homely."

"No harm in giving a place a bit of personality, right? Unlike your house." I arch an eyebrow. "No offence, but apart from Finn's room, it looks like a show home. How long have you been there?"

"Four years. Before that, I was on Corraig." He nods toward the window, where the island looms faintly on the horizon. "Grew up there. I moved here when . . ." He trails off.

I hesitate. Should I let it go? That'd probably be wise, but apparently I'm not wired for wise. "Finn's mom?"

He nods. "We were childhood sweethearts. After she passed . . . well, I needed a change of scene. Couldn't face staying on the island."

97

The confession blindsides me. Lachlan's a widower. That changes things. Explains the gruffness. Doesn't excuse it—not entirely—but suddenly I see the man differently.

I'd assumed he was divorced. Why did I jump to that conclusion? Because it was easy to imagine his prickliness driving a woman away? Probably. But it might also have been because there aren't any traces of a woman in his house. Not a single photo of his childhood sweetheart, Finn's mom. Not that there are pictures of Lachlan or Finn up either—only Finn's drawings on the cork board.

Some doors you barge through. Others, even I can see they should stay shut, at least for now. So I don't dig into the absence of photos. Instead I tip my head and say, a little curiously, "Let me get this straight. You left Corraig for a change of scene, and yet you sail to it every day?"

"Aye." His mouth twists ruefully. "Don't worry, the irony isn't lost on me."

His phone buzzes on the table, the lock screen lighting up with a photo of Finn and his gap-toothed grin. Oh, that's too sweet. Say what you like about Captain Grumpypants, he adores that kid. And Finn? He's thriving. That's all down to Lachlan.

"You can check that if you want," I say.

"Och, it'll just be Struan and Douglas, fellow single dads." He taps the notification anyway, then smirks and turns the phone toward me. The screen shows a kids' bedroom so buried in toys, I couldn't tell you what colour the carpet is.

> DOUGLAS
>
> Told them to play quietly. This is what I came back to after doing the dishes. 😩

"Good God," I say. "Forget bedtime. That's a war zone."

Lachlan's phone buzzes again and another photo comes in. This one shows a little girl fast asleep in a perfectly neat room.

STRUAN

> Meanwhile . . . like butter wouldn't melt.
> Parenting is a breeze, eh, lads?

Lachlan's lips twitch. "Struan only has his daughter at weekends, and she's an angel. He likes to rub our noses in it, but it's all good fun." He sets his phone back down, and as he does, his gaze lands on my notepad. "Old school. Most people use a device these days."

"Oh, that. Just dabbling with some story ideas. There's something about the feel of pen on paper."

"You write your own stories? Aye, that makes sense. Explains why Finn thinks you're the greatest storyteller alive."

The compliment warms my chest. "I'd *like* to write my own stories," I correct. "I've been brainstorming ideas but nothing's grabbed me yet. I thought about doing something with dragons—Finn would love that—but I can't think of a unique take. Besides, it has to appeal to me too, and honestly? Dragons don't fascinate me nearly as much as they do a certain six-year-old boy."

Lachlan nods then cocks his head and regards me like he's turning over a puzzle piece. "Stories, publishing, nannying. Bit of a mix, eh? At the interview I never did ask why you left New York to come here."

Ah. The dreaded question. I take another sip of Scotch—still awful, but maybe less so than before—and buy myself a second to think. "I needed a break," I say carefully. "Publishing can be pretty cut-throat, and I . . . burned out. My grandmother passed away earlier this year, and she always told me stories about growing up here. She lived in the house your friend Douglas is in now. Coming to Scotland felt right somehow."

All true. Just not the whole truth. I'm not ready to tell him about the app, the firing, the spectacular way my career went up in flames.

"So *that's* why you were peeking in Douglas's window the first time we met."

"Peeking is such an ugly word. I was . . . curious. Which is basically the same thing, I know, but it sounds way less creepy. Anyway, I'd love a proper tour at some point. You think Douglas would mind?"

"Nah, not at all. I'll introduce you. He's the one who sent through the photo of his kids' carnage."

"Yeah, I noticed the name. Pretty sure it didn't look like *that* when my granny lived there. She loved fun, but she wasn't a fan of mess, not that she was as much of a stickler as you are. I actually met Douglas's parents the other day at the playground. The twins too. Those two are wild, but they keep things interesting." They'd given their grandparents heart attacks by jumping from the top of the jungle gym. After that got banned, they moved on to launching themselves off the swings mid-air.

I finish off my Scotch, and this time I only slightly grimace.

Lachlan chuckles and nods at the bottle. "I take it you aren't for a top-up, then?"

"You know what? It might just be growing on me." I push my glass across the table. "Hit me. But you have to join me. I want to see what you're like when you're not all tense and in dad mode."

That earns me a proper laugh, and God help me, it's nice. Lachlan looks younger when he laughs, the worry lines smoothing away. For once he's just . . . a guy, not Captain Grumpypants.

"Careful," I tease. "Hide that smile before someone sees it. You'll lose your shot at the Grumpiest Man of Ardmara award."

Shaking his head, he refills our glasses.

"How old are you anyway?" I ask. A bit blunt, maybe, but I want to know.

"Thirty-one."

Only four years older than me. That's less of an age gap than I'd thought.

And now that I'm really looking at him . . . wow. His eyes are even greener than I realised, like sea glass caught in sunlight. No, not just green, but flecked with gold near the centre. His lashes are ridiculously dark for a man, his beard a whole ginger-brown situation, and the way his shirt stretches across his chest . . .

God, he's . . . something.

I'm staring. Definitely staring. *Abort, abort.*

I grab for my newly refilled glass, desperate for cover, and end up knocking it sideways instead. Scotch splashes across the table.

Smooth, Blair. Real smooth.

"Careful!" Lachlan reaches for the toppled glass at the same time I do, his hand covering mine, warm and rough. Distractingly so. My pulse spikes. He rights the glass then withdraws, leaving my skin tingling.

"You could've just said no to another drink," he jokes, standing to grab paper towels. "No need for theatrics. Or is the whisky hitting you already? Do you see one of me or two?"

"One of you is plenty," I mutter, my cheeks hot. *Especially now I've noticed just how damn attractive you are.* Time to change the subject to something safe and dull. "Uh . . . washing machine. Do I have borrowing privileges?"

He mops up the Scotch with swift, no-nonsense movements. Which, annoyingly, makes the muscles in his forearm flex in a way

I'm trying very hard not to notice. He really shouldn't look this good while cleaning up a spill.

"Oh, aye, of course. This place was a holiday let once. I thought about continuing that when I moved in but never got round to it. It's only set up for short stays, so no washing machine. Use the one in the house whenever you like."

He tosses the wet paper towels in the trash and reclaims his seat. "I've got a gym set up in the garage too. If you ever fancy a workout, go ahead."

Well, that explains the broad chest. And the arms that make wiping a table look like foreplay.

"Since you managed to spill your second glass before you even had a sip, I'd best top you up." He uncorks the bottle.

"Actually . . ." Hard liquor plus sudden awareness that Captain Grumpypants is kind of sexy? Dangerous combo. Better not. "On second thought, I'm good, thanks."

"Ah. Right, then." For a beat he looks disappointed. Then he drains his own glass, pushes back his chair, and stands. "I'll let you get back to your evening. Good night, Blair."

And then, unprompted, he smiles at me. An unguarded smile that hits me harder than the Scotch.

"Uh . . ." I swallow. "Good night."

And just like that, he's gone, leaving me with a flickering candle, the faint scent of Scotch in the air, and the startling thought that there's more to my grumpy boss than I realised.

CHAPTER ELEVEN

BLAIR

I wake up to sunlight streaming through a gap in my curtains—actual Highland sparkle, not the gloomy drizzle we had yesterday. Everything feels quiet, like the world's still deciding whether to wake up or roll over for another hour.

I sit up and yawn. Despite last night's Scotch experiment, my head is clear. I guess I did only manage one before christening the table.

Which reminds me . . . the way Lachlan's hand covered mine when we both reached for the glass . . .

Nope. Not going there. Fresh air, that's what I need.

Jeans, sweater, sneakers. Notebook, pen. Five minutes later I'm crunching across the pebble beach, the air so sharp and clean it practically exfoliates my lungs. I feel *awake*, and I've not even had a coffee yet.

I perch on a boulder that's just the right height for writing. It's like the Highlands want me to be productive. Pen, paper, waves. Zero algorithms, no tech-bro slogans about "minimum viable product" or other nonsense. Just me and my thoughts and a story waiting to be found.

I'm scribbling random observations—about how the water glitters like it's auditioning for a jewellery commercial, and how the seaweed looks like mermaid hair—when movement catches my eye. Something sleek and dark emerges from the water and onto a nearby rock.

No way.

An otter.

My jaw actually drops. I'm staring at a legit wild otter, water dripping off its whiskers. It shakes itself, droplets spraying in a perfect arc, then flops down to groom.

I freeze. Do. Not. Move. Apparently, I've been chosen by the otter gods, and I'm not about to blow it. For a good two minutes I watch this little guy roll in the sunshine, completely ignoring me. Then—*splash*—it's gone, leaving behind only a widening circle of ripples.

Okay, wow. That was . . . yeah. Magical.

I jot it all down. Sleek fur. Whiskers. The ripple-ring thing. Maybe my story will have an otter in it. Maybe—

"Blair!"

Finn barrels down the path from the house in his pyjamas, waving at me, Gus galloping ahead of him.

"Morning." I snap my notebook shut, just in case Gus decides it's his new chew toy, then give him a good scratch when he comes over to say hello. No sign of Lachlan. "Are you two allowed down here by yourselves?"

"Aye." Finn beams at me. "So long as we stay where my da can see us from the kitchen window and don't go too close to the water. Besides, we're not by ourselves. You're here!"

"True."

He sits himself down beside me and glances at my notebook. "What're you writing?"

"Just some ideas for a story. I think it might have an otter in it. I literally just saw one, right there." I point out the spot, and Finn's face goes through a whole journey of emotions: excitement, wonder, then something that looks suspiciously like outrage.

"You saw an otter? A real one?"

"Yeah, it came right up on that rock and—"

"I've lived here since I was two and I've never seen one. You've been here, like, a week!" Then, in a mutter: "So unfair."

I have to bite back a smile at his indignation. "Hey, I just got lucky. They're shy. Right place, right time."

"I suppose," he says, but he still doesn't look happy about it. After a moment, though, he perks up. "I know it's the weekend, but seeing as we did something together yesterday, do you think we could do something together again today?"

"Aw, Finn." His hopeful face just about kills me. "I'd love to, but I've already got plans. Ellie's offered to take me to a secret local spot she says tourists don't usually see."

"Oh."

"But hey, from tomorrow we've got the whole week together, right?"

"Aye." He picks up a stone and flings it into the water, watching the splash. "Will you at least tell me where Ellie takes you? So I can know about the secret spot too?"

"Absolutely. I'll even take photos."

"Okay." He stands. "I'm going to go get breakfast. Come on, Gus. Bye, Blair!"

They head up the path, Finn turning once to wave. I wave back then return to my notes.

So, a story about an otter. And maybe . . . a boy who's lived by the sea for years but never seen one?

◆ ◆ ◆

I pull up outside Ellie's cottage. She's waiting in her little front yard, which looks like something straight out of a lifestyle blog. Flowerbeds, neat paths, the whole deal. Puts Gerald to shame.

She hops into the passenger seat with a canvas bag slung over her shoulder. "Hi, Blair. Okay, head for the main road. I'll direct you from there." She buckles her seat belt. "Fair warning, it does get a bit narrow when we're off the main road again."

"Narrow?" I laugh, pulling out. "Ellie, I drove here from Glasgow. I've already redefined my relationship with the word 'narrow'."

Twenty minutes later I'm eating those words.

"This isn't a road," I mutter, gripping the steering wheel as we bump along. "This is a hiking trail that someone accidentally paved. Badly. If another car comes toward us, what do we do then? Duel?"

Ellie points to a wider bit of road ahead. "You pull into the nearest passing place and let them by. It's all very civilised."

"Right. Civilised." I navigate around a pothole that could swallow a small child. "In New York this would be considered a war crime against automobiles."

The road—and I use that term very loosely—winds up through increasingly wild countryside. Stone walls give way to open hillsides dotted with sheep.

"Park there," Ellie says, pointing to a pull-off beside a wooden gate. "We're on foot from here."

I manage to wedge the car into the space without scraping the gatepost, though it's a close thing. "Please tell me the walk is less terrifying than the drive."

"Only if you don't mind mud and sheep poo," Ellie says

cheerfully, giving my white sneakers a once-over. "I did warn you to wear a good pair of walking boots."

"Don't own any. But I promise I'll buy some before our next adventure."

We grab our bags and head through the gate, following a footpath that meanders alongside a stream. The water chatters over smooth stones, while the air smells of heather and something fresh and wild.

The path leads us into a glen—I'm learning the Scottish words—where the hills rise on either side like protective arms. Gnarled trees lean over the stream, their roots twisted into the banks, and everywhere I look there are shades of green I didn't know existed.

"This is gorgeous," I say, pulling out my phone to snap a photo. "How is this not crawling with tourists?"

"Most visitors stick to the easier walks closer to town." Ellie steps carefully over a boggy bit of path. "Plus, it's not easy to find unless you know where you're going."

The path starts to climb, winding up the hillside through bracken that brushes against our legs. My city-soft muscles protest a bit, but it's the good kind of protest, the kind that reminds you your body was designed for more than sitting at desks and riding subway cars.

After what feels like a proper Scottish workout, the path levels out and we emerge onto a plateau. And there, arranged in a rough circle like sentinels that have been waiting centuries for company, stand ancient stones, tall and weathered.

I stop dead. "Oh. Wow."

They're maybe twice my height, their surfaces etched with lichen and time. Some lean at odd angles, as if bowing toward the centre.

"How old are they?" I whisper, though I'm not sure why I'm whispering.

"Over four thousand years."

I move closer, my sneakers silent on the springy turf. The stones seem to hum with something I can't put a name to—not sound, but presence. Like they're holding secrets in their granite hearts.

"This is what people call a thin place," Ellie says.

"A thin place?"

"You know how sometimes you go somewhere and it just feels . . . different? Like the boundary between our world and something else isn't quite as solid?"

Anywhere else, a line like that would sound woo-woo. But here it makes perfect sense.

"Yeah, I feel it too." A shiver runs over my arms, then I shake it off. "Although if this turns into a time-travel situation, I want advance notice so I can fix my hair before meeting Jamie Fraser."

Ellie laughs, and the mood eases. She sets down her bag and starts unpacking: sandwiches wrapped in tinfoil, a flask, a couple of apples. It's simple, but out here, surrounded by hills and history, it feels like a feast.

"Wow, Ellie. This is amazing. Meanwhile I brought . . . an appetite. Next time, though, the food is on me."

We tuck in, and after a while Ellie says, "So, how are things going with the brooding and monosyllabic ferry captain?"

"Turns out he's not as brooding or monosyllabic as I first thought. He came over last night to apologise that he and Finn cut into my day off, which I didn't mind at all. We ended up having a drink. Scotch." I glance at the looming stones uneasily, then lower my voice. "Not my favourite."

"Careful," Ellie says, grey-blue eyes alight with mischief.

"Saying that too loud in Scotland could get you exiled. And yet, whisky with Lachlan Munro? That sounds . . . cosy. You're not developing feelings for your grumpy boss, are you?"

I almost choke on my sandwich (cheese and chutney because apparently that's a thing here—surprisingly good). "As if! I'm only saying he's not as much of a grump as I first thought, not that I'm attracted to him." *Though he's not exactly unpleasant to look at*, I add silently. "Getting involved with him would be unprofessional. Complicated. Stupid. And that's not me."

Time to redirect before Ellie gets too smug. "What about you, huh? No secret someone you've got your eye on in this charming town?"

Ellie makes a face but there's a blush creeping up her cheeks. "Not really."

"Oh, come on." I lean in. "You must at least have a crush. Who is it? Spill."

She laughs, a shy little giggle that's about as un-Ellie as I've seen her. "Well . . . I do quite like a certain man who lives in a house with roses climbing up the walls."

"Douglas? As in the father of the twins? Are you a glutton for punishment?"

Her giggle turns into full-on laughter. "I know. They're adorable, but after their last trip to the library I needed paracetamol."

We both crack up at that. When the laughter dies down, though, Ellie sobers, her smile gentler now. "It's a lost cause anyway. Douglas's wife, Leah, is in and out of the picture. Sometimes gone for months then suddenly back again. No matter how long she's been away, he always takes her back. So, yes, maybe I *am* a glutton for punishment. But we can't help who we're attracted to, right?"

Immediately, unhelpfully, my mind serves up an image: Lachlan across from me at the little table in the granny flat. The intensity of those green eyes. The rare smile tugging at his lips. His shirt clinging to his chest in ways I had no business noticing. And those forearms—seriously, forearms should not be allowed to be that distracting.

Ellie's right. You *can't* help who you're attracted to. Even if that person happens to be your broody, infuriating, ridiculously hot boss.

◆ ◆ ◆

". . . and then, Mary Poppins-style, Ellie produced these perfect little sandwiches, cheese and chutney. Nothing fancy, but out there it tasted like a five-star picnic."

On the laptop screen, Mom laughs, eyes crinkling. Dad tilts his head. "Standing stones and cheese sandwiches. You're living the dream, kiddo."

I'm back in the granny flat, catching up with my parents by video call.

"I'm telling you, it's magical here. I saw an otter this morning too. On the beach. Just hanging out, like, 'Hey, welcome to Scotland.'"

"You sound so happy," Mom says. "It's good to see you smiling."

Dad nods then clears his throat. "I know you're there to take a breather, and this nanny thing sounds great, but . . . are you keeping an eye out for jobs back here?"

"Michael!" Mom elbows him. "She went there to escape all that, remember?"

"Right, right. It's just, Blair was so passionate about her career . . ."

I smile, even as something tightens in my chest. "Nope, I'm not looking for a job back home. Not right now anyway. I'm going to give Scotland my full attention for a while."

"That's exactly what you should be doing," Mom says. "Don't rush. You'll figure things out when the time's right."

Dad lifts his hands in surrender. "Point taken, no career talk. But as your dad, I reserve the right to ask about this ferry captain. He's treating you okay, right?"

"Uh, yeah. He's nice enough." I leave out the part about Scotch and candlelight. Some things my parents don't need to know.

We chat a little longer before saying our goodbyes and promising to speak soon. After ending the call, I put on the kettle to make myself a tea—I really *am* getting the hang of life in Scotland—then glance through the scribblings in my notebook. I've already written down my story's title, *The Otter and the Boy*. Now to actually write the story itself.

One thing, at least, is clear. Today's trip to the standing stones made it click. The very best children's stories always have a touch of magic, even when they're otherwise rooted in the real world. Mine's going to be no different.

Time to get comfy. Tea, pyjamas, notebook, and a writing sprint.

I yank the curtains closed—just for privacy, it's still light out—then peel off my jeans, unhook my bra, and toss it onto the chair. Bliss! After a whole day strapped in, a little boob freedom is proof that happiness really is found in the small things. I glance down. And, yep, they really are small things. But perky. Cute, even. Ellie's are like the Highlands, majestic and impossible to ignore. Mine are more like a "wee glen". Petite, but still worth the hike.

The kettle clicks off. Okay, tea first, pyjamas later. I pad over, pour the hot water into my mug, dunk the teabag, and breathe in the steam. Look at me, practically a local. All I need now is a tartan blanket and a shortbread addiction.

Something catches my eye. A thin stripe of daylight glows where the curtains don't fully meet. Oh. Should probably fix that.

I cross the room and reach to tug the fabric together—

And freeze.

Because outside Lachlan is trudging toward the trash can, a black bag dangling from one hand, and he's just noticed me.

Our eyes meet. His go wide. Then his gaze drifts down. The bag slips from his grip and hits the ground.

Apparently my boobs have the power to halt a grown man in his tracks. Who knew?

I yelp and dive out of sight, skin on fire, my heart hammering so hard I can feel it in my throat.

Oh my god. Oh my god. Oh my god.

Well, there goes my dignity, straight into the trash with Lachlan's garbage.

CHAPTER TWELVE

LACHLAN

I sit on the edge of my bed, mug of coffee in one hand, half-eaten slice of toast in the other.

Can't stop thinking about last night. About her. About what I saw through that gap in the curtains.

I shouldn't be thinking about it. Definitely shouldn't be thinking about the curve of her small breasts, or how her rosy nipples looked in the evening light . . .

"Stop it," I mutter, setting down the mug harder than necessary. Coffee sloshes onto my bedside table.

I'm her employer, for Christ's sake! She's here to look after my son, not to star in whatever dirty film my brain is playing. It was an accident. She was mortified. And I bloody well should be too. Should *not* have lain awake all night replaying it like some randy teenager.

I finish my toast then stand and tug down my pyjama shorts. Time to get dressed, except my body has other ideas. My cock is stubbornly stiff, threatening to turn the simple act of getting dressed into an obstacle course.

I glare down at the problem like it's personally insulted me.

"I'm her boss, you daft prick," I tell it sternly.

But apparently my cock doesn't give a damn about professional boundaries.

I manage to wrestle my boxer briefs on, though it's more of a struggle than it should be. Then come the trousers. I get them up easy enough—sort of—then I get my shirt on. But when I try to do up the button of my trousers, there's no chance. Bloody thing won't reach. My cock is still refusing to play by any rules except its own.

I suck in my gut and try again. Still nothing. I twist sideways, yanking at the waistband like maybe sheer force will help me win this particular battle of willpower versus anatomy. My elbow smacks the lamp, nearly toppling it.

"Brilliant," I mutter. Nothing like starting your day by fighting your own bloody trousers—and losing.

This is ridiculous. I'm supposed to be the captain of a ferry, and I can't even control my own body? I don't have time for this nonsense. I can't be late.

Think about something else. Paperwork. Tide charts. Weather reports. The safety briefing I have to give every morning.

Finally, my cock gets the memo and decides to calm down, allowing me to wrangle everything into place.

All right, Lachlan, deep breath. You're professional. Responsible. Not a total shambles.

I head to Finn's room, where he's still curled up under his duvet like a hibernating bear. I set his school uniform out on the chair—grey trousers, white shirt, navy jumper—then give his shoulder a gentle shake.

"Morning, lad. Time to get up."

Finn opens one eye, peers at the clothes, and frowns. "Da, it's the summer holidays."

Shite.

"Right. Of course it is." I force a laugh that comes out more like a bark. "Just making sure you're awake."

Finn frowns, baffled.

I rummage through his drawers for more appropriate summer clothes. From downstairs, a voice calls up, "Hello?"

Blair. Already inside. Must've let herself in through the back door, like I told her she could.

My stomach does something complicated.

"I'll be right down," I call back, then I grab Finn some shorts and a T-shirt. "Pop these on then go down for breakfast. Have a great day, okay?" I kiss him on the forehead and head downstairs, steeling myself for normal conversation. Professional interaction. Not thinking about last night.

Blair's in the kitchen, looking annoyingly put-together for someone who's about to spend the day chasing after a six-year-old. Hair sleek, a touch of make-up, and unless I'm imagining it, perfume. Does she really need to make such an effort just to look after Finn?

Not that I can complain about it. It doesn't interfere with her job. It only distracts *me*, and I should bloody well know better.

"Morning," I manage, not quite meeting her eye.

"Good morning!" She's bright and cheerful, though there's something forced about it. Like she's trying just as hard as I am to pretend last night never happened. "Beautiful day, isn't it?"

"Aye. Should be good sailing weather." Attempting to follow her lead and act normal, I take a step towards the work surface— and trip over Gus, who's planted himself at my feet.

I stumble but catch myself. "Shit! Sorry, boy." His tail thumps hopefully. "Hey, don't look at me like that. You've already had your breakfast."

Except . . . has he? Christ, I honestly can't remember. Between the sleepless night and this morning's trouser fiasco, my brain feels like porridge.

"Er . . ." I don't want to overfeed the daft beast, but I also don't want him going hungry. Better safe than sorry. I scoop out another portion and dump it in his bowl.

Gus wags his tail like Christmas has come early.

"Finn will be downstairs in a moment," I tell Blair. "He's just getting dressed. Have a good day."

And with that, I escape into the sea breeze, already rattled and the morning hasn't even properly started.

This is going to be a long bloody day.

◆ ◆ ◆

The familiar outline of Corraig grows larger through the bridge windows as I ease the *Calabrae* into the final approach. Same rocky headlands I've known since I was a bairn. Same cluster of white cottages hugging the harbour. Same weathered pier where I used to fish on summer evenings.

I bring her in by muscle memory—throttle back, adjust for the cross-current, let her drift in gentle as a kiss. The engines rumble to a stop, and I feel the satisfying bump as we settle against the pier fenders.

Below, car engines start up. Foot passengers shuffle ashore. The usual controlled chaos of arrival.

Once the last of them is off, Kenneth's voice crackles through the intercom. "All clear on deck, skipper. Next sailing's not for a while. Fancy stretching your legs and grabbing a coffee?"

"Not happening."

"Aye, thought not. Worth a shot, though."

Silence returns, broken only by the lap of water against the hull. Through the glass, I watch the last stragglers vanish into the village, heading home or to visit family or to explore the island's walking trails. Twice a day, five days a week, I bring folk here. And every time I sit in this spot, staring at the island I grew up on. The island I can't set foot on. Too many ghosts in those streets.

I drag in a breath and shove the thought away. My mind goes to something just as unwelcome: the gap in those bloody curtains. A flash of skin. Blair's—

Christ. Not again.

I scrub a hand over my face but it doesn't help. I need to get a grip.

◆ ◆ ◆

The front door clicks shut behind me and Gus bounds into view, his whole backside wagging with the force of his tail. I crouch to give him a proper scratch behind the ears.

"Hi, Gus. Good to see you, lad."

"Da!" Finn appears at a run, nearly bowling me over with the force of his hug. "You're home!"

"Aye, I'm home." I ruffle his hair, and for a second my shoulders drop, the day's weight easing.

Then Finn says, "Da, Blair started writing a story." And the tension returns because, of course, we're not alone.

"It's a proper one, like the books we read, but she's making it up herself." Finn tugs my hand. "C'mon!"

He leads me through to the living room, where Blair's straightening cushions. She glances up with a smile that's maybe just a touch too bright, and the awkwardness rushes back in.

"Hi. How was your day?"

"Fine. Much the same as always."

"Oh. Well, we had the best day, didn't we, Finn?"

He nods eagerly. "Blair's story is called *The Otter and the Boy*. I drew a picture of the otter. Look!"

He drags me to the coffee table, where there's a crayon drawing—a stick figure boy standing beside a brown blob. Not sure I'd have been able to identify it as an otter if he hadn't told me, but it's Finn's, and that makes it perfect.

"This is great, Finn."

"Tell Da about the story," Finn says to Blair.

Blair laughs, and the sound does something warm and unwelcome in my chest. "It's about a boy who finds a young otter caught in a fishing net on the beach. The otter's weak and can't hunt properly, so the boy has to help him—bring him food, keep him safe. But here's the thing: the otter only comes out for the boy. When his dad comes down to the shore, the otter hides. So the dad doesn't even know if the otter's real or if his son's making it all up."

"The boy has to take care of the otter all by himself," Finn adds.

"Sounds like a good story."

She's brilliant with him. Patient and creative and exactly what he needs. So why can't I just leave it at that, instead of replaying last night on a loop? It was only a moment—a few seconds at most—and yet I've spent every bloody hour since thinking about it.

I should join in, ask more about the story, keep the conversation going. Instead I feel hot under the collar for no good reason. *Idiot.*

"Back in a sec. Need some water."

I escape to the kitchen, but before I can fill a glass, my gaze catches on a laundry basket by the back door. Blair's washing, neatly folded, ready to be carried back to the granny flat.

I shouldn't look.

I look anyway.

Christ.

On top, a pale pink bra, lace edging visible. Beneath it, what might be matching knickers, simple but soft and feminine. My hand lifts before I even register the movement, drawn by the delicate lace—

I snatch it back like I've been burned.

What the hell is wrong with me?

"Thanks for letting me use the washer, Lachlan." Blair's voice makes me spin. She's followed me through, as has Finn. Did they see? I don't think so.

"I'll get that out of your way," Blair adds.

"Right." My voice comes out sharp. Clipped. "Good. And it's Lach-lan, not Lock-lan. Remember?"

She blinks, startled. "Oh. I—"

"It's fine." I rub at my temple. "Sorry, bit of a headache. Anyway, you don't need to hang about. I'll see you tomorrow."

It's a very clear dismissal, and Blair's cheeks flush. "Right. Okay." She picks up the basket. "Bye, Finn."

"Bye, Blair," Finn says quietly.

She doesn't look at me as she leaves, and after the back door closes, the silence stretches until Finn breaks it, his voice small. "Why were you mean to Blair?"

I run a hand through my hair, guilt sitting heavy in my gut. "I wasn't mean. I was just . . . tired. Like I said, I've got a headache."

"You were mean," he insists. "She was being nice and you were mean to her."

No mercy from him. And he's right. I *was* mean.

"I'm sorry, lad. Sometimes grown-ups get grumpy when they're tired, just like kids."

But Finn's not buying it and neither am I. He wanders off and I'm left in the kitchen, furious with myself.

You're making this worse. You're making it weird. Stop it.

She's doing nothing wrong. Nothing except being kind to my son and living in my space and looking like—

Stop.

Tomorrow I'll be better. Polite but professional. Detached.

I'll lock it all away where it belongs. No excuses.

CHAPTER THIRTEEN

BLAIR

The morning is overcast and cool as I cross the small yard from the granny flat, arms wrapped tight around myself. I'm still smarting from yesterday's dismissal, the sting of it clinging harder than it should.

Finn must've spotted me through the window because he yanks the back door open before I can knock. Gus barrels out, a furry tornado circling my legs.

"Blair! Guess what? I dreamed about otters last night, and one of them could talk, and he told me his name was Gerald, just like your plant!" Finn insisted I give him a tour of the granny flat yesterday, and that's when he met Gerald in all his leafy glory.

"That's amazing, buddy. Did Dream Gerald have any good stories to tell?"

"He did! He said—"

"Finn, let Blair in," Lachlan interrupts, appearing behind Finn, looking every inch the stern ferry captain in his crisp uniform.

Finn scoots back to make room, and I step inside. "Morning," I offer, aiming for neutral.

"Morning." Lachlan doesn't look at me, focusing instead on filling Gus's food bowl. At the sound of kibble rattling into the dish, Gus hurtles over and drops into a perfect sit, eyes locked on the prize, tail sweeping the floor.

Finn dives back into his dream, words spilling out in a rush I try to follow while I slide bread into the toaster. Behind us, Gus is already crunching his breakfast like it's the best thing he's ever tasted. Lachlan clears his throat and, more gently this time, interrupts his son.

"Sounds like a fun dream, Finn. But why don't you go and get dressed? I've laid out some clothes on your bed—don't worry, not your school uniform this time." The corner of his mouth quirks before he adds, "That way you and Blair can get started on your adventures as soon as breakfast is done."

Finn accepts the logic without question and bounds upstairs, leaving me alone with his father, Gus's noisy crunching the only sound in the kitchen. After a moment Lachlan turns to me, his green eyes guarded. "Listen. I wanted to apologise for being short with you yesterday evening. That wasn't . . . professional of me."

Not professional? Try all-out mean.

"It's fine," I lie, because what else can I say? That his hot-and-cold routine is giving me whiplash?

He nods curtly, like he's checked that apology off his mental to-do list. The toaster pops and I busy myself pulling out the slices then reaching for the jam and a knife. I'm not in the mood for more conversation with Lachlan, but he isn't rushing off like I thought he would. Instead, he pours Finn's orange juice, something he'd normally leave to me.

"I was wondering if you and Finn might want to head to the Pit this morning?" he says at last. "Struan's got Isla—he'll have her a bit more than usual over the summer holidays. And Douglas is taking the twins. His parents are under the weather."

I glance out the window at the sky, thick with clouds that look ready to spit rain any second. The Pit sounds a lot more appealing than any of my other plans for today.

"Yeah, sure. We'll head over there."

"Great. I'll let the dads know to expect you." Lachlan taps out a quick message on his phone then adds, "You should ask Douglas to give you a tour of his house. I'm sure he won't mind showing you around."

It takes me a second to realise what this is: an olive branch in grumpy Scotsman wrapping paper.

"I will, thanks." And damn it, my mouth even tugs up despite myself. But only a little.

He gives me one of his patented brisk nods and pockets his phone. "Right, then. I'll go say goodbye to Finn and leave you to it."

◆ ◆ ◆

The Pit is pure chaos: shrieks ricocheting, slides thudding, kids swarming the jungle gym like a beehive. My ears are already begging for mercy. And the smells? Yikes. Spilled juice boxes, hand sanitiser, that *eau de sweaty sock* funk. Consider my senses officially assaulted.

It's not exactly the Highlands idyll I've been soaking up these past days, but here I am on a plastic chair that's seen better years. Maybe better decades. Most of the adults are clustered at tables on this side of the room, while a few unlucky ones have been dragged into the mayhem by their energetic offspring.

"So, Blair . . ." Douglas leans across the sticky table, raising his voice to compete with the noise. "How are you finding Ardmara?"

"I, uh, love it," I say, though the words come out distracted. Because honestly? I'm still trying to locate Finn. We arrived mere minutes ago, and the second he caught sight of his friends, he bolted straight into the giant maze of tunnels and slides.

Douglas follows my gaze. "Don't worry, Finn's a sensible lad. They look out for each other in there. Mostly."

As if summoned by our conversation, Finn's dark head appears at one of the little bubble windows. He grins and waves madly but before I even get the chance to wave back he's gone again. He seems happy enough, though.

"Um, Douglas, my grandmother actually lived in the house you're in now. It's one of the reasons I wanted to come to Ardmara in the first place."

"Oh, aye, my parents mentioned that. Said they met you and Finn at the park the other day. I can let you have a look around at some point, if you'd like?"

"That would be great. Thanks."

"I'll need to give the place a clean before you come around, though," he adds. "Seeing as it was your grandmother's home, I'd like you to have a decent impression of it."

"I don't want to put you to any trouble." But the photo Lachlan showed me the other day flashes in my mind: post-play carnage in the twins' room that looked like a bomb had gone off.

He waves it off. "It's fine. It is a bit easier when they're at school, though. Over the summer my folks help with childcare, but only at my place. Which means when I get home from work, I'm the one tidying the chaos." He runs a hand through his scruffy ginger beard, then glances toward the ball pit, breaking into a broad smile at the sight of Rosie "swimming" through the multicoloured balls, laughing delightedly. "They drive me daft, but I love them."

"Here we go!" Struan reappears with a tray of coffees, juice boxes, and sweet treats. I met him briefly when I came in, before he went off to grab drinks for us all. The contrast between the two men strikes me again. Douglas is solid and steady, a little rough round the edges. Struan is taller, leaner, younger. And with that tousled man bun and breezy posture, he radiates carefree charm.

"One Americano for the lady," he says, winking as he slides a cup in front of me.

That's the other thing about Struan: total flirt. He hugged me like we were old friends when I arrived. Gorgeous, sure, but he doesn't do it for me. Maybe instead of flirty and in-your-face, I prefer my Scots grumpy and complicated. Preferably in a ferry captain's uniform.

Seriously, brain? That's where you go? Considering how that grumpy Scot's been treating me, I really shouldn't find him attractive. Not even remotely.

"How much do I owe you, Struan?" I ask, forcing myself back to the here and now.

"Don't be daft." He drops into a chair. "Fair warning, you'll want sugar. The coffee's dire."

He isn't wrong. One sip nearly makes me gag, and I'm diving for the sugar. God. Nothing like the coffee at the Lighthouse Café.

"So," Struan says, "what do you think of our five-star establishment?"

I glance around. "It's . . . lively. The kids seem to love it."

Struan gives me a look that says he knows I'm being diplomatic.

Douglas chuckles. "This place certainly takes a bit of getting used to. But when your kids are wee and it's dreich outside, it helps keep you sane." A rogue plastic ball from the pit bounces off his head. He doesn't even flinch. "Well, sane-ish."

We spend the next twenty minutes enduring dreadful coffee while making up for it with the treats Struan brought over: shortbread and "snowballs", chocolate-coated marshmallow puffs rolled in coconut. The kids swoop in and out, pausing only long enough to sip from juice boxes before tearing off again.

In one of the pit stops, I finally meet Isla. She marches over with her chin up, tawny curls bobbing, and says, "Hi, I'm Isla. Finn says you're the American nanny." While her dad pricks her finger, she explains, very matter-of-fact, that she has diabetes and he's checking her sugars.

In between the kids' flyby visits, I learn what the dads do. Douglas is a fisherman in a line of fishermen going back generations. Struan runs Walker Builds, a construction firm, with his father. Back home, it feels rare for work to be passed down like that. Here, it seems woven into the fabric of the place.

Finn's voice carries across the play area. "Blair, watch me do this!" He's perched at the top of the fire pole, grinning like a daredevil. He shoots down it in one quick blur.

"Great job, buddy!" I give him a thumbs-up. He beams then vanishes back into the chaos.

"You and Finn are hitting it off," Douglas observes.

"Finn's great," I say. *Unlike his grumpy father*, I add in my head.

Struan stretches his long legs out in front of him, his grin lazy. "You know, I'm the one you should be thanking for landing this nanny job."

"Oh yeah?"

"I'm the one who suggested Lachlan put out an ad for a nanny." He quirks a brow. "So? How's it been living in close quarters with the man himself and having Lachlan as a boss?"

I take a bracing sip. Tastes like regret and burnt rubber. Am I supposed to lie? Is it wildly inappropriate to rant about your boss behind their back? Then again, it's also inappropriate for your boss to be unfairly dismissive and snarky.

"Honestly? It hasn't exactly been easy." I roll the mug between my palms. "And I know this is unprofessional, but . . . he's just so moody all the time." God, it feels good to admit it out loud. And apparently I'm not done because the next words tumble out too: "You both seem normal enough. How do you put up with him?"

Struan and Douglas exchange a look.

"Maybe his grumpiness has something to do with a very pretty young American suddenly living in his back garden." Struan waggles his eyebrows meaningfully.

I snort before I can stop myself. Still, my stomach flips at the idea. "Right. If he liked me, he'd actually talk to me like a human being instead of brushing me off."

As Granny would've put it, I'm simply not the man's cup of tea.

"Lachlan's always been private," Douglas offers. "Work, home, his boy, his dog. That's his world. Other than these Pit meetups, he's not really integrated since he moved here. Maybe the gruffness is just him adjusting to someone new in his space."

Right, so he's private. Likes his own space. Still doesn't give him the right to be rude.

"Maybe you could coax him out more," Struan suggests brightly. "You know, socialise the beast."

Inwardly, I scoff. Yeah, definitely not in my job description.

I'm saved from replying when pandemonium erupts, courtesy of the twins. Rosie ignores the golden rule of one-off-one-on and barrels down the slide on Isla's heels, colliding with her and bumping the glucose monitor on her arm. At the same time Logan decides to scale the jungle gym from the outside and manages to wedge his foot straight through the netting.

For a few frantic minutes we're all scrambling. Struan checks Isla's sensor, carefully peeling back the adhesive to make sure it's still secure—it is. I steady Logan while Douglas frees his foot and gets him down. Then Douglas gives both twins a firm scolding. They mumble what sound like apologies before skipping back into the fray, unfazed.

"Those two, honestly," Douglas mutters as he drops back into his seat. "The holidays have barely started and already they've worn my folks ragged. Summer's off to a flying start."

I remember Ellie saying his wife comes and goes as she pleases, which basically means Douglas is raising two mischievous kids as a single parent. Can't be easy.

A tap on my shoulder pulls me from my musings. I turn to find Finn grinning at me, slightly out of breath.

"Tig, you're it!" he announces. "Catch me if you can!"

Before I can protest, he's off like a shot, Logan, Rosie, and Isla shouting for me to give chase as they tear after him.

You don't need to be a linguistic genius to guess that "tig" must be what I'd call "tag". I know how this game works.

"Oh, you better believe I'll catch you," I call, pushing back from the table and charging into the fray.

"Good luck!" Douglas shouts after me.

"We'll send in backup if you get stuck!" Struan adds with a laugh.

And despite the mayhem, the awful coffee, and the sticky

floors, I'm grinning as I run after four giggling children through the play maze.

Maybe the Pit isn't so bad after all.

◆ ◆ ◆

The bell over the library door gives a polite little jingle as we troop inside. After the Pit, the hush in here feels like air conditioning for my ears.

"Blair! What a nice surprise," Ellie says from the desk, smiling. "And you brought company today. Welcome, everyone."

The kids chorus a distracted "hi" before bolting for the children's section. Struan and Douglas nod their greetings then peel off toward the shelves. I go over to chat with Ellie.

"I've actually got something to show you," she says. She ducks below the counter and comes up with a black-and-white printout from an old newspaper, which she slides across to me. "Found this yesterday when I was poking through the digitised archives."

A school photo fills most of the page: three neat rows of children, girls in pinafores and cardigans, boys in blazers and shorts. Their names are printed below in faded typewriter font.

"Oh my God," I say. "Is that my—"

"*This book is all about bogies!*" Logan's voice booms across the library like a foghorn.

Douglas winces. "Indoor voice, mate!" Then, in a quick whisper toward the desk, sheepish as anything, "Sorry, Ellie."

Ellie's cheeks go pink as she waves it off—adorably flustered—and I catch the way she fusses with a pile of bookmarks. Huh. Sweet.

But then my gaze drops back to the photo, and I see her.

Front row, second from the left. My granny. Pigtails, gap-toothed grin, mischief glinting in her eyes. A fragment of her life from long before she could have imagined emigrating to Canada.

"That's her!" I say, surprised at how choked up I feel. "Oh my God, Ellie. Thank you so much for finding this."

Finn appears at my elbow, a picture book tucked under one arm. "What're you looking at?"

"A photo of my granny when she was little, about your age." I point her out. "She went to the same school you go to."

"Really? Maybe she drew pictures just like I do and they're still on the walls somewhere!"

"Um, maybe. Probably not, but she'd have played in your schoolyard, maybe even sat in your classroom."

"Wow," Finn says. "That's cool."

"What have you got there?" Ellie nods at the book Finn is carrying.

"*Wallace the Wildcat of Wick*. I want Blair to read it to me and the others. She's *really* good at reading."

"Is she now?" Ellie shoots me an amused glance. "Well then, Blair better get reading."

I carefully slip the sheet into my bag and thank Ellie again before Finn tugs me toward the children's section. He leads me to the bay window seat and settles beside me. Isla and the twins have already plopped themselves down on beanbags and now they watch me expectantly.

All right, not just Finn this time. A whole audience. Let's do this.

I open to the first page and begin. "Wallace the wildcat woke in his wee den, whiskers twitching and tummy rumbling . . ."

I don't make a production out of it, just enough rhythm to keep them hooked. But within a minute, two kids I don't know drift over and plop themselves down, listening in like it's Story-time at Barnes & Noble. Then another joins. Guess I'm the entertainment today.

And it's not just the kids. Struan leans against a bookshelf, watching me, amused. Douglas looks grateful for a few minutes of peace. Ellie, at the desk, props her chin in her hand and listens, soft smile in place.

When I finish, there's a collective little sigh, which in library-speak is basically applause.

"Blair's writing her own story," Finn proudly announces to the group. "It's about an otter."

"Can we hear that one now?" one of the kids I don't even know asks.

"Um, no, because it's not finished yet. I'm still working on it."

"She's read the start to me, though," Finn says.

Logan scowls, affronted on principle. "How come Finn gets to hear it and we don't?"

"Finn's my test pilot. When it's ready, you guys can hear it next."

Logan nods, apparently satisfied with this.

◆ ◆ ◆

I'm at the kitchen counter preparing a snack for Finn while he sits at the table, tongue caught between his teeth as he draws. His hair is still windswept and his cheeks flushed from our walk on the beach with Gus.

The furball himself sits by my feet, amber eyes fixed on the package of crackers I'm opening.

"Nice try, Gus. I literally fed you an hour ago." But when he lifts one paw and tilts his head—pure canine innocence—I give in. "Oh, fine. You're too cute for your own good."

I toss him a cracker, which he snaps from the air with impressive precision. He then trots off into the hallway to eat it like he's afraid I might change my mind. *Not a chance, buddy. That ship sailed the moment it hit your mouth.*

I set Finn's plate—crackers with cheese and apple slices—on the table and sit beside him with a mug of camomile tea. It's already past two. Less than two hours until Lachlan gets home.

"That's a brilliant drawing, Finn." I peer at the house he's sketching—clearly his own, complete with the path down to the pebble beach. "Though I'm curious, why no colours? Your pictures are usually so bright. This one's all grey."

"I'm making it black and white, just like your granny's picture. Then maybe I can trick Da into thinking it's an old photo too."

My heart does a little flip. His mission is impossible, sure, but if cuteness could bend the rules of reality, we'd be in business.

"That's a great idea."

"You know how the library had a picture of your granny?" Finn says, shading the front door now. "Do you think they might have photos of my mum too?"

Oh.

Finn's never mentioned his mother to me before. I set my mug down carefully.

"I'm not sure, buddy. Maybe."

"We have a photo album with pictures of Mum, but Da never takes it out." He stops drawing and looks up at me hopefully. "Maybe you and I could look at it?"

"Oh, sweetheart . . . maybe that's something you and your dad should do together."

Finn's face falls. "He won't want to. He doesn't like looking at old photos."

The defeat in his voice is heartbreaking, and I have no idea what to say. It's not my place to show Finn pictures of his mom, but it hurts to see him like this.

He nibbles at his snack and draws, and the mood slowly rights itself. I think we've moved past it. But when I return from a quick trip to the bathroom, I find the kitchen empty, Finn's drawing abandoned on the table.

"Finn? Where are you?" I check the living room—nope. "Gus?" I call.

At the sound of his name, Gus pads down the stairs. "Where's Finn, boy?"

He seems to understand because he turns and heads back up. I follow him to the room I know to be Lachlan's bedroom, though I've never set foot in it before. Finn sits on the floor by an open closet, a photo album in his lap.

"Finn . . ." I pause at the threshold, aware this is Lachlan's space, not mine. "That's a special book. Maybe you should look at it with your dad, yeah?"

He doesn't acknowledge me, just keeps on looking at the album, his expression awed, almost reverent. But sad too.

I step into the room, following Finn's gaze to a photograph of a young woman with dark hair and warm brown eyes cradling a baby Finn. He traces the curve of her hair with one small finger.

"Your mom was beautiful," I say softly.

Finn nods. Gus sinks to the floor beside him and nudges his knee with a damp nose.

"She had your eyes."

"You think so?"

"Definitely."

He turns the page. "Look, Da doesn't have any grey hair." Lachlan beams at the camera, a breeze ruffling his hair as he holds infant Finn by the sea. He looks so much younger, though it can't have been more than six years ago.

Finn keeps flipping through the album. I know it isn't my place to look at these pictures with him, yet I can't bring myself to stop him.

"I don't remember much about my mum," he says after a while, unprompted. "But sometimes I smell something and it reminds me of her. Like when clothes come out of the washing machine—that smell reminds me of her. And sometimes when I'm falling asleep, I remember her singing to me, but I don't know if that's real or just something I made up."

He studies another page. "I wish . . . I wish I knew more about her."

My throat goes tight. All I want is to scoop him up and promise him answers, stories, memories—anything to fill that gap. But I can't. That's something only his dad can give him.

I don't probe but I get the impression Lachlan hasn't told Finn much about his mom. And that feels wrong. Even if Finn's own memories are fuzzy, he deserves to know her through his father's stories.

CHAPTER FOURTEEN

LACHLAN

Finn and I are settled on the sofa with Gus sprawled across our feet like a furry blanket. I've got my arm around my son, and he's tucked into my side, watching the telly. This is our time. No distractions, no complications. Just us.

His programme comes to an end, so I reach for the remote and switch off the TV. "All right, wee man. Let's go run your bath."

"Okay," Finn says, his voice quieter than usual. Then: "Da?"

"Aye?"

"What was Mum like?"

The question hits me sideways. "What?"

"Mum. What was she like?"

My chest tightens. We don't talk about Leanne. Not really.

"She was . . ." The words stick. Christ, I don't even know where to start.

Finn tilts his head, waiting.

I clear my throat. "She was kind," I manage finally. It comes out rough, too small a word for the whole of her, but it's all I can give him right now. "A good mum. Why are you asking, lad?"

He shrugs. "Just wondering."

Just wondering? Finn doesn't "just wonder" about his mum. Not after four years of carefully not asking, of learning that these conversations make his old man go quiet and distant.

"Finn, what's brought this on? Have you been thinking about Mum today?"

Another shrug. "Maybe."

"Has someone been talking to you about her?"

His eyes dart away, a dead giveaway. "No."

"Finn."

"Well . . . maybe a bit."

The pieces click into place, and my jaw tightens. "Blair."

He nods reluctantly. Of course it was Blair. I'd decided to keep her at arm's length, to be polite and professional. And yet here she is, somehow getting under my skin anyway by crossing lines I thought were bloody obvious.

"What exactly did Blair say to you?"

◆ ◆ ◆

I give one sharp knock but don't wait for an answer. Too wound up for politeness, I push open the door to the granny flat and find Blair at the little table, notebook open, a mug of tea steaming beside her.

She looks up, startled. At least she's properly dressed for once—jeans and a soft blue jumper that brings out her eyes. Not that I notice. Not really.

"Lachlan! I—"

"We need to talk." My voice is sharper than I mean it to be, but I don't soften it. "About what happened today with Finn."

She closes her notebook slowly, buying herself time. "If this is about the photos, I can explain—"

"Explain what? That you went through my personal things? You had no right."

"I didn't go through anything!" She stands, colour rising in her cheeks. "Finn wanted to see pictures of his mom. He got the album out himself, and I—"

"You should've told him to put it back. Said it was something for him and his father to do together."

"I tried! But he looked so sad, and—"

"It wasn't your call to make, Blair." I'm pacing now, heat rising under my skin, the small space feeling even smaller. "You don't get to decide what's best for my son. That's my job."

For a long beat she just looks at me. Something hardens in her eyes, and her apologetic expression slips away. What replaces it is steelier.

"You're right," she says quietly. "I should've handled it differently. But Lachlan, would it be the worst thing to have a few photos and mementoes of Finn's mom in the house? Or to tell him a story about his mom now and then?"

"That's not—"

"Finn barely knows anything about her," she pushes on, her voice gaining strength. "And the only way he will is if *you* tell him. Stories matter, Lachlan. Not just the ones in books. The ones we share about the people we love. Yes, she's gone, and that's awful, but that doesn't mean you can never talk about her."

"I'm trying to protect him," I snap.

"Are you really protecting Finn? Or just yourself?"

I freeze. Words desert me. The anger that carried me here flickers out, leaving only the truth I don't want to face.

She's wrong. She has to be.

"Just . . ." I rake a hand through my hair, suddenly exhausted. "Leave the past where it is, Blair. Please. You're brilliant with Finn and I appreciate that. I do. But you're here to look after him when I can't, not to dig up what's gone."

Her mouth opens like she wants to argue but I'm already turning away.

"We'll see you tomorrow."

The door clicks shut behind me, but her words stick, following me across the garden. *Are you really protecting Finn? Or just yourself?*

◆ ◆ ◆

Back in the house, Finn's quiet through his bath, through brushing his teeth. Normally, I'd be telling him to stop talking with his mouth full of toothpaste foam. Instead, he goes through the bedtime motions without his usual chatter. I want to blame Blair for this, for bringing up something that was none of her business, for making my boy sad. But the words she threw at me keep circling back. Am I protecting Finn? Or, as Blair suggested, just myself?

When I tuck Finn into bed, he looks small against the pillows. "Da?" Those brown eyes—Leanne's eyes—watch me.

"Aye, lad?"

"Will you . . . will you tell me about Mum? Just one story?"

Bloody hell. He's not giving up. I almost deflect, almost suggest we read *Zog* instead. But the way he's looking at me, the careful way he's asking—like he's not sure I'll say yes—breaks something loose inside me.

I sit on the edge of his bed, hands clasped between my knees. Where do I even start?

"Your mum . . ." I clear my throat. "She loved stories. Always had a book in her hand. Didn't matter what kind. Love stories, adventures, mysteries, she read them all."

It sounds flat. Dull. Like I'm reciting facts instead of talking about the lass I loved. I want to tell him about how she'd lose herself in those pages, how she'd cry happy tears at the endings, how she'd insist on telling me all about what happened to these fictional characters, even if I didn't always listen with rapt attention.

But the words stick. None of it comes out right.

Christ, if Blair had known Leanne, she'd know how to do this properly. She'd paint pictures with her voice, make Leanne come alive again.

I glance down, half expecting Finn to look bored or confused. Instead he's staring at me, wide-eyed, soaking up every word like it's gold.

The tightness in my chest eases just enough for me to go on. "She'd stay up too late reading. Way past when she should've gone to sleep. But she got lost in the stories, you see. Said they made the world seem bigger, full of magic."

"Like you and me, Da," Finn whispers, a sleepy smile spreading across his face. "And Blair. We like stories too."

"Aye, we do." I smooth his hair back from his forehead. "And she loved reading to you when you were wee. Had her own way of telling them, made you hang on every word."

His smile grows wider. "Tell me more?"

So I do. I tell him about how she'd hum while she cooked, how she collected smooth stones from the beach, how even a drizzly day couldn't stop her from dragging us out for picnics. The words come easier now, and Finn drinks them in like he's been thirsty for them his whole life.

"Thank you, Da," he murmurs when his eyelids finally grow heavy. "For telling me about Mum."

"Sleep tight, wee man."

I wait until his breathing evens out before I head through to my bedroom and, from my wardrobe, pull out a photo album. My hands shake slightly as I flip through the pages, past images I haven't looked at in years.

Finn in his pram, Finn on a blanket, Finn in my arms. Leanne took nearly all of them, so she's noticeably missing from them. Her eye is everywhere, though, in the way she caught the light, the angle, the little notes she scribbled underneath.

Then—there. Leanne cradling Finn when he was only a few weeks old, her smile so bright, both of them perfect and whole and mine.

I take the photo to the kitchen, to the cork board where Finn's drawings live in bold, chaotic colour. Carefully I pin Leanne's picture right in the centre, among the dragons and dinosaurs and stick-figure families. Her face shining out through Finn's messy colours.

"I'm trying, Leanne," I whisper to her smile. "I've made mistakes but God knows I'm trying."

Of course there's no answer. But looking at her there surrounded by our boy's artwork, I think maybe—just maybe— she'd understand.

CHAPTER FIFTEEN

BLAIR

I cut across the backyard from the granny flat, my stomach tight with dread. I'm later today, deliberately so. I've tried to time it so there's no chance of any small talk before Lachlan has to leave for the ferry. Two mornings in a row I've walked to this house feeling like I'm heading into battle instead of work. This is not what I came to Scotland for. I didn't fly four thousand miles just to get steamrolled by some brooding Highlander with a chip on his shoulder.

If Lachlan gives me any more grief this morning, I'm done. Simple as that. I'll pack up Gerald and my dignity—what's left of it—and find somewhere else to figure out my life. Edinburgh, maybe. Or back to New York, tail between my legs.

The back door is unlocked, as always. Gus is first to greet me, nails scrabbling across the floorboards, tail wagging like we haven't seen each other in weeks. Lachlan stands at the counter in his ferry captain uniform, gulping coffee like it's medicine.

"Morning," I say, my voice flat and professional. No smile. Just the bare minimum of politeness.

His eyes flick to mine, and for a second something passes

across his face—regret, maybe, or uncertainty. But then he's checking his watch and grabbing his keys from the counter.

"Blair, I—"

"Da, Da, Da!" Finn bounces into the kitchen in his pyjamas. "Tell Blair about the picture!"

Lachlan hesitates, caught between whatever he was going to say and his son's enthusiasm. But in the end, the ferry schedule wins. "I've got to go. We'll talk later, aye?" He ruffles Finn's hair, gives me a brief unreadable look, then he's gone.

"What picture, buddy?" I ask, my voice softening. My anger belongs to his father, not him.

"Right there!" Finn points to the cork board. Among his colourful artwork is a photo of a baby Finn and his mother. She's looking down at him with such pure, radiant love it makes my chest ache.

"Da put it up last night," Finn says. "And he said it's just a first step. We can get a frame to display it properly and put up more pictures too."

Tension drains from me like air slowly leaking from a tyre. Lachlan heard me. Despite his anger, despite storming out of the granny flat, he listened.

"It's beautiful, Finn. She looks so happy."

"Da told me a story about her," Finn continues, settling at the kitchen table. "About how she loved reading books. Just like us!"

I pop a couple of slices of bread in the toaster. "Oh?"

"Yes." Finn goes on, telling me how she'd cry even at happy endings and stay up late to finish books. And he doesn't stop, repeating things I can only assume Lachlan told him last night after our argument.

With each detail Leanne becomes more real to me. Not just

the beautiful woman in the photographs, but a person with quirks and habits and passions. Someone who would have understood my love of stories, who might have become a friend if circumstances had been different.

"She really does sound amazing," I tell Finn when he finishes.

"Aye, she was," he says confidently.

Yesterday I accused Lachlan of protecting himself instead of Finn, and maybe I was right. But Lachlan took those hard words and did something with them. He didn't just put up a photo. He gave Finn back a little piece of his mom.

◆ ◆ ◆

The kitchen table is a mess of newspaper and Finn's beach treasures: smooth pebbles, tiny periwinkle shells, even a bit of sea glass glinting in the light. Carefully he daubs glue along the edge of a plain wooden photo frame.

We stopped at the little craft shop in town earlier, and of course he spotted the frame. I hesitated before buying it—yesterday's fight with Lachlan still too fresh—but Finn's hopeful grin undid me. So we came home with the frame and the promise of an afternoon project. Technically, Lachlan's schedule says "drawing", but this is close enough, right? Besides, this week I've been treating the schedule as more of a guideline than gospel anyway.

"Here, Blair, you do this one." Finn nudges a shell toward me. His fingers are sticky with glue but he couldn't care less.

I pick it up. *It's just a frame*, I remind myself. What goes in it, that's Lachlan's decision.

Twenty minutes later Finn sits back to admire our handiwork. "It's perfect," he declares.

It is beautiful. A little chaotic, sure, but beautiful all the same.

Finn jumps off his seat and walks over to the cork board, reaching for the photo of him and his mum. "Now we just need to—"

"Whoa, hold on. The frame needs to dry first. If we don't let the glue set properly, all your pretty shells will fall off."

"Oh. How long does it need to dry?"

"A few hours at least. Let's wait until your dad gets home, then you and him can put a photo in. That photo, or a different photo . . ." I really don't want to be accused of overstepping again.

"Okay." Finn is clearly disappointed but he doesn't argue. Instead he studies the frame critically. "Do you think Da will like it?"

"Your dad is going to love it. You made it with your own hands, and that makes it incredibly special. Now, let's go do something else while we wait for your masterpiece to dry."

◆ ◆ ◆

We're in the backyard when Gus's ears prick at the sound of a car in the driveway. He barks once, sharp and eager, before tearing off around the side of the house. Finn bolts after him, yelling, "Da!"

I gather up the scattered toys—plastic dinosaurs, a ball Gus slobbered half to death—and drop them in the storage boxes by the back door. By the time I step into the kitchen, Finn is already tugging Lachlan through from the hallway, Gus dancing around their legs.

"Here it is!" Finn announces, pointing at the table. "A photo frame for Mum's picture. Blair helped me make it."

My stomach tightens. *Here we go again.*

Lachlan studies the decorated frame, then his eyes flick to me. I can't read his expression, so I jump in before he can say anything.

"We made *a photo frame*," I clarify. "There isn't a picture in it yet, and it's up to you what goes in it. But Finn was very keen to decorate it and make it look nice, and, well, I didn't want to discourage his creativity."

The silence stretches. Finn looks between us, his enthusiasm dimming as he picks up on the tension.

Lachlan steps closer to the table and runs his fingers along the frame's shells and sea glass. "You did a great job. It's brilliant, Finn."

Finn brightens. "Really?"

"Really." Lachlan goes over to the cork board, takes down the photo, and carefully slides it into the frame. "There. Perfect."

Finn beams. Then, hopefully, he asks, "Can I make more? For other pictures?"

"Aye, if you and Blair want to make more frames, go right ahead. It'd be nice to put up a few more photos around here. Make it less like a show home." He throws me a look as he says this last bit, quoting my own accusation back at him, but there's a teasing curve to his mouth. He's not mad at me. For once.

Lachlan's gaze shifts to the window. Outside, late-afternoon light spills across the water like melted gold. "I know from this amazing frame that you've already been to the beach today, Finn, but fancy another stroll?"

"Aye!" No hesitation. In Finn's world, no one in their right mind would say no to more beach time.

Lachlan looks at me. "Blair? Would you like to come? No pressure," he adds quickly. "Only if you want to."

It's as though last night's argument never even happened.

"Okay," I say uncertainly. "That sounds nice."

Minutes later, the three of us are crunching across the pebbles while Gus hurtles after the stick Finn keeps throwing for him.

After a few more tosses, Lachlan says, "Finn, could you take Gus down to the water and play fetch with him there? I want to have a grown-up chat with Blair."

"Sure." Finn whoops and charges off, stick in hand, Gus galloping beside him.

Lachlan and I stand for a while, saying nothing, watching Finn shriek with laughter while Gus acts like every toss of the stick is the best thing that's ever happened.

Eventually Lachlan runs a hand through his hair. "Blair, I . . . Christ, this is hard."

I wait. Not going to throw him a lifeline, but not twisting the knife either.

"I owe you an apology," he says. "For last night. For . . . well, for being a right bastard. You were right. About all of it." The words seem to cost him. "I wasn't protecting Finn. I was protecting myself. Because talking about Leanne, remembering her properly . . . it hurts."

Down by the water Finn flings the stick and Gus plunges into the shallows after it, splashing wildly.

Lachlan's jaw works. "It was gallstones. She'd had pain after meals for months but kept brushing it off. Said it was just stress, or eating too fast with Finn underfoot. By the time she finally went in, the doctor said the gallbladder had to come out. Laparoscopic, nothing major. Might even be home the same day, he said."

I can guess how this story ends but I let him tell it.

"There was a complication during surgery. Rare. One in

thousands. Her heart just . . . stopped." His gaze fixes on the horizon. "We had our lives mapped out. And then . . ."

"I'm so sorry," I say softly.

"Her parents passed away before Finn was born, mine too, so it's not even like there are grandparents who can tell him about her. That's on me. And you're right, he needs to know who she was. He deserves those stories."

Gus bounds back up the beach, stick clenched in his mouth. Lachlan takes it. "You're playing with Finn, you daft mutt, not me." He hurls the stick down to the shore, and Gus tears after it, back to Finn.

"I know I haven't been easy to work with. But Blair, what you've done for Finn already . . . he's different. Happier. I'd like you to stay on, if you're willing. And I promise I'll try to do better."

I cross my arms, buying myself a second. Don't want to make this too easy for him. "I'll be honest. Last night and this morning, I was pretty close to packing it in."

Something flickers across his face. Fear, maybe.

"But," I add, "I accept your apology. And I'll stay." I glance toward Finn and Gus. "Besides, Finn's wormed his way into my heart. Gus too, surprisingly. And I suppose you're not so bad either."

I give him a cheeky smile, and after a moment he smiles back. Really smiles, not the stiff version he usually manages.

The sea breeze lifts his hair, and his green eyes catch the golden light reflecting off the water. When he's not scowling or looking like the weight of the world is on his shoulders, Lachlan Munro is downright breathtaking.

CHAPTER SIXTEEN

LACHLAN

Sweat clings to me, the low thud of bass from my Bluetooth speaker filling the garage. I lower the barbell onto the squat rack, legs burning from the last set, and wipe my forehead with the back of my hand. This is what I need. The sting of exertion, the ache building in my shoulders, the blessed simplicity of weight and resistance and nothing else.

No complicated emotions, no awkward conversations, no thoughts of—

"Oh! Sorry. I'll, um, come back another time."

Bloody hell.

Blair stands in the doorway, water bottle in hand, black leggings painted on, fitted sports top hugging every slim curve. Her hair is pulled back into a ponytail. She's ready to work, to sweat, and the sight knocks the breath clean out of me.

"You don't have to go," I manage, reaching for my own water bottle to buy myself a moment. "I said you could use the gym."

I'd meant when I'm not in it, but I can hardly turf her out now.

"Are you sure? I don't want to get in your way."

She's not even trying to be sexy but my brain doesn't give a damn. Those leggings. That top. The way it clings to her flat stomach and small breasts . . . *Christ, look somewhere else.*

"It's fine. Just mind the weights. Some of them are heavier than they look."

She steps inside and surveys the cramped space. It's not much. A bench, some dumbbells, squat rack shoved against the wall, a pull-up bar mounted in the doorway. Basic kit for a basic routine. Nothing fancy, just enough to work off the day's frustrations and keep myself in decent shape.

"Thanks for letting me crash your workout," she says, setting her water down and reaching for a pair of lighter dumbbells. "I promise I won't judge your routine too harshly."

I snort. "Generous of you."

Ducking back under the bar, I line it up on my shoulders then lift it and start another set of squats. A moment later Blair mirrors me, dumbbells tucked against her chest. The garage suddenly feels even smaller, the scent of her perfume mixing with sweat and metal. Every time she dips, it throws my focus off, wrecking my concentration.

"So this is where you come to hide from the world?" she asks between reps, slightly breathless.

"I don't hide."

"Right. You just happen to have built yourself a fortress of solitude in your garage."

There's teasing in her voice, but also understanding. Like she gets it. The need for a space that's yours alone, where you can strip everything back to its simplest parts.

"Something like that," I admit.

With a groan she sets down the dumbbells then watches me

while I do a few more reps. "Trying to keep up with you should come with a warning label," she complains.

"That was barely a warm-up. Besides, you're still standing, aren't you?"

"For now. If I collapse, you'll have to carry me out."

The mental image that conjures up—Blair in my arms, her body pressed close—nearly makes me drop the bloody bar. I carefully lower it back onto the rack.

The music changes and suddenly Marvin Gaye's "Let's Get It On" fills the garage.

Oh, for fuck's sake.

I lunge for my phone, fumbling to skip the track. "Bloody algorithm," I mutter, heat crawling up my neck. "Never plays what I want. Christ knows where that came from."

Blair's trying not to laugh, I can tell. Her lips are pressed together but her eyes are dancing with amusement. "Technology, huh? So unreliable."

"Aye, well . . ." I clear my throat and select something more appropriate. Something without lyrics about getting it on. Foo Fighters, that should do.

We work in comfortable silence for a few minutes, the tension easing. Then, between sets, she says, "So, about hiding from the world . . ."

"Aye?"

"Guess I'm hiding too." She gives me a quick, shy smile that doesn't quite reach her eyes. "From New York. From everything, really."

"What happened?"

So she tells me. About her dream job in children's publishing, about a storytelling app that went sideways, about how she took the fall. I let her talk, don't interrupt. She finishes with, "I wanted to come somewhere I didn't think anyone would know about the app. Or about me."

"Aye. That makes sense. Only thing is, that story? It reached us even here."

Her eyes widen in horror. "You're kidding?"

"Nope. Struan sent me a link to an article about it a while back. I think I said . . ." I get my phone and check. "Aye, my exact words were, *What pillock thought this was a good idea?*"

"You . . . you actually said that?"

I show her the message, unable to hold back a grin. "Sure did. But folk lap up a scandal, don't they? From all you've said, sounds like you got dealt a shite hand."

Her shoulders loosen a fraction. "So you're not going to fire me for being publishing's public enemy number one?"

"No. You've more than proved yourself. Mind you, if you'd told me all that at the interview, there's no way I'd have hired you. Maybe it's just as well you kept it to yourself." I pause. "And if I ever meet your old boss, he's getting a black eye."

She laughs. "Thank you. That means more than you know."

And just like that, something shifts between us. She's opened up and I didn't turn away. We're both running from something, and that understanding hangs in the air between us.

We get back to our workouts, but I find myself watching her more openly now. The way she bites her lip when she's concentrating. Blows at her blonde fringe when it gets in her eyes. Pushes herself even when she's tired. She's stronger than she looks, this lass. Losing her dream job, having her reputation torn to shreds, that would break most people. But she hasn't let it knock her down.

She moves to the mat and lies on her back, knees bent. Then she lifts her hips.

Glute bridges. Christ almighty.

I freeze, deadlifts forgotten, watching the smooth, controlled movement of her body. The way her back arches, the tilt of her hips, the flex of her thighs, the gentle curve of her—

I snap my gaze away.

Focus, you bloody idiot. She's exercising. It's not sexual. Except my body hasn't got the memo because my cock decides now is the perfect time to wake up. Cheers for that.

I slap a couple more plates onto the bar and attack my deadlifts harder than sense dictates, hauling the weight like it's to blame. But every time she moves, every soft exhale she makes, it's like someone's turned up the heat in the garage.

Think about something else. Anything but the way she's moving on that mat.

But it's no use. Four years I've kept this part of myself locked away, and now it's roaring back to life with the subtlety of a bloody freight train. I can feel my shorts getting tighter, and panic sets in because there's nowhere to hide in this cramped space.

"Okay, I'm done." Blair collapses flat on the mat and fans herself with her hand. "If I do another set, my glutes are going to mutiny."

Thank Christ.

"Could you pass me my water? I can't feel my legs."

Ah. I risk a quick glance down. Bit tight, but nothing obvious. Should be okay.

I grab her bottle, being very careful not to let our fingers brush when I hand it over. Can't risk even that much contact right now.

She sits up to drink and I turn away, pretending to organise weights that don't need organising.

"Right," she says after a few moments, "I'd better head back. Grab a quick shower."

Unhelpfully, my brain conjures up an image of Blair in the shower, water streaming down bare skin—

"Then straight to bed," Blair adds.

Oh, come on. This really isn't helping my shorts situation.

"See you tomorrow," I manage roughly. "Good workout."

She stands, stretching. I keep my back turned.

"Night, then," she says. But instead of going, she adds, "Lachlan, are you all right?"

Bloody hell. She's moving closer to me.

"Fine," I say without turning around.

"You sure?"

Her voice is quiet now. Close. Too close. If she reaches for my arm, touches me, I'm done for.

I cough, desperate to end this before I make a mistake I can't take back. "Aye. I'll see you in the morning."

There's a pause and I can feel her watching me. Finally she says, "All right. Sleep well, Lachlan."

I wait until the garage door clicks shuts before I let myself breathe again. I've kept this part of myself buried so deep I thought it was gone for good. Now, thanks to her, it's back with a vengeance.

God help me.

CHAPTER SEVENTEEN

BLAIR

"Your turn, Blair," Finn says, passing me the dice.

I'm sitting cross-legged on the living room rug. Finn kneels opposite me, and Gus is to the side. He's appointed himself official game supervisor, which apparently means drooling on the *Snakes and Ladders* board and nudging the little counters with his nose.

"Hey, Gus, stop moving things around!" I rescue my counter and put it back where it belongs.

Finn giggles. "He thinks everything's a toy." Reaching over to scratch behind Gus's ears, he adds loyally, "But we love him anyway, even if he is silly."

I roll the dice—a two—and land on a snake's head. "Ugh!" Back home it's chutes, here it's snakes. Just another minor cultural difference. Either way, it means I'm going back a *lot* of squares.

Finn whoops with delight at my misfortune, then the front door opens with a creak. Both Gus and Finn snap their heads toward the sound. Gus is first to bolt for the hallway, paws skittering on the hardwood. Finn's right behind him, abandoning our game without a second thought.

Lachlan's low chuckle reaches me from the hallway, followed by, "Aye, hello to you too, you daft mutt. Miss me, did you?"

"Da, guess what!" Finn's words trip over themselves in his rush to tell his father the big news. "Logan's invited me to his house for a sleepover! Isla's going to go too. There's going to be a boys' room and a girls' room. Can I go? Can I?"

I step into the hallway to find Finn bouncing at his father's side like a human pogo stick.

"Douglas is taking tomorrow off to look after the kids," I explain. "His parents can't do tomorrow for some reason."

Lachlan glances my way and raises an eyebrow. "Aye? And he seriously wants two more kids to look after? Four kids total?"

"That's what I said, but Douglas assured me Logan and Rosie are easier to manage when they've got friends to keep them busy—and to stop them fighting with each other."

"Rather him than me," Lachlan mutters.

I notice he's not looking at me directly, and there's something careful about the way he's holding himself. Controlled. Familiar. Frustrating. I thought we were past this after yesterday's beach conversation.

Then again, something was off last night in the garage too. He'd been distant, almost twitchy, like he couldn't wait for me to leave. Almost like he was . . . no, it couldn't have been that.

"Well, I suppose that's all right, Finn. Just so long as you don't let Logan lead you astray. You know how he likes to get up to mischief. Be on your best behaviour for Douglas, please."

"Woohoo!" Finn takes off down the hallway, pumping his fists in the air.

"I can pick him up in the morning," I offer. "It'll give me an opportunity to finally see inside Douglas's house."

Lachlan nods, his gaze skimming past me again. "Aye. Thanks, Blair. That's good of you."

The politeness in his voice grates. After all that progress yesterday—the apology, the honest conversation on the beach, the way he'd smiled at me—he's putting the walls back up again.

It's like one step forward, two steps back with this man.

◆ ◆ ◆

From my window in the granny flat, I watch Lachlan, Finn, and Gus walk along the road toward Douglas's house. Finn's practically skipping with excitement, no doubt chattering away to his father about all the games they'll play at the sleepover.

Twenty minutes later Lachlan and Gus trudge back alone. Lachlan's shoulders are set in that familiar tense line, and even from this distance, I can tell he's wound tight.

I pace around the small space, Gerald the only witness to my growing frustration. This hot and cold routine of Lachlan's is driving me crazy. One minute we're having breakthrough conversations on the beach, the next he's keeping me at arm's length like I'm radioactive.

Well, enough is enough. Finn's not here to overhear whatever awkward conversation we're about to have, and I'm done tiptoeing around whatever's eating at him.

I march across the backyard and knock hard enough to make the door rattle. Lachlan opens it, surprise flickering across his face. He's in dark jeans and a soft grey henley that clings to his chest in ways that do nothing for my concentration.

Gus trots over, tail wagging. I give him a distracted pat, eyes still on Lachlan.

"Hi," he says. "Washing machine? Gym?"

I fold my arms. "Do I have a load of dirty clothes with me? Am I in gym gear? No. I'm here to talk."

"Oh. Right." He steps back stiffly. "Best come in, then."

I brush past him into the kitchen. He hovers by the counter, hands shoved in his pockets. Gus curls up in his dog bed.

"Tea? Coffee?" Lachlan offers.

"I'm good." I fix him with a look. "Talk to me, Lachlan."

"About what?"

"About why you're acting so weird around me! Are you avoiding me? We were finally getting somewhere, and then suddenly it's like we've hit rewind."

"I've no idea what you're on about," he mutters, but there's no conviction in it.

"Oh, come on. I thought we were past this yesterday after your apology on the beach. But today you can barely look at me, and last night in the garage you got all weird on me at the end." I take a step closer. "What's going on?"

He runs a hand through his dark hair, leaving it mussed. "Blair . . ."

"I'm looking after your son five days a week. I'm right next door. I'm here for another month. If this is going to work, I need to know what the deal is."

"It's not . . ." He stops, swallows. It's like a war is playing out on his face. "You didn't do anything wrong."

"Then what?"

His jaw tightens. Finally, quietly: "Last night. In the garage. What you were wearing . . . and those exercises you were doing . . ."

Heat floods my cheeks but I don't back down. "The glute bridges?"

He nods, not meeting my eyes. "Aye. They were . . . distracting."

I fold my arms. "Please. Every morning I have to look at you in that uniform. Ever think about that?"

He scoffs and finally looks at me directly. "Aye, but you're a beautiful woman. I'm—"

"A handsome man," I cut in.

The words hang in the air between us. Lachlan stares at me like I've just claimed the moon's made of cheese, disbelief etched on every line of his face.

"Blair . . ."

"What?" I step closer, close enough to catch the clean, masculine scent of his soap. My pulse skips. "You don't think you're attractive? Because newsflash, Captain Munro, you are."

Surprise flickers in those green eyes, then it melts into something darker. Hotter. Dangerous.

I step closer still, tilting my face up toward him. His breathing's shallow, his pulse thudding at the base of his throat.

"Don't," he rasps.

I pause, lips inches from his. "Why not?"

"Because if I start, I won't be able to stop."

Heat spirals through me. I drink in the conflict tightening every muscle in his face, the way his fists clench like he's fighting himself.

Screw it. I press my lips to his.

For a heartbeat he goes still. Panic spikes—have I pushed too far?

Then his hands are in my hair and he's kissing me like he's starving, desperate, stealing the breath from my lungs. When I open for him, his tongue slides against mine, rough and demanding, and the sound he makes is broken, guttural, like a man in pain.

"This is a bad idea," he mutters against me, even as his hands slide down to grip my hips.

"I know," I breathe, tugging him closer anyway.

He backs me against the wall, his body pressing against mine, and I feel him hardening through his jeans. The realisation jolts through me. I fist my hands in his hair, marvelling at how soft it is, how good he smells this close.

His hands move over me, charting every curve, and when he cups my tit through my sweater, I arch into his palm with a soft moan that drives him wild.

Across the room Gus lifts his head at the commotion then huffs and flops back down, as if deciding humans are hopeless.

"Bedroom," Lachlan growls, the rough command sending a shiver straight to my core.

We stumble toward the stairs, pausing every few steps to kiss, hands roaming, pulling at clothes. My sweater hits the floor somewhere between the kitchen and the bottom step. His henley follows soon after, and I get my first look at his chest—broad, solid, a landscape of dark hair that makes my fingers itch to touch. *Tom Selleck, eat your heart out.*

By the time we reach his bedroom, I'm breathless, my bra hanging loose. I don't even know when he unhooked it.

Lachlan stops just inside the doorway, hands poised to push the bra off my shoulders. "Tell me to stop."

I meet his eyes, seeing the conflict there, the vulnerability. "I don't want you to stop."

The bra slips off and hits the floor.

For a moment he just stares, like he can't believe I'm real. "So fucking pretty," he says hoarsely. Then his hands are on me again, rough, greedy palms closing over my tits, thumbs teasing my nipples until I'm gasping his name.

When he lowers his head to take one nipple into his mouth, the scrape of his beard against me is exquisite torture. I thread my fingers through his hair, holding him there as he devours me, teasing first one nipple, then the other until I'm squirming.

"My turn," I manage, pushing him back just far enough to fumble at the button of his jeans. After wrestling both them and his boxers down, I have to stop and stare. Because Jesus, he's gorgeous. Thick, hard, flushed, and mine to touch. My mouth actually waters.

Then I spot the detail. Uncircumcised. Huh, that's new. All my exes were cut.

"Interesting," I murmur, and before he can so much as blink, I'm wrapping my fingers around his cock and exploring the way the skin shifts under my touch, sliding back to bare his glistening pink head then forward again to hide it.

He sucks in a sharp breath. "Christ, Blair. You're not shy, are you?"

"Nope." I grin up at him, cheerful as anything, and keep going. Every stroke makes him twitch and groan. When a bead of pre-cum gleams at the tip, I drag my thumb across it just to see what he'll do. The low, broken sound that rumbles out of him is pure sin.

But then his big hand clamps around my wrist, halting me.

I raise an eyebrow. "Hey, I was just starting to have fun down here! And don't even try to pretend you're not enjoying this. Trust me, captain, I can feel how much you are."

"I'm enjoying it too much," he growls, his Scottish accent

thicker than usual. "It's been years, Blair. If you keep going, I'll lose it right here. Leave my cock alone and let me taste you."

He makes quick work of my leggings and panties then guides me onto the bed. When he settles between my thighs, I brace for him to be frantic, as desperate as his kisses.

Instead, he slows down. His big hands spread me open, his thumbs parting me with maddening care, and the look on his face makes my breath hitch. He's studying me like I'm a treasure he's been denied for years.

"Beautiful," he murmurs, and then his head dips.

The first stroke of his tongue rips a cry out of me. That mouth that's been so stingy with smiles, so quick with sharp words—God, it knows exactly what to do to my pussy. He licks and sucks and teases until I'm writhing, fists buried in his hair.

He eats me like a starving man, like he can't get enough, tongue flicking over my clit until I'm babbling his name. The noises spilling out of me are obscene, but I don't care.

His grip on my thighs tightens, holding me open for him as I climb higher. His breathing grows rougher, punctuated by deep, guttural sounds that vibrate against me until I can't hold back any longer.

When I come, crying out his name, his fingers dig into me hard enough to bruise. I feel the scrape of his teeth as he groans, his whole body trembling like he's unravelling right along with me.

For a second I just lie there, dazed. Then my brain catches up. Wait . . . did he—

I prop myself up, panting, and glance down between us. Sure enough, his cock is twitching, a creamy drop leaking from the tip. "Oh my God. Did you . . . ?"

Colour rushes up his neck, flooding his cheeks. I can't stop the grin that spreads across my face.

"That's kind of hot," I tell him. "Proof of how much you wanted me. Who knew Captain Grumpypants could lose control like that?"

He groans, mortified, but I don't care. I draw him down onto the bed beside me. When my eyes snag again on the drop of cum still clinging to him, I don't even think. I just lean down and lick it away, tasting salt and him.

His hips twitch and he makes a throaty sound. His cock is slowly softening, and I watch with interest as his foreskin slides forward, covering him. Curiosity sparks, and I press a kiss to the soft, velvet skin.

"Christ!" he gasps.

"That got your attention." I pull his foreskin back and kiss the head directly.

This time his hips jerk, and his moan is low and ragged. I laugh softly. "Who knew foreskins could be this much fun?"

He gives me a roguish smile. "Trouble. Pure trouble, that's what you are, Blair."

But for the first time since I've known him, Lachlan Munro looks completely relaxed—wrecked, but relaxed. And I have to admit, I kind of love being the one responsible for it.

Grinning like an idiot, I curl into his warmth. He gathers me close without a second thought.

For a few minutes neither of us says anything. We just lie there, bodies tangled, catching our breath. I'm still floating, replaying every filthy, wonderful second.

Then Lachlan's phone buzzes on the nightstand. He reaches for it immediately, glances at the screen, and goes rigid.

"It's Douglas," he mutters, already swiping to answer. "What's wrong? Is Finn all right?"

I push up onto an elbow. His voice is clipped, urgent, like he's bracing for disaster. Has losing his wife conditioned him to always expect the worst?

But Douglas's reply, faint but clear in the quiet room, is calm. "Nothing's wrong. Finn just wanted to say good night."

And then Finn's small voice: "Night, Da. Love you."

Lachlan exhales, shoulders sagging. "Love you too, lad. Sleep well."

He ends the call and sits on the edge of the bed, naked, staring at nothing.

After a moment he says, "This was a mistake. A terrible mistake. I'm your boss. I had no right—"

"Relax." I sit up beside him. "There's no HR department here." My gaze drops: his cock is fully soft now, lying heavy against his balls. I give it a little poke like I'm testing if an avocado is ripe. "Pretty sure you're safe from a sexual harassment complaint."

But he doesn't laugh. Instead, he drags a hand over his face. "You're my son's nanny, Blair. This can't happen again. Ever."

The words knock the wind out of me. Heat prickles my skin, and not in a good way. *Great. Best orgasm of my entire life and now he's acting like we just opened Pandora's box.*

I want to laugh at the absurdity. How could something that felt so right be wrong? But the laugh won't come. Because the truth is, I don't want that to have been a one-time thing. Not now I've felt what it's like to be wanted with that kind of hunger.

CHAPTER EIGHTEEN

BLAIR

I wake alone in the granny flat to the hush of the sea and the cries of gulls overhead. Peaceful enough—for a moment. Then my thoughts tumble back to last night.

God, the way he'd eaten me out was like . . . like his life depended on it. I've never experienced anything like it. My cheeks flush just thinking about it. But then afterward . . . the way he'd shut down, called it a mistake, acted like we'd committed some kind of crime against humanity.

I roll over and check my phone. Nearly nine o'clock. Normally I'd have been with Finn for an hour by now, but with him at Douglas's, I had the luxury of sleeping in. It also saved me from having to face Lachlan before he left for work. Small blessing.

After a quick shower I head into the main house, pat a very excited Gus, then clip his leash to his collar. "Come on, boy. Let's go collect your favourite little human."

Naturally, Gus stops to sniff every streetlight and front gate, but before long we reach Braeview Drive. The sounds of chaos spill out Douglas's house before I even knock: kids shrieking with laughter, feet thundering across floors, and what sounds like a wrestling match in progress.

Douglas answers the door looking like he's survived a natural disaster. His red hair is sticking up at odd angles, and there's a dusting of flour on his shirt.

"Blair! Perfect timing. I was just about to send up a flare for rescue services."

Behind him, Logan streaks past wearing nothing but underwear and a superhero cape. Rosie barrels after him in full princess regalia, brandishing a wooden spoon like a sceptre.

A beat later Finn and Isla appear together, looking almost civilised after the storm that just blew through. When Finn spots me, he grins so wide it nearly splits his face. "Blair! You're here!"

"Hi, buddy. Good to see you—and fully dressed! Unlike some."

Finn giggles then drops to his knees for a Gus reunion. The dog smothers him with wet kisses.

"Hi, Blair," Isla says to me, calm as you please, like we've been friends for years. Then she turns and races off after the twins, yelling, "Logan, capes don't make you invincible!"

"Have you had a good time?" I ask, tousling Finn's already messy hair.

"The best! We stayed up until ten thirty, and Logan taught me how to make armpit farts, and we built a spaceship and flew to Mars, and—"

"All right, lad," Douglas interrupts with a chuckle. "Maybe save some stories for the walk home. Blair, would you like the grand tour? Fair warning, though, I'd planned to have the place spotless for you, but with four kids staying over . . ." He gestures helplessly at the chaos around us.

"I'd love to see it, and don't worry about the mess. I'm just impressed you're all still alive and accounted for."

While Finn and Gus tear off after the twins and Isla, Douglas leads me through the house, making jokes about the various disasters that befell each room during the sleepover. The living room, which I glimpsed through the window my first day in Ardmara, is now a minefield of Lego. Douglas warns me to watch where I'm going—says there's no pain on earth worse than stepping on Lego. The kitchen, meanwhile, still bears the scars of what he drily calls "the pancake fiasco".

It's a lovely house, warm and lived-in. But as we move from room to room, I keep waiting for that moment of connection, that sense of "this is where Granny grew up".

It doesn't come.

At first I think I'm maybe too distracted by last night. But no, that's not it. I just . . . don't feel her here. And I shouldn't be surprised, really. The house probably looks nothing like it did when she was young, not with the modern appliances and Douglas's furniture, and with toys scattered everywhere.

But as we head back downstairs, I think of what I told Lachlan, about how important it is to tell stories about the ones we've lost. He listened—he told Finn stories about his mom—so maybe it's time I take a leaf out of my own book.

Douglas leads me back into the kitchen, where the four kids are clustered around the table, picking at leftover pancakes, Gus positioned strategically for any dropped crumbs.

"You know," I say to the kids, "my granny once told me a story about something that happened in this kitchen when she was your age."

Four pairs of eyes snap to me. Even Douglas looks intrigued.

"When my granny was little, it was normal for families to

keep chickens in their yards. Some even had a goose or two. Not pets exactly, more like noisy alarm systems that also laid eggs."

"Geese are mean," Isla says with authority.

"Well, one day my granny forgot to latch the back gate. The neighbour's goose spotted its chance. It waddled into the yard, marched through the open kitchen door, and suddenly"—I spread my arms wide and flap them, honking loudly enough to make the kids jump—"HOOOONK!"

The kids squeal with laughter.

"My granny and her mom were shrieking, running in circles while this great big goose flapped and chased them around the kitchen table. They tried to shoo it out, but it just hissed and flapped harder, until finally her mom grabbed a broom and chased it out the door."

Rosie's eyes are wide. "And that happened in *this* kitchen?"

"In this very kitchen," I confirm. "And guess what? Granny never forgot to latch the gate again."

The four kids look at each other, grinning, then Logan sticks out his elbows, flaps like mad, and shouts, "HONK! HONK!"

The others dissolve into laughter and join in. Gus, excited by the noise, bounces around them, barking like he's part of the flock.

Meeting Douglas's amused eye, I bite my lip. "Sorry!"

He chuckles. "Don't be. That was a brilliant story. But aye, Logan and Rosie are going to be honking the rest of the day now."

I giggle, but inside something settles into place. I came here hoping to feel my granny in these walls. Instead, I brought one of her stories to life for a new set of children, and maybe that's even better.

♦ ♦ ♦

Finn's tongue pokes out as he concentrates on drawing a lopsided dragon with way too many teeth. He's beside me at the kitchen table, and I'm half watching him, half watching the clock. Any moment now—

Right on schedule the front door clicks open. Finn's head snaps up like a meerkat's. "Da's home!" He abandons his picture and bolts for the hallway, though Gus gets there first.

Okay, time to make myself scarce. Already got my shoes on— always be prepared for a quick exit.

"Hi, Lachlan," I call toward the hallway as I edge for the back door. "That's me off!"

I'm one second from freedom when his voice stops me. "Wait!"

Damn it. Wasn't quick enough.

"Blair, I wanted to say"—his voice grows louder as he approaches—"you can stay for dinner tonight, if you want. Or not. Up to you."

Before I can even process this unexpected invitation, Finn comes tearing back into the kitchen.

"Yes! Please stay, Blair! Please!" He bounces on his toes, eyes wide with hope. "It's fish and chips night. Da's the best at making them, honest!"

My hand is on the door handle, escape within reach. But then Lachlan follows his son into the kitchen, and for once he doesn't avoid my gaze. He looks straight at me, steady and direct. Still in his ferry captain uniform, crisp white shirt and dark trousers, all authority and command.

"Well?" he prompts. "You staying?"

A beat passes. The kitchen feels too small, the air too thick.

168

Finn's hopeful face. Lachlan's unwavering gaze. The memory of his hands on my skin, his mouth on my—

"Okay . . . yeah, I'll stay," I hear myself say.

Lachlan's face transforms. A real smile spreads across it, wide and genuine, the kind that makes him look years younger and dangerously attractive.

"Perfect." He rubs his hands together. "Why don't you two relax next door and watch some telly? I'll sort dinner."

Finn blinks up at his father in amazement. "I don't have to help?"

And he's not the only one who's surprised. Lachlan suggesting screen time? Outside of the sacred schedule? Is it a blue moon?

"Well, you were at a sleepover last night," Lachlan says reasonably. "I imagine you're tired. You can relax for the next wee while, then tell me all about it when we're eating."

Fast-forward a few minutes, and I'm on the couch with Finn, watching some cartoon about talking vegetables while he provides running commentary on every single plot point. To be honest, after the emotional whiplash of the past twenty-four hours, mindless kids' TV is exactly what I need.

"Dinner!" Lachlan calls from the kitchen a while later.

We head through to find the table set and Lachlan changed into a soft grey T-shirt and black sweatpants, his feet bare. In casual clothes he looks . . . human. Approachable. Definitely not the stern ferry captain. More like the man who held me in his arms last night, however briefly.

As I approach my chair, he pulls it out for me. The unexpected chivalry catches me off-guard, and I glance at him in surprise, but he's already settling into his own seat as if it were nothing.

The fish and "chips"—french fries, not a bag of Lay's—are perfectly golden. There is, however, a suspicious green blob on the side, which I eye warily.

"Uh . . . is that baby food?"

"They're peas," Finn says. "They're supposed to look like that. They're mushy peas."

"If you say so, buddy." I try them. Soft, buttery, a little salty. Not nearly as tragic as they look.

As we eat, Finn launches into an exhausting play-by-play of every moment of his sleepover. And I mean *every* moment. What time they went to bed (ten thirty!), what they had for breakfast (pancakes that looked like spaceships!), how Logan can burp the alphabet (but only got to M before his dad told him to stop).

I'm grateful for Finn's chatter. It fills the silence between Lachlan and me, all the things we can't say with little ears listening. But even as I nod and smile at Finn's stories, I'm hyperaware of Lachlan across the table. The precise way he cuts his fish. The way his mouth quirks when Finn describes the "epic pillow fight that nearly destroyed the universe".

Finn yawns hugely, rubbing his eyes even as he keeps talking. Poor kid's running out of gas.

"Here, let me help," I murmur, reaching over to cut his fish into smaller pieces. The gesture is so automatic, so natural, I don't think twice about it—

Until my gaze catches on the photo of Leanne in the frame Finn and I decorated. She's looking down at baby Finn with such love, and suddenly I feel like an imposter. Today I'm cutting up her son's fish. Last night I was in her husband's bed.

No wonder my stomach twists.

"And then," Finn continues around another yawn, "we played the floor is lava, and in the end it was between Logan and

170

Rosie, but Logan fell in, so Rosie crowned herself queen of the lava and made us bow to her."

"Sounds like you had quite the adventure, lad," Lachlan says. "I'm amazed Douglas survived it."

Finn giggles. "He said next time he's sending us all to Struan's house."

"Poor Struan doesn't know what's coming for him."

I force a smile, but I catch Lachlan looking at me a moment too long before he glances away. The air between us is charged.

By the time we finish eating, Finn can barely keep his eyes open. He's swaying slightly in his chair, fighting sleep with the determination of a tiny warrior.

"Right then," Lachlan says, standing to clear the plates. "Someone clearly needs an early night. I'll go run you a bath."

"Can I have a bath tomorrow instead?" Finn mumbles.

Lachlan considers, then nods. "Aye, that's fine. In that case, it's time to get into your jammies. Let's go upstairs."

Finn slides off his chair and gives me a sleepy wave. "Night, Blair."

"Night, buddy. Sweet dreams." As they head for the stairs, I add, "I'll sort the dishes."

"Leave them," Lachlan calls back. "You're a guest tonight. I don't want you lifting a finger."

When Lachlan comes back downstairs ten minutes later, I'm at the sink, elbow-deep in soapy water.

"Finn asleep?" I ask, glancing over my shoulder.

"Out like a light. He barely made it through—" Lachlan stops mid-sentence when he spots me. "Oi, I told you not to do that."

"You cooked, I'm cleaning up. That's fair." I set a plate in the drying rack. "Besides, I'm almost done."

The kitchen falls quiet except for the gentle splash of water and the soft clink of dishes. Lachlan hovers nearby, hands shoved in his pockets. The room feels crowded with everything we're not saying.

Finally, he clears his throat. "Blair, about last night. The things I said afterward . . . I'm sorry. I panicked."

I pause, a glass halfway to the rack. "It's okay."

"No, it's not." His voice is rough around the edges. "The thing is . . . it's not just that I haven't been with anyone since Leanne passed. It's that I was never with anyone before her. There was no one else."

The glass nearly slips from my hand. I set it down carefully then turn to face him. The raw vulnerability in his expression squeezes my chest.

"Oh," I manage finally.

"We got together in our teens," he adds, like he needs to fill the silence. "So . . . I know what we did last night probably doesn't mean as much to you as it did to me. You're from New York. *Sex and the City* and all that."

I blink, then a smile tugs at my lips. "Wow, your references are so up to date. You do realise that started airing in the nineties, right?"

His cheeks flush but he presses on. "My point is, it's none of my business, but I imagine you've had multiple sexual partners. You didn't grow up on a small Scottish island like me. So, last night . . . well, it meant something to me."

The earnestness in his voice brings my teasing to a screeching halt. I dry my hands on the dish towel then step closer to him, laying my palm on his arm. "It meant something to me too," I say simply.

Relief flashes across his face, softening into something

warmer. For a moment we just stand there, my hand on his arm, the kitchen hushed around us.

"Anyway." I give his arm a gentle squeeze before letting go. "Finn's not the only one who's pooped. I'm going to head back."

Disappointment flickers in his eyes. Before it can linger, I lean in and press a soft kiss to his cheek, breathing in his clean, masculine scent.

"Good night, captain."

I slip toward the back door, aware of his gaze following me, my heart doing something fluttery and ridiculous in my chest.

◆ ◆ ◆

Back in the granny flat, I go through my usual bedtime routine on autopilot—face wash, moisturiser, brushing my teeth. But my mind keeps circling back to our conversation in the kitchen, especially that moment when his voice cracked slightly as he said, "There was no one else."

The raw honesty of it. The way he'd looked at me like he was bracing for rejection.

I spit out toothpaste, rinse, then shuffle toward bed, saying goodnight to Gerald. I've only just lain down with my notebook and pen when there's a knock at the door.

I open it and there he is, in an old grey T-shirt and navy pyjama bottoms, his hair mussed.

"I just realised," he says quietly, "you kissed me goodnight . . . and I never kissed you back."

The world stutters to a halt.

"So I wanted to fix that."

He steps closer and cups my face in his hands. His mouth is warm, gentle against mine, nothing like the desperate passion of last night. His beard grazes my skin, his breath carrying the faintest hint of mint. And then, too soon, he's pulling back. It was only the briefest of kisses, but it leaves me swaying.

"Goodnight, Blair."

"Uh . . ." I swallow. "Goodnight, captain."

He turns and leaves me in the doorway, my lips still tingling.

CHAPTER NINETEEN

LACHLAN

Saturday morning, and the house feels lighter somehow. Maybe it's the sun streaming through the kitchen windows, or maybe it's the sizzle of bacon and sausages in the pan, the smell of toast. I may have a rigid meal routine, but Saturday's our cheat morning. Start of the weekend and all that.

My phone buzzes on the work surface. The Dadventurers group chat.

> **DOUGLAS**
>
> Usual time at the Pit today, lads?
>
> **STRUAN**
>
> Aye, Isla and I will be there.
>
> Lachlan, why don't you invite that nanny of yours along? She was a laugh the other day. Bonny too.

A sharp, unwelcome spark fires low in my belly. *Bonny too.* Aye, she is. But the thought of Struan's easy charm working on Blair, of him making her laugh the way he does with all the mums at the Pit . . .

No. Not today.

LACHLAN

Nah, too sunny for soft play. Finn and I have other plans. Next time.

I plate up the food and carry it to the table. Finn's already sliding into his chair, eyes bright, smacking his lips. Gus hovers close, tail swishing.

"Dig in, lad."

He needs no encouragement, squeezing ketchup onto his plate before attacking his bacon. I add brown sauce to my own plate then cut a bit off a sausage and toss it to Gus. He catches it midair.

Finn munches away with gusto, but between mouthfuls he's already thinking ahead. "I can't wait to play with Isla and the twins later. Maybe we'll finish the superhero game we were playing at the sleepover. It was so—"

"We're not going to the Pit today."

"What?" His fork clatters against the plate. "But we always go on Saturdays!" His lower lip juts out, full pout engaged.

"Aye, usually. But I thought we could go to Traigh Bàn instead." I pause, letting this sink in. "And invite Blair along."

The transformation is instant. The pout vanishes like it was never there. "Really? We can invite Blair even though it's the weekend and it's not her job to look after me?"

"We can invite her but I can't guarantee she'll say yes. Why don't we see what she thinks?"

"Now?" He's halfway off his chair already.

"Finish your food first."

He demolishes it in record time then bolts for the back door,

Gus bounding after him. I follow at a more reasonable speed, but I'm no less eager than he is.

Finn pounds on the granny flat door with all the subtlety of a battering ram. "Blair! Blair, it's us!"

The door opens, and there she is. Hair sleep-ruffled, an oversized jumper slipping off one shoulder, but just as breathtaking as ever. She looks surprised but pleased to see us.

"We're going on an adventure today, and you're coming too!" Finn announces.

"Only if you want to," I add quickly. "No worries if you've got other plans."

That smile of hers—bright, unfiltered—hits me square in the chest. "Sounds like fun. I'm in."

Finn whoops with delight, already tugging on her hand. "Can we go now? Can we? I'll get my bucket and spade."

Outwardly I'm calm, but truthfully I'm just as pleased as my son. Maybe more.

"Give Blair a chance to get ready first," I tell him. Then, to Blair, "We'll head off in an hour?"

"Perfect."

◆ ◆ ◆

The drive to Traigh Bàn, Gaelic for "white beach", takes twenty minutes. Finn chatters about sand castles and buried treasure the whole way, Blair occasionally punctuating his monologue with a delighted exclamation when the coastal road grants us a particularly spectacular view.

When we crest the final hill and the beach spreads out below us—miles of pristine white sand kissed by turquoise water—Blair breathes, "Oh my God. This place is beautiful."

I pull into the small car park. The moment I turn off the engine, Finn rockets out of the car, Gus bounding after him towards the dunes. Blair and I follow at a more leisurely pace. I carry the rucksack with our supplies while she has the picnic blanket tucked under one arm.

When we reach the beach, we kick off our shoes. The sand is soft beneath my feet, the air carrying that familiar tang of salt, only today it tastes sweeter somehow. The breeze teases Blair's sundress and tugs at her blonde hair, half clipped up but already coming loose. I have to shove my hands in my pockets to stop myself from reaching out and tucking a stray strand back behind her ear.

"Look, Da!" Finn shouts from ahead. "I can see forever!"

He's not wrong. The beach stretches endlessly in both directions. A few families are scattered in the distance, but we might as well have the place to ourselves.

"Wow. Back home in New York a place like this would be packed on a day like today."

"Aye, well. That's why I live here and not there." I shoot Blair a half-smile. "Not a big fan of crowds."

"You don't say? And here was me thinking you were a people person."

I smirk. Then, spotting a pair of black and white birds picking their way along the shoreline, I point them out. "Oystercatchers. Listen."

Their sharp, piping calls carry on the breeze, and Blair tilts her head to catch the sound. "Beautiful view, dramatic birdsong . . . you're really spoiling me, captain."

We spread the blanket near the dunes, far enough from the tide line to stay dry but close enough for Finn to dash between us and the water without me worrying. The idea is that he and Gus might play by themselves for a bit, but of course Blair and I have only just sat down when Finn unzips my rucksack, rummages about, and pulls out a ball. "C'mon, you two! Let's play!"

So, up we get again, and we have a fun game of catch for a few minutes—until Gus intercepts the ball midair and races off with it in his mouth. We all chase after him, Finn shrieking with delight, Blair's dress flying, me trying hard to focus on the dog and not that dress.

We get the ball back—slobbery but intact—but now Finn wants to head down to the water. He yanks off his T-shirt without a second thought, and I throw Blair a wry smile before tugging mine off too, stripping to my shorts. I give Finn a five-second head start before chasing him to the shore. When I catch him, I hoist him up onto my shoulders and race through the shallows, Gus splashing alongside us. Finn whoops, his arms spread out like wings, and Blair's laughter carries across the beach as she cheers us on.

I run a hundred metres or so before turning and racing back again, then I haul Finn down from my shoulders and dangle him over the water. He squeals, kicking his legs, trying to cling to me.

"Nooo, Da, don't you dare!"

I grin and plonk him straight in.

He goes under with a splash and comes up sputtering, hair plastered to his forehead, laughing so hard he can barely breathe. Then, with a battle cry, he launches himself at me, skinny arms locking round my stomach.

"Got you now!"

I let him knock me backwards into the surf, water closing over my head. When I surface again, he sits on my chest like he's just slain a monster, triumphant grin splitting his face.

"Victory!" he crows.

Once he's milked the moment for all it's worth, Finn finally clambers off my chest, water dripping from him in streams. Gus shakes himself beside us, spraying both of us with even more. I haul myself up, raking a hand through my hair and wringing out my shorts, then together we make our way back up the beach.

Blair's been watching the whole spectacle, amusement written all over her face. She's sitting on the blanket, arms wrapped round her knees, sundress fluttering in the breeze.

When Finn gets close, he grins wickedly and holds out his dripping arms. "Wet hug!"

Blair lets out a mock scream and scrambles to her feet. "Don't you dare, mister!"

Finn charges straight for her, giggling, while she races across the sand, laughing and protesting. Gus thinks this is a great game and tears after them, barking like mad.

I stay where I am, watching, chest still heaving from the run and dunking. And it hits me. *This.* This is what's been missing. Laughter. Joy. The way Blair makes everything lighter, makes even an ordinary Saturday feel like a holiday.

Blair, with Finn not far behind, doubles back to the blanket, snatches up a towel, and whirls to face him. "Now I'm going to get you!"

Finn turns tail and runs, but Blair catches him, wraps the towel around him, and squeezes him tight. "One hug, just as requested! Only I get to stay dry."

He squeals, wriggling, then finally surrenders, turning to face her and grinning as she gives his upper half a quick rub dry. They make their way back to the blanket together, Finn now swaddled like a burrito.

I unpack the rucksack: sandwiches, juice cartons, fruit, and the flapjacks Flora dropped round earlier despite her broken wrist. Blair picks one up, takes a bite, and closes her eyes in appreciation. "These are incredible. How on earth did she make these with her arm in a sling?"

"Stubbornness, mostly," I reply. "Woman's got more determination than sense sometimes."

"Her Empire biscuits are my favourite," Finn chimes in. "I can't wait till her arm's better so she can make them again." He licks his lips in anticipation.

We eat, and after a while I notice Blair's gaze flicking my way. Her eyes linger on my bare chest, wet shorts, the sand stuck to my skin. She looks up quickly, meets my eyes, and gives me a smile that feels warmer than the sun overhead.

Then, suddenly: "Oh! Sun cream." She rifles through her bag.

Finn groans. "Do I have to?"

"Yes, mister. You'll thank me when you don't look like a lobster later." She squeezes some onto her palm and pats the space in front of her. "Come here."

He shuffles over reluctantly, plonking himself down cross-legged. Blair peels his towel open, freeing his arms and shoulders, then rubs the lotion in with gentle but thorough strokes while he squirms and pulls faces.

"Hold still, buddy," she scolds lightly. "You want the seagulls to mistake you for a tomato?"

Finn giggles, and I find myself chuckling too, more at his glee than the joke. Watching them together, so easy, so natural . . . it does something to me I can't quite name.

It doesn't make sense. A woman like her—smart, beautiful, with her whole life ahead of her—and me. A broken widower with more baggage than sense. She deserves better than someone who's spent four years hiding from the world.

Then again, she's not here to stay. She's only here for the summer. It's temporary.

The thought sends an odd pang through my chest. Because what happens when she leaves? What will that do to Finn, who's already so attached? And what will it do to me?

I catch myself before the spiral can take hold. *Live in the moment*, I tell myself firmly. *Don't ruin this.*

"Da, can I borrow your phone?"

I hand it over without thinking, then watch as Finn fiddles with it for a moment before holding it up at arm's length.

"Say cheese!" Gus bounds over, shoving his sandy nose into the shot, and Finn laughs as he snaps the picture.

"Let me see," I say, taking the phone back.

Bloody hell.

There we are—Finn beaming in the centre, Blair's arm draped casually around his shoulders, me on the other side with something approaching a smile, and Gus's golden head poking into the bottom of the frame. We look . . . right together. Too right. Natural. Like a family.

And that's what makes it dangerous.

I shut down the thought before it can take root.

The afternoon stretches on, perfect and golden. Finn builds a sandcastle, Gus digs holes, and we all lie on our backs spotting shapes in the clouds.

When Finn and Gus wander off to do some paddling, Blair settles beside me on the blanket. She follows my gaze across the water to where Corraig rests on the horizon, a green jewel in the sea.

"Have you ever taken Finn there?" she asks gently. "To see where he spent his first few years?"

I shake my head. "To be honest, even though I sail there ten times a week, I never get off the ferry myself."

She's quiet for a moment, not pushing. It's one of the things I'm learning to appreciate about her. She knows when to speak and when to let silence do the work.

"Well," she says finally, "maybe it'd be nice for you to go together one day. And if you'd like some emotional support, I'd be more than happy to join you."

The offer is simple, no strings attached. No judgement for my cowardice, no pressure to decide right now. Just support, if I want it.

"Thanks," I say. "I'll think about it."

By late afternoon Finn admits defeat to exhaustion and curls up on the blanket with his head pillowed on my thigh. Gus flops down beside him, equally knackered from a day of hole digging and ball chasing.

Blair and I sit in comfortable silence, watching the light change on the water. Her hand rests on the blanket between us, close enough that I could reach out and cover it with mine, if I had the courage.

For the first time in four years, I'm not trying to be happy for Finn's sake. I just . . . am. The weight that's been pressing on my chest for so long has lifted, just for today. I can breathe.

"This has been perfect," Blair says softly.

I look down at my napping son then meet her eyes and nod. "Aye. It has."

CHAPTER TWENTY

LACHLAN

After Finn drifts off—exhausted from sun and sand—I find myself at my bedroom window, staring across the back garden towards the granny flat. A soft glow spills from Blair's window, and though I can't see her from here, I know she's still awake.

I should go to bed. Let today end on the perfect note it's already struck. Maintain some bloody boundaries.

Instead, I pad barefoot through the house and out the back door, the night air cool against my skin. My pulse quickens as I cross the garden and knock on her door.

She opens it almost immediately, like she was waiting. She's in soft cotton shorts and a vest, her hair loose around her shoulders. And her eyes . . . warmth, mischief, a dare I can't resist.

"You here to give me another goodnight kiss?" she asks, that American directness I'm coming to love threading through her voice.

"Aye," I rasp.

Our kiss isn't innocent like last night's. I frame her face with my hands and take her mouth, hungry for the sweetness I've been thinking about all evening. She melts against me, fingers fisting in my shirt.

We stumble backwards into the flat. I kick the door shut, lips never leaving hers. She tastes of heat and salt air, and I can't get enough.

"The curtains!" she gasps. "Can't get up to mischief in front of Gerald." With a cheeky wink, she goes over to the window, where that plant of hers still sits on the sill, and yanks the curtains closed.

I chuckle, heat thrumming low. "Looks like you've learned your lesson. Close the curtains first, *then* get your tits out." I catch the hem of her vest top, tugging it upwards. "Or rather, let *me* get your tits out."

She laughs as I tug the vest over her head, and Christ, the sight of her bare chest nearly stops my heart. Four years I went without this hunger, without touching or wanting like this, and now she's all I crave.

Her tits are perfect, small and pert, nipples already erect in the cool air. I can't stop myself from cupping one, marvelling at the soft weight of it, the firm peak jutting against my hand.

"Lachlan." Just my name, but breathless, needy—and it makes my cock strain hard against my joggers, the thin fabric doing nothing to hide what she's doing to me.

I back her against the wall, mouth at her throat, her collarbone, the sweet spot where neck meets shoulder. She tastes of clean skin and faint soap, better than any whisky, and I want to devour every inch of her.

Her hands are busy too, tugging at my T-shirt until I have to break away long enough to pull it over my head. When her palms flatten against my chest, fingers tangling in the hair there, a low groan rumbles out of me.

"Time to lose these," I mutter, hooking my thumbs into the waistband of her shorts. I slide them down her legs, and fuck me, seeing her naked again knocks the breath from my lungs.

She's beautiful. Pale silk skin, curves and hollows my hands itch to explore. A neat triangle of golden hair between her thighs. The rise and fall of her chest, quick with need. I've already tasted her, but the sight of her like this still makes me feel half-wild, undone.

"You're staring," she says softly, but there's no self-consciousness in it. Just heat.

"Can you blame me?" My voice comes out gravelly. "You're . . . Christ, I've no words."

And I really don't. No words do justice to what I'm seeing, what I'm feeling. So I kiss her instead, deep and hungry, my hands greedy on her body. The curve of her waist, the flare of her hips, the soft skin of her inner thighs . . .

When I cup her pussy, she's already wet. "Please," she whispers against my lips, and I don't need to be asked twice.

I slide one finger through her folds, finding her clit, and she arches against the wall. She's slick and ready, and when I circle that sensitive bundle of nerves, her hips buck against my hand.

"More," she gasps, and I ease one finger inside her.

Christ. She's tight, hot, gripping me like a fist. I have to close my eyes for a moment to keep from losing control. When I add a second finger, she cries out, head thudding back against the wall.

I work her slow but steady, thumb on her clit while my fingers curl inside, finding that spot that makes her writhe. She's making sounds that wreck me—gasps, moans, broken little cries. And now she's rocking against my fingers, working herself on me. Fuck, watching her chase her own pleasure is enough to break a man.

"Lachlan, I'm—"

"That's it," I murmur against her ear. "Let go for me."

And she does. She shatters, crying my name as her body clenches around my fingers. I nearly come myself just from watching her. The flush across her chest, the way her mouth falls open, the tremor that runs through her whole body—it's sexy as hell.

She sags against the wall afterwards, breathing hard, eyes glazed with satisfaction. Then she focuses on me, lips curving in a dreamy smile. "That was . . . incredible." Her smile twists into something cheekier. "And how about you? Did you . . . ?" She tugs at the waistband of my joggers, peeking down. "No! You didn't blow your load. Well done."

I let out a rough laugh. "Barely. Another minute of that and I'd have been finished."

She smirks at that, then yanks my joggers down, freeing my cock. Her hand closes around me—her skin warm, her rings cool—and a hiss rips from my throat. Christ!

"Still getting used to hands that aren't your own?"

I nod, not trusting my voice as her fingers explore. She focuses on my head, tugging my foreskin down and sliding it back up, clearly fascinated. I chuckle despite the fire racing through my veins.

"Again?" I manage.

She shrugs, grinning. "It's still a novelty for me. Just trying to get used to all these differences. You Scots drive on the left, we Americans drive on the right. You say chips, we say french fries. Your cock's uncut, my exes' weren't."

The casual way she says it—like she's listing off travel guide tips—actually makes me laugh, even though I'd rather she didn't mention her exes while her hand's driving me out of my mind.

"Anyway," she continues, giving my shaft a squeeze that blurs my vision, "I'd like this inside me now, please. It's been a whole minute since my last orgasm and I'm getting a bit impatient."

"Of course," I rasp, then reality crashes back. "Oh, shit. I've . . . well, I've no condoms. There's been no need for them. And, well—"

She cuts me off with a laugh. "It's fine. I'm on the pill, Lachlan, and clean. And based on what I know about your sexual history, I'm going to say you're clean too. So . . ."

She moves to the bed, lying back and spreading her legs, offering me a view that makes my mouth water and my cock twitch desperately. Pink, glistening, so fucking perfect it makes my head spin.

"Come over here."

For a moment I just stand there, drinking her in. Blair, spread out on rumpled sheets, a feast laid out for me. Then my body takes over, and I'm moving towards her like a man possessed.

I climb onto the narrow bed, settling between her thighs. My cock is so hard it's almost painful, pre-cum beading at the tip. I grip myself at the base, line up with her entrance, and push inside in one slow, steady stroke.

We both gasp at the same time. The sensation of her surrounding me—hot, tight, perfect—is almost too much. I have to stop, buried deep inside her, just breathing.

"Okay?" I manage, searching her face.

"More than okay," she whispers, and when she smiles up at me, something in my chest cracks wide open.

I start to move, slow and careful, watching her face for every reaction. The way her eyes flutter closed when I hit the right angle. The little gasps when I go deeper. The flush spreading down her throat to her chest.

"Still holding out on me, captain," she teases breathlessly. "Impressive."

I grunt, fighting to keep my rhythm steady. "Aye, but I'm not far off. That's why I'm taking it slow."

It's true. Every stroke, every clench of her around me pushes me closer to the edge. But I want this to last. Want to keep her wrapped around me as long as I can.

When her breathing hitches, when her nails dig into my shoulders, I know she's seconds away. "Come for me," I say. "Want to feel you."

And she does, breaking around me with a cry that's music to my ears, her body clenching and fluttering in waves that drag me over with her. I manage three more desperate thrusts before my balls tighten and I'm coming hard, spilling inside her with a groan torn from somewhere deep.

For a long moment we just lie there, gasping, hearts hammering against each other. Then, while I'm still buried inside her, I find her mouth with mine, kissing her soft and deep.

When I finally pull out and collapse onto the bed, she curls into my side like she belongs there. No awkwardness this time, no panic about crossed lines or mistakes. Just contentment, warm and golden in my chest.

"Stay a bit longer?" she murmurs against my shoulder.

I should go. Pretend there are still some boundaries. Remember my bed is in the main house with my son and my dog.

Instead, I tighten my arms around her. "Aye. A bit longer."

We lie there in comfortable silence, her fingers tracing lazy patterns on my chest, my hand stroking her hair. For once my head is quiet. I'm just here. Present.

Eventually, though, the pull of sleep tugs at me, and I know I need to go back to the house before I drift off in her bed.

"I should head back," I murmur reluctantly.

She nods, understanding, and I force myself to sit up, to pull on my clothes. When I'm dressed, I lean over her one more time, pressing a soft kiss to her lips.

"Goodnight, Blair."

"Night, captain."

I step outside, the night air cool against my skin, but her warmth lingers with me back to my own bed and follows me into sleep.

CHAPTER TWENTY-ONE

BLAIR

I wake to the soft sound of waves against pebbles and a delicious ache between my thighs that brings last night flooding back in vivid detail. I'm smiling before I'm even fully awake.

Lachlan. His hands exploring every inch of my body. The way he'd looked at me—reverent, hungry, completely undone. The feel of him finally inside me, moving with careful control until it broke into something raw and desperate.

I stretch languidly in the bed, savouring the pleasant soreness, the echo of pleasure still warming me. Even afterward, the way he just held me, like he couldn't bear to let go . . .

Rolling over, I squint at my phone. Nearly nine. I pad to the kitchenette in my PJs, putting the kettle on for coffee.

As I wait for it to boil, reality creeps in, cutting through the afterglow still clinging to me.

What the hell am I doing?

The thought hits me as I'm spooning instant coffee into a mug. I came to Scotland to escape complications, to live simply for a few months while I figured out my next move. Instead, I've somehow gotten myself tangled up with a widower and his six-year-old son.

This isn't some breezy summer fling with a charming local. He lost his wife. His son lost his mom. This is real-life heartbreak territory—with a ticking clock because eventually I'll have to leave.

The kettle clicks off, and I pour the boiling water, watching the coffee crystals swirl and dissolve. I take a tentative sip, then another.

Ugh. I never drink instant at home. Thought I might get used to it after a few days here, but nope. It's just not good. Better than nothing, though, and the caffeine does bite through the fog.

Do I regret last night? God, no. How could I regret sex that good? But standing here alone in the morning light, I can't shake the feeling that I'm in way over my head.

My phone buzzes.

ELLIE

Still on for our Sunday adventure? x

BLAIR

Absolutely. Need it more than you know x

Maybe a day away from this place, from Lachlan and all these messy feelings, could help me get my head straight.

◆ ◆ ◆

The to-go coffee from the Lighthouse Café is a godsend. Proper coffee, none of that instant crap. That's more like it.

Ellie and I follow the coastal path that winds above Ardmara, the town spread out below us, so pretty it almost looks fake. The wind whips my hair across my cheeks while gulls wheel overhead, crying.

"The view from up here is amazing," I say, pausing to look back at the harbour.

"Mm-hmm," Ellie says absently, then hums a melody under her breath.

"Okay, I have to ask, what's with all the humming? You've been at it since we left the café."

Ellie winces. "Have I? Sorry. I've got the summer festival coming up, and I can't stop running through songs in my head."

"You perform? That's amazing. What do you play? Please tell me it's the bagpipes."

She laughs. "Fiddle. I'm in a wee band with a couple of guys. One of them is Struan. You know, grin, curls, thinks he's irresistible."

I snort. "Flirty Struan, of course. Not a bad guy, though—when he's not wiggling his eyebrows. But I bet you wish it was Douglas in the band instead." I nudge her with my elbow. "Right?"

"Blair! You're terrible. Anyway, seems I'm not the only one with a creative streak. At the library Finn said you're working on a story."

"I am. Or I was." I sip my coffee, watching a fishing boat carve across the water. "Been a bit distracted lately."

"Oh? You did say something in your text about needing this walk."

I think about deflecting, but who am I kidding? I've never been great at keeping my mouth shut. And being here, far away from anyone who knows the New York version of me, makes it way too easy to overshare.

"I had sex with Lachlan. Twice."

Ellie nearly chokes on her coffee. "You what?"

"Well," I plough on, because apparently my mouth has decided we're doing this, "the first time was all him on me. Best oral sex of my life." I let my head fall back and stare dreamily up at the blue sky. "But then last night we went the whole way, and . . . let's just say that man knows what he's doing." I bring my fingers to my mouth in a chef's kiss. "Could barely walk straight this morning."

When I glance at Ellie, her cheeks are the colour of ripe tomatoes.

"Too much?"

"No!" she says quickly, then laughs at herself. "God, I'm like a shy librarian cliché, aren't I? Trust me, I've dog-eared plenty of spicy chapters in my time. I'm just not used to *talking* about such things quite so openly."

I quirk an eyebrow. *This* is openly? Ellie should hear the director's cut running in my head. But maybe in a small Highland town, people are a bit more reserved than I'm used to. Pretty sure Lachlan would sooner discuss tide charts than fingering techniques. Which just goes to show, you don't need to be able to *say* something to be very, very good at it. Last night he hit every spot like he had a map.

Ellie leans closer, almost conspiratorial. "I'll admit, Lachlan struck me as more . . . schedules and rulebooks than bedroom acrobatics."

I grin. "Oh, he's disciplined, all right. Just in the fun ways too. I mean, if he wanted to lay down the law, I'd obey."

"Blair!" Ellie squeaks, clapping a hand over her mouth. And then we both lose it, laughter spilling out and carried away by the wind. A nearby sheep looks up mid-chew, fixes us with a judgemental stare, then goes back to grazing like our conversation is beneath its notice.

We keep walking, our laughter trailing off as the path curves around a headland and the coastline stretches wide and glittering in front of us.

"But honestly?" I say. "It's complicated. He's a widower, Finn lost his mother, and I'm only here for a short time. Also, sure, the sex is great, but there's something else too. Behind all that gruff ferry captain stuff, there's a side to him that gets under my skin. Yesterday we spent the whole day at this beach—Traigh Bàn—and it was just . . . perfect. He was relaxed, Finn was happy, and I kept getting these stupid little butterflies in my stomach." I shake my head. "Which is ridiculous. I didn't come here for butterflies. I came here for escape."

Ellie is quiet for a moment, her expression thoughtful. "Well, if we got to pick who we fancied, life would be a lot simpler. I'd have picked someone a little less complicated. As for Lachlan, I think he probably needs someone to shake him out of his grief. If it's helping him, and you're enjoying yourself, what's the issue? So long as Finn's not stepping over discarded clothes in the hall, it seems harmless enough."

She gives a little self-deprecating smile and tucks a lock of dark-blonde hair behind her ear. "Listen to me, pretending I know about these things. But if it feels right, maybe it *is* right."

I consider this as we walk, then link my arm through hers. "You know what, Ellie?"

"What?"

"You're pretty wise for someone who blushes at sex talk."

◆ ◆ ◆

By the time I get back to the granny flat, it's late. I insisted on treating Ellie to dinner at the Ferryman's Rest, payback for the meal she made me my first night here, and the picnic she packed for our standing stones adventure. We may have lingered for a drink or two after we finished eating.

I should just crawl into bed. Instead I find myself padding across the yard. It's long past Finn's bedtime, and the main house is lit soft and low. I knock lightly at the back door. After a moment it opens, and there's Lachlan, in a soft T-shirt that hugs his chest and shoulders, and grey sweatpants that hug plenty too, if you catch my drift.

"Blair." The corner of his mouth curls. "Wasn't sure if I'd be seeing you before tomorrow." He leans in a fraction, nostrils flaring. "Is that wine I smell?"

"Do you have a captain's hat?" I ask, ignoring his question.

His brow furrows. "Aye. But I don't usually wear it. More of a special occasion thing."

My gaze drifts down his body, slow and deliberate, pausing shamelessly at the bulge in those sweatpants. He really does fill them out nicely. When I finally drag my eyes back up, a wicked smile tugs at my mouth. "I'd like to see you in it. And only it."

I lay my hand on his firm chest, feeling the steady thud of his heart through cotton, and push him back a step into the kitchen. I slip in after him, nudging the door shut with my heel.

"Can you sort that out for me, captain?"

His half-smile stretches into something darker, hungrier. "Aye."

CHAPTER TWENTY-TWO

BLAIR

Monday

When the front door clicks open at four o'clock, Gus is up like a shot, paws scrabbling as he barrels into the hallway to see Lachlan.

"Da!" Finn leaps up, scattering Lego everywhere. "Come and see what we built!" He bolts out of the living room too, returning moments later, dragging his father by the hand. And, yep, there it is again, that unfair little hitch in my chest when I see Lachlan in uniform. Crisp shirt, epaulettes, the whole package. Apparently ferry-captain chic is my kryptonite.

"Blair." Lachlan gives me a nod, a glint of warmth in his eyes.

"Lachlan," I return, aiming for casual. Mostly succeeding.

"Look, Da!" Finn points proudly at the Lego creation on the coffee table. "It's Ardmara pier. We didn't have enough white bricks for the lighthouse, so some of it's yellow."

"Very impressive." Lachlan crouches to study the uneven little tower like it's architectural genius. Meanwhile, I gather up stray Legos and pop them back in the box.

"Oh," Finn says. "Do we have to tidy up already?" You'd

think he'd know the routine by now. When Lachlan gets home from work, that's when I skedaddle.

But Lachlan surprises us both by saying, "Not just yet. Blair, I was wondering if you'd like to stay for dinner tonight?"

"On a weekday?" Finn asks.

"Aye, on a weekday," his father confirms, straightening. Then, to me, "What do you think?"

It takes me all of two seconds to decide. "Sure. I'd like that a lot."

Finn whoops and does a victory lap around the coffee table, arms out like an airplane. Gus, catching the mood, snatches up a ball and parades around, squeaking it over and over.

Lachlan's lips twitch. "Great. I'll go start the chilli."

And just like that, the celebration dies. Finn groans, flopping onto the couch in exaggerated despair. Gus drops the ball and sinks onto the floor, ears drooping in solidarity.

"Chilli con carne," Finn says sadly. "My least favourite meal."

◆ ◆ ◆

Tuesday

I'm sitting at the little table in the granny flat, with only Gerald and a book for company, when movement across the yard catches my eye. Lachlan appears in the kitchen window and lifts his hand in a crisp salute.

Our signal. That means Finn's asleep. All clear.

I grin and salute back before shoving my feet into sneakers. No time to waste. Not when there's a sexy ferry captain waiting.

The back door opens as I reach it, and Lachlan steps aside to let me in. He's swapped his uniform for jeans and a grey henley, and honestly, he looks just as devastating dressed down as he does in epaulettes.

"Evening," I say lightly as I slip past him, only to yelp when his palm lands squarely on my ass and gives it a squeeze.

"Lachlan!"

He doesn't apologise. In fact, he has the nerve to claim the other cheek too.

Before I can swat him, Gus pads over, tail wagging. I ruffle his ears quickly, laughing. "Sorry, buddy. This doesn't concern you." Then I catch Lachlan's hand and tug him down the hallway. "C'mon. Let's go, captain."

"So impatient, Blair," he says with a dark chuckle, his voice husky.

I toss a look over my shoulder as I climb the stairs, then give my hips a deliberate sway. Predictably, his hands find my ass again.

"You really do have the most glorious arse," he murmurs. "I could watch you go upstairs all day."

Laughter fizzes in my chest but I bite it back.

The second his bedroom door shuts behind us, Lachlan grabs a hold of me and presses me back against it. His mouth claims mine. Hot, insistent, no preamble.

"Now who's impatient, huh?" I manage against his lips.

He laughs low in his throat, his tongue teasing mine, and I melt into the kiss. His hands roam me like he can't decide which part of me he wants most. Waist, breasts, hips, all of me fair game.

I tug at his henley, desperate for skin, and he whips it over his head in one move. My sweater follows, and when his gaze drops to the lace beneath, hunger flashes in his eyes.

He makes quick work of the clasp and then the bra too drops

away. His mouth is on me at once, greedy and eager. I arch into him, gasping, my fingers threading through his hair.

◆ ◆ ◆

Thursday

Gus snores between Finn and me, warm and heavy, his body pressed against both of us. It's early afternoon, and the three of us are curled on the living room couch while I read Finn the latest instalment of *The Otter and the Boy*.

When I finish, silence lingers. Finn blinks, and for a second I worry I maybe didn't get this part right. Then his face breaks into a grin. "It's *so good*!" He claps his hands and bounces on the couch, jolting Gus awake. The dog huffs before settling again.

My chest swells, light and tingly. Kids don't fake this kind of enthusiasm. If Finn was bored, he'd be wriggling or begging to do something else. Instead he's here, bright-eyed, completely swept up in my little story.

"I'm really glad you liked it."

"I did! What happens next?"

"Um, well, I haven't written the next chapter yet."

Finn folds his arms, the picture of indignation. "Then you better write it soon. I need to know what happens!"

I nod gravely. "Message received, sir. I'll have the next chapter on your desk by morning."

◆ ◆ ◆

I water Gerald, pluck a couple of yellowing leaves, then check the main house again. There he is, at the kitchen window, a grin curving his mouth as he lifts his hand in our familiar salute.

Tonight, though, I don't return it. Instead I let my robe slip from my shoulders, satin pooling at my feet, and press a hand to my mouth in a mock *oops*.

I already flashed Lachlan once through this window. Tonight I figured, why not do it again? Only on purpose this time.

From the shock on Lachlan's face, you'd think he'd been struck by lightning. I turn and slowly bend to scoop up the robe. When I straighten, he's dragging a hand down his face like a man in agony.

A giggle bubbles out of me as I shrug back into the satin, the thin fabric clinging to every curve. It doesn't hide much, and that's exactly the point.

When I reach the main house, I discover Lachlan's sweatpants don't hide much either. The outline of his cock is clear as day against them, and wow, is he hard. *Mission accomplished, Blair.*

"Naughty girl," he growls. He shuts the back door, snaps the blinds closed, then hauls me against him, his cock pressing into my hip. He gives my ass a smack hard enough to make me gasp. Then, crouching down on his haunches, he shoves the robe up around my waist and mutters a rough, reverent, "Fuck."

No panties. Nothing at all. Just me, bared for him.

In one swift move he tears the robe off me and tosses it aside. "Turn around and pick it up. I didn't get the full view last time. Bloody Gerald was in the way."

Smirking, I do as I'm told. Only as I straighten, he pushes me back over again.

"Uh-uh. Not so fast. I'm not done looking yet."

I bite back a giggle. "Planning to gawk all night, captain? Or are we taking this upstairs?"

◆ ◆ ◆

Saturday

We're back at Traigh Bàn and the beach is ours alone, just miles of white sand and the sharp tang of salt in the air. Our shoes lie abandoned by the picnic blanket, and we're lined up ready for a race. To make things fair, Lachlan carries me on his back, his hands hooked under my thighs, my arms looped around his shoulders.

"That's the finish." Finn points at a chunk of driftwood about a hundred yards away. "Ready?" He bounces from foot to foot. Beside him, Gus lets out an eager whine, every bit as excited as Finn.

Lachlan tightens his hold on me and leans forward.

"Three . . . two . . . one . . . GO!" Finn shouts, and we take off across the sand.

Gus rockets into the lead, of course, while Lachlan matches Finn's pace stride for stride. The boy's little arms and legs pump furiously, his face scrunched with determination.

Halfway there, Lachlan eases off just enough for Finn to pull ahead, and I can't hold back my grin. Even with me clinging to his back, I know fine well Lachlan could outrun a six-year-old, but he wants his boy to win.

I play along, patting his shoulder like a jockey. "Giddy up, horsey!"

"He's just . . . so fast," Lachlan pants loudly enough for Finn to hear.

Finn glances back, grinning, then puts on an extra burst of speed. He reaches the finish, leaps over the driftwood, and throws his arms in the air in triumph.

◆ ◆ ◆

Sunday

I sit cross-legged on Lachlan's bed in one of his soft cotton T-shirts and nothing else. Lachlan stands in front of me, completely naked except for the captain's hat perched cockily on his head. Broad shoulders, defined chest, that trail of hair leading down to where he's already hard again, despite everything we've done tonight . . .

"What is it with you and this bloody hat?" he asks.

I drag my gaze up from the obvious focal point to find his green eyes glinting with amusement. "I find it sexy. Can't help it. Besides, I've realised something. Last time I asked you to wear nothing but it, I missed a trick. See, I only ever saw what you looked like with it up here." Sitting up, I pluck the hat from his head and turn it over in my hands. "Not down here."

With exaggerated care, I balance the hat on his cock then lean back on my hands to admire my handiwork. It's basically the world's most inappropriate hat stand. My shoulders shake as I fight to keep from bursting out laughing.

Lachlan glances down at himself then back at me, one brow lifting, caught somewhere between humour and heat.

At the look on his face, I lose it, laughter bubbling out of me. A soft chuckle rumbles from him too.

"You always find a way to surprise me, Blair."

"My pleasure, La*ch*lan." I roll the *ch* just right, the way I've rehearsed it a hundred times.

His eyes widen. "Wait, did you just say my name right?" He glances down at himself, then back at me. "Now? Out of all times, you pick *now*?"

"I've been practising hard. La*ch*lan went to Lo*ch* Ness. When he saw the Lo*ch* Ness Monster, he said, 'O*ch* aye the noo!'" I deliver the tongue twister like I've just nailed a Rubik's Cube blindfolded.

Lachlan stares at me for a moment then lets out a full-bodied laugh that shakes his shoulders and lights up his whole face. The hat wobbles dangerously but somehow stays put. "Nobody actually says 'Och aye the noo.' That's pure tourist nonsense. But . . ." His grin softens. "Good pronunciation of 'och.' I'm impressed."

I reach out to straighten the crooked hat then trace the taut lines of his abs, his skin hot beneath my fingertips, muscles tightening in response. His breath hitches.

"Now that I've impressed you with my pronunciation," I whisper, fingers drifting higher, through the dark hair on his chest, "how about I impress you with something else?"

I lift the hat with a flourish and settle it back on his head. Then I wrap one hand around the base of his cock, marvelling as he stiffens even more in my grip. My other hand cups his balls, giving them a slow, teasing squeeze.

"You're all mine now, captain."

Then I take him into my mouth, and the groan that rips from him—raw, desperate—sends heat pooling deep and urgent between my thighs.

◆ ◆ ◆

"Do you have blonde hair?" I ask, peering over my board.

"Nope."

I flip down all the yellow-headed cartoon faces, the plastic tiles clacking into place. Finn and I are sprawled on his carpet, deep into a game of *Guess Who?* while Lachlan freshens up after work. Funny how different things are now. In the early days of looking after Finn, I'd make a quick exit the moment his father came home. Now I stay for dinner each evening like it's the most natural thing in the world. Finn doesn't even comment on it anymore, just expects it. And Gus, who usually parks himself at my feet during mealtimes, seems equally convinced I belong.

Finn taps his chin, staring at his board. "Hmm . . . do you wear glasses?"

"Yep."

He flips down the characters without glasses, gives a little sigh, and drops his chin into his hands. Not exactly the picture of enthusiasm, and that's not like him.

I push myself upright. "What's wrong, buddy?"

"It's Monday." He lets out another sigh, this one worthy of a Shakespearean tragedy, and rolls onto his back like life is just too heavy to bear. "That means chilli."

"Oh yeah? Well, not tonight. Because *guess who's* making dinner?"

Finn peers up at me, brow furrowed. "You?"

"Me. And I'm not making chilli. I'm making pizza."

He blinks, then flips onto his stomach and scrambles up, his whole face lighting like I've just promised him a trip to Disney World. "Pizza? Homemade pizza?"

"Yep. Dough and everything. Want to help me make it?"

Finn squeals, and Gus lifts his head, ears pricked, gaze darting between us like he's desperate not to be left out.

Footsteps creak on the landing then Lachlan fills the bedroom doorway, hair damp from the shower, looking ridiculously good in a long-sleeved white T-shirt and dark sweatpants.

"Da!" Finn bounds over to him. "Blair says she's making dinner. Is that okay?"

Lachlan strokes his beard like he's giving it serious thought, even though he and I already agreed this. "Hmm. Breaking tradition, are we? I suppose . . ." His lips twitch. "I'll allow it."

Finn whoops, and Gus joins in with a couple of happy barks.

"Shall we get started?" I ask Finn.

"Yes!"

◆ ◆ ◆

Wednesday

Lachlan's bed rocks with a relentless rhythm as he drives into me from behind, his grip fierce on my waist, fingers biting into my skin. Each thrust sparks through me, winding the tension tighter and tighter until I can barely keep it together. A moan slips free before I can stop it. He feels so damn good, so deep like this.

"Shh," he growls in my ear, slowing just enough to make me ache. "How many times do I have to remind you to be quiet?"

I glance back over my shoulder. "Sorry. I just can't help it." I tilt my hips in shameless invitation.

He shifts, pressing his hand between my shoulders, guiding me down until I'm braced on my elbows, ass tipped high. The new angle has him slamming deeper, and with every hard thrust I come apart.

The moan that tears out of me is louder this time, helpless as my climax crashes over me in waves. My body clenches around him, every nerve ending on fire.

"Blair!" he tries to scold, squeezing my ass, but the breathless way he says my name betrays him. He picks up the pace, hips snapping harder until, with a broken groan, he comes. I feel every hot pulse of him, milking him for all he's worth until we're nothing but trembling limbs and ragged breathing.

Later, tangled in his sheets and held close against his chest, reality tiptoes back in. "I should go," I murmur.

But when I shift to move, his arm tightens around me, possessive. "No. Stay with me tonight."

"But Finn—"

"I'm up before he is. You can slip back then."

The warmth of his bed, the strength of his embrace . . . it's too tempting to resist.

"Okay," I whisper, sinking back into him.

◆　◆　◆

Saturday

"Logan Fraser, get your sister's foot out of your mouth this instant!" Douglas bellows across the chaos.

I'm at a table with him and Struan, watching the mayhem in the ball pit unfold. The familiar cocktail of warm plastic, sugary snacks, and overheated kids hangs in the air, underscored by a symphony of squeals and crashes.

Logan releases Rosie's foot with a guilty grin. All four kids are deep in some elaborate shark game, with Logan taking his predator role very seriously. Finn surfaces nearby, giggling as he splashes through the multicoloured balls. Isla, meanwhile, perches on the edge, apparently playing the lifeguard—not that she's doing much to stop the shark attacks.

"So, Blair," Struan says, leaning closer to me. "Is our boy Lachlan still being his usual grumpy, moody self with you?"

"Um . . . no, actually. He's been fine lately."

Douglas and Struan exchange a look.

"He *has* been in a good mood recently," Struan agrees. "Almost like he's finding some kind of release that's putting him in a better state of mind."

My cheeks flame as the implication hits home. Oh God. They know. They absolutely know what's going on between us.

"What did I miss?" Lachlan asks, returning with a tray laden with juice boxes and cups of the barely drinkable coffee.

"Um . . ." I clear my throat, avoiding his eyes. "Well, I think the secret is out."

Lachlan looks from Douglas to Struan, both smirking like they've uncovered the scoop of the century.

"Brilliant," he sighs, setting down the tray.

◆ ◆ ◆

Friday

My fingertips trace lazy patterns in the hair on Lachlan's chest, his heartbeat racing hard beneath my hand. We're a tangle of limbs on his bed, both of us still breathless from the night's exertions.

"Well," I murmur, pressing a kiss to his collarbone, "someone was particularly enthusiastic tonight."

His chest rumbles with quiet laughter. "Aye? And what about

the lass who was gripping the headboard like her life depended on it?" His fingers trail down my bare arm, teasing.

I'm about to reply when footsteps sound in the hallway. We freeze, listening. The soft pad of feet, moving closer to the bedroom door.

"Shit," Lachlan whispers, lunging for his pyjama bottoms.

I dart for the bathroom, snatching my robe from the floor as I go and pulling the door shut behind me. It's pitch black inside—I don't dare risk the light.

The bedroom handle rattles. "Da?"

I go still, hardly daring to breathe, as Lachlan answers in that gentle, soothing tone he uses only with Finn. I can't make out the words but his low murmur threads through the quiet.

I edge back a step and bump the counter. Something wobbles then topples—a shampoo bottle, maybe, hitting the tile floor with a dull thud. I wince, braced for Finn's small voice: *What was that noise, Da?*

But there's only Lachlan's soft tone, calm and reassuring.

A few long minutes tick by before the bathroom door cracks open.

"Blair?" Lachlan whispers. "The coast is clear. Bad dream, but he's settled now."

I blow out a breath and slip back into the bedroom. "That was close."

"Aye." But his voice is strained now, the easy intimacy gone, replaced by tension.

I hesitate, then say, "Maybe I should head back to the granny flat tonight. In case he wakes again."

"Aye, that might be wise. Just for tonight."

The words hang heavy between us, a stark reminder of how

quickly passion can turn complicated with a six-year-old down the hallway.

CHAPTER TWENTY-THREE

LACHLAN

The kitchen smells like cheat-morning indulgence. Pancake batter sizzles in the pan while bacon pops and crackles beside it. Gus sits beside me, nose twitching at every delicious smell, a thread of drool dangling from his jowls. Finn's at the table in his pyjamas, working on some elaborate drawing of what looks like a dragon fighting a pirate ship.

I stack the first batch of pancakes on a plate and start the next round, humming under my breath. Christ, when did I start humming?

"Fancy nipping over and asking Blair if she wants pancakes?" I ask Finn.

"Sure." He hops down from his chair, bare feet slapping against the wooden floor, but slows halfway to the back door. "Da?" Even in just that one word, there's a careful note to his voice, like he's testing the waters.

"Aye?"

"I was wondering . . . was Blair in the en suite last night?"

Shiiiiitttttt.

"Why do you say that?" I manage, buying myself time while

my brain races. Christ. He's six. Too young for this. Way too young.

"I thought I heard her," Finn says matter-of-factly. "When I came into your room after my bad dream."

Fuck.

I switch off the hob and draw a steadying breath. "You might've done," I say slowly, turning to face him properly. "Tell you what. How about just us lads have breakfast this morning? You and me. And we can have a proper chat."

Finn shrugs and wanders back to the table, resuming his drawing. As if he hasn't just turned my world upside down with one innocent question.

I finish plating up the pancakes, hands steadier than they've any right to be. What do I say? How much is too much? And how little is too little? Douglas and Struan already know. If I brush Finn off now and something slips out at the Pit . . . no, better he hears it from me. Straight from his da.

I set his plate down and slide into the chair opposite him. "There you go."

He takes a bite. "It's yummy. Do we have maple syrup? Blair says nothing's better than maple syrup on pancakes. It comes from Canada. Did you know that? That's where Blair was born, even though she lives in New York."

So much for easing into this. He's steered us right back to Blair. I'd rather have planned this conversation. Talked it through with her first. But here we are.

I cut into my own pancakes, buying myself another moment. "No maple syrup, I'm afraid, but I can pick up some next time I'm at the shops. Anyway, about last night . . ." I clear my throat. "Aye, you did hear Blair in the en suite, Finn."

He looks up at me, fork suspended halfway to his mouth, waiting.

"You like Blair, right?"

He nods decisively, no hesitation there.

"And I like Blair too. But sometimes when two adults like each other . . . that can turn into something more than being just friends."

His brow furrows like he's working through a tricky sum. "You mean like wanting to kiss each other?"

Christ, he's sharp. "Aye. Like wanting to kiss each other."

"And . . ." He tilts his head, studying me with those serious brown eyes that are so like his mother's. "Have you kissed Blair, Da?"

My throat feels tight. "Aye. I have."

Finn considers this. The silence stretches, broken only by the tick of the kitchen clock and Gus's panting. Finally, he nods. "Okay."

That's it? Just . . . okay?

I wait, expecting more questions, protests, confusion. But he just goes back to his pancakes like we've been discussing the weather.

"Do you have any more questions?"

He pauses mid-chew. "I don't think so."

"Okay. Well, let me know if you think of anything else. But Blair and I . . . we're still figuring this out, all right? Nothing's changed between you and her. She's still your nanny, and she's still going to be looking after you while I'm at work."

Another nod, another bite. Then, around a mouthful: "I like it when Blair's here. You smile more."

His words catch me off-guard. I have to swallow hard before I can speak again. "She makes both of us smile, eh?" I reach out and ruffle his dark hair.

Well, that went better than expected. Much better. But now comes the next challenge: telling Blair that Finn knows.

◆ ◆ ◆

A little while later, Finn, Gus, and I are outside the granny flat and Finn is pounding on Blair's door. My palms are damp, which is ridiculous. I've captained ferries through Force 8 gales, but telling a woman that my six-year-old knows we've been kissing? Terrifying.

Blair opens the door, looking a little puzzled. "Hi. Everything okay?"

I understand her confusion. The last two weekends, we knocked on her door bright and early, inviting her over for breakfast. Today we didn't and she's probably wondering why.

"Aye," I say. "We're going for a walk into town. Fancy joining us?"

"Of course. Just give me a minute to get my shoes on."

Soon we're walking along by the harbour. The sky's overcast, pewter clouds hanging low, and the sea's choppy, white caps breaking against the harbour wall. There's tension in the weather that matches what's twisting inside me.

Boats bob in the water. Mooring lines strain and creak, and Gus snuffles hopefully at empty fish crates. Finn skips ahead, fascinated by a boat unloading the day's catch, silver scales glinting in the grey light.

Right. No more putting this off.

"When I was making breakfast, Finn asked me if you were in the en suite last night."

Blair falters mid-step. "Oh. Wow." She glances at me. "And . . . what did you say?"

"I was thrown by it. But I didn't want to lie. So I told him, aye, you were."

A beat of silence. Then a woman passing with a shopping bag calls, "Morning!" and leans down to ruffle Gus's ears. Blair returns the woman's greeting with an easy smile, but as soon as we move on, the smile falters. "What else did you say?" she asks quietly.

"I said . . . well . . ."

Christ, this is awful. *I* don't know how to define this thing between me and Blair, yet now I have to tell her what I told my son about us? Awkward as fuck.

"I said sometimes, when two adults like each other, it turns into more than friendship. Kept it simple."

Her expression doesn't give much away. At last, though, she nods. "I think that's okay."

"He also asked me if that means we've kissed. I said yes."

Another pause. Ahead, Finn runs to the Fisherman's Memorial, a bronze figure of a man hauling a net, face set to the sea. Finn circles the base, balancing along the edge as if it's a tightrope.

"I know this complicates things," I say. "I didn't plan it. I just didn't want to lie to him."

"Yeah. I understand that. It's fine."

"You sure?"

She lets out a quick, unconvincing laugh. "Yes! I'm sure." Then her smile slips again. "I just don't want Finn thinking I'm taking his mom's place. And . . . you know, I'm only here for the summer."

A knot tightens low in my gut. "Aye. Adult relationships are a bit of a mystery to him, but I told him we're still figuring things out, and he seemed to get that."

"He is clever for six." Her smile reappears, more certain now. "I think you did the right thing. Best to be honest with him."

Her smile coaxes one out of me, and I blow out a breath. "Right, then. How about takeaway coffees from the Lighthouse Café? And a top hat for Finn while we're at it."

"Please! I had to have instant this morning. I hate that stuff so much."

We collect our drinks and Finn's marshmallow treat, then Blair and I settle on a bench at the play park while Finn runs off to join some other kids on the swings. Our conversation moves on to lighter things as we watch him pump his legs, hair flying, then race over to the climbing frame and clamber up it. Once the coffees are done and Finn is all played out, we head back to the house.

When we're almost there, and there's no one else in sight, Blair says, "If Finn knows we've kissed, presumably we can hold hands?" And without waiting for an answer, she slips her hand into mine. It's warm, soft, and fits perfectly.

Up ahead, Finn glances back. His eyes flick to our linked hands and for a moment he stares. I tense, braced for more questions.

Instead he smiles, bright and uncomplicated, then turns and races on, Gus bounding beside him.

After that, with every step home, the knot in my gut eases.

CHAPTER TWENTY-FOUR

BLAIR

Finn is wedged between Lachlan and me on the couch, a bowl of microwave popcorn sits on the coffee table, and *Spider-Man: Homecoming* plays on the TV. Gus has claimed the spot at our feet, though he keeps lifting his head every time someone reaches for the bowl. The sneaky golden retriever already managed to snag a few kernels when Finn got distracted during the ferry scene.

"You used to take that ferry to work? That's so cool!" Finn had said loudly, after I whispered that fact to him. Then, when the entire ferry was split in half lengthwise: "Bet you're glad you didn't take it that day!"

It was when Iron Man flew in to save the day, and Finn jumped to his feet whooping, that Gus went for the popcorn.

Now the camera sweeps across the Manhattan skyline, glass and steel reaching for the clouds, and my chest tightens unexpectedly. Those familiar streets, the yellow taxis, the constant hum of eight million people living their lives . . .

That's home. This—Scotland, Ardmara, this cosy living

room—is just temporary. A summer adventure before I figure out how to rebuild my life back where I belong.

But then Finn shifts against me, his small body warm and trusting, and it feels so natural, so *right*, that for a moment I can almost forget this isn't my real life.

Almost.

My gaze drifts to the mantelpiece, where a new photo sits: Leanne holding tiny Finn's hand, steadying him as he wobbles on chubby legs. Finn and I have been busy recently—more crafting sessions, more trips to the beach for decorating materials—and Lachlan has filled the new frames with pictures of his late wife.

But looking at the photo, I can't help but think, *What am I doing?* I'm snuggled up with this woman's husband and son, playing house like I belong here.

Earlier, when Lachlan told me Finn knew about us, I said it was fine. And maybe it is. But it *has* changed things. Made this whole situation feel more real, more serious. More like something that matters instead of just a summer fling with convenient accommodations.

Then, though, a hand slips across the back of the couch—Lachlan's, reaching over his son like it's the most natural thing in the world. His hand rests on my shoulder, and its warmth melts away my doubts.

By the time the credits roll, Finn is practically boneless against his father, eyes heavy-lidded and blinking slowly.

"Someone's sleepy," Lachlan observes. He leans in and theatrically sniffs his son. "Hmm . . . not too bad. All right, if you're tired, you can skip your bath tonight, but you absolutely have to have one tomorrow. Deal?"

"Deal." Finn yawns hugely then turns those drowsy brown eyes on me. "Blair? Will you tuck me in tonight?"

I glance at Lachlan, unsure about the boundaries of this new dynamic. He gives a small shrug, leaving the choice with me.

"Okay, sure." I pat Finn's knee with a smile. "I'd love to."

◆ ◆ ◆

Upstairs in Finn's bedroom, I settle into the chair beside his bed with *The Day the Crayons Quit* in my lap. We picked it up from the library yesterday. I thought it'd be perfect for a kid who's always drawing.

"This one's about crayons going on strike," I tell him as he pulls the blanket up to his chin.

"Mmm," he murmurs, already sounding half-asleep after our cosy evening on the couch.

I open the book and begin reading through the funny complaint letters Duncan finds from his crayons. Red Crayon is overworked from colouring fire engines and strawberries. Yellow and Orange have fallen out because both think they should be used to colour the sun.

Normally, Finn would be giggling at their silly gripes, but tonight he just looks at the pictures, lids drooping, a small smile playing at the corners of his mouth. By the time I get to Pink Crayon lamenting about being underused (except by Duncan's little sister), his breathing has gone slow and steady.

I close the book softly and lean forward to smooth the covers. "Sleep tight."

I'm about to stand when his eyes open again and he says, "Are you staying in our house tonight?"

"Oh. Um, I think so, yes."

A sleepy smile spreads across his face. "I like the idea of you being here with us rather than all by yourself in the granny flat."

Something warm and complicated ripples through me. This little boy, who's already lost so much, wants me here. Wants me to be part of his small family unit instead of the outsider looking in.

"Love you, Blair."

His words zing straight past my defences, right into the softest part of me. Love. For a six-year-old, it's simple: you care about someone, they make you happy, so you love them. No complications. No questions. Just love.

But I'm not six. And yet, looking down at this sweet boy who's somehow claimed a piece of my heart without me even realising it, I can't bring myself to deflect or downplay his words.

"Love you, Finn," I whisper back.

His smile lingers for a moment before his eyes drift closed again. Soon his breathing evens out into the deep rhythm of sleep.

◆ ◆ ◆

I find Lachlan in his bedroom, sitting on the edge of his bed, waiting for me.

There's no sneaking around tonight. No tiptoeing through the house or slipping out before dawn. For the first time since this started, I can just walk down the hallway and into his room like it's no big deal.

The thought should be liberating. Instead, it makes something flutter nervously in my belly. Because without the secrecy, this feels dangerously close to . . . well, to real life. To being part of this family instead of just visiting it.

He stands and moves closer, his hands framing my face, his thumbs brushing over my cheekbones. I lean into the touch despite the warning bells in my head. *This is going too fast. Getting too complicated. I'm supposed to be here temporarily, figuring out my life, not falling for a widower and his son.*

But then Lachlan's mouth finds mine, gentle and sure, and my doubts blur at the edges. His hands slip to the hem of my sweater, lifting it over my head with careful reverence, like he's unwrapping something precious.

"So beautiful," he murmurs against my collarbone, pressing soft kisses to the hollow of my throat, the curve of my shoulder. When he unhooks my bra and takes my breast into his mouth, tongue circling my nipple, I arch into him with a soft gasp.

This is what I need. Not thinking. Not worrying. Just this. His hands on my skin, his mouth making me forget everything except how good he makes me feel.

He strips off my leggings, my underwear, until I'm naked in the lamplight. Then I'm reaching for his belt, fumbling with the button of his jeans, desperate to feel him against me, inside me.

"Easy," he chuckles, but his breathing is already rough.

I push his jeans and boxers down to his knees—not bothering to get them all the way off—then push him back onto the edge of the bed. I climb onto his lap, knees bracketing his hips, then sink down onto his cock. We both gasp.

"Christ, Blair . . ."

Any last questions in my head scatter like startled birds. There's only this. The stretch and fullness of him inside me, the way his hands grip my hips, the heat building between us. This feels so right, nothing else matters.

CHAPTER TWENTY-FIVE

LACHLAN

I'm standing at the top of the stairs, one hand resting on the banister, listening through the open door of Finn's bedroom. Blair's voice drifts out, animated and warm.

For the past four nights, she's taken over the bedtime routine completely. I should probably feel put out about it. After all, those quiet moments before Finn drifts off have always been ours, just the two of us. Well, three if you count Gus curled up and listening in. It does sting a wee bit, standing here while someone else claims that special time.

But Christ, she's good at it. Natural. The way Finn leans in, utterly spellbound, whenever she opens a book says everything.

Tonight's a bit different, though. Not one of Finn's usual books. Her own words, by the sound of it.

"The otter's whiskers twitched as he watched the boy approach the water's edge," Blair says, her voice carrying the gentle rhythm of a born storyteller. "His coat had grown thick and glossy again, and when he slipped into the water, he moved like liquid silver."

Ah. *The Otter and the Boy*. The story she's been working on.

I edge closer to the doorframe, drawn in despite myself. Through the gap Finn is propped up on his pillows, eyes fixed on Blair's face, hanging on every word.

"The boy felt his heart swell with pride," Blair continues. "He'd done it. He'd helped the otter get better. But then . . ." Her voice drops, weightier now. "He saw something that made his stomach twist into knots."

"What?" Finn whispers.

"Another otter. A female, sleek and beautiful, gliding through the water toward his friend. And when the two otters touched noses, greeting each other with soft chirps, the boy suddenly understood what this meant."

Bloody hell, even I want to know what happens next.

"His otter friend was better. Completely healed. Which meant . . ." Blair pauses dramatically.

"He might leave?" Finn's voice is small, worried.

"The boy watched them swim together, diving and playing, and he felt happy for his friend. But he also felt something else. Something that made his throat tight and his eyes sting. Because if the otter was truly better, if he'd found his own kind again, then maybe he wouldn't need a human boy anymore."

She's good. Really good. The story's simple enough for a child, but layered with something heavier: love, loss, letting go. Hits harder than it should.

When Blair closes her notebook, Finn sits up straighter. "Is that the end? Do the otter and the boy not see each other anymore?"

Blair's smile is warm, reassuring. "No, it's not the end. There's more to come."

"How many more chapters? And how long will it take you to write them? Because I need to know what happens!"

Blair laughs and tucks the duvet under Finn's chin. "I'm working on it as fast as I can. But stories are like plants. They need time to grow."

"Like Gerald."

"Exactly like Gerald."

Satisfied, Finn sinks back against his pillows, his eyes already heavy, the thrill of the story giving way to sleepiness. "Night, Blair."

"Sweet dreams, Finn."

I step back from the doorway as Blair slips out. She jumps when she spots me. "What are you doing lurking out here?" she whispers.

"I heard some of your story and it sucked me in. Couldn't stop listening."

She shakes her head, embarrassed. "You don't have to say that."

"I'm not just saying it. It's bloody good."

I ease past her into Finn's room, where he's already drifting off. Leaning down, I press a soft kiss to his forehead. "Love you, lad."

"Mmm. Love you too, Da."

Downstairs in the kitchen, I pour myself a dram of whisky and lift a questioning brow at Blair.

"Oh, go on then."

I pour her a glass too and we settle at the table.

"That story of yours," I say after a sip. "It really is good. You should do something with it. Get it published. You must have contacts."

Her smile falters. "Thanks, but . . ."

"I'm not just being polite," I cut in. "You heard Finn. He's desperate to know what happens next, and that boy doesn't fake enthusiasm. That was real. Other people make a living telling stories. Why not you?"

She turns her glass in her hands, her gaze on the table. "Because I torched every bridge in publishing. And this . . ." She shrugs. "It's just something I've always wanted to try. Doesn't mean I'm any good at it."

"Bollocks," I say flatly. "What about self-publishing?"

"At Everhart & Greene we . . . well, we didn't think much of self-publishing. We saw ourselves as gatekeepers, you know? Making sure only quality books reached the shelves. These days, people can put whatever they like up for sale."

I lean back, studying her. "I read an article once about some self-published author making good money. Better than a lot of the ones with big publishers. And you've got the experience, haven't you? Why not use it for yourself? Keep more of the profits instead of giving them away?"

Blair runs a finger around the rim of her glass, thinking it over, then a small smile plays at her lips. "That sounds like something I should look into. Tomorrow." She tips back her glass, finishing the whisky in one go, and sets it down with a decisive clink. Standing, she circles the table and comes up behind me. Her fingers brush my shoulder, then trail down to the top button of my shirt. She slips it open, then another, her fingertips toying with the hair on my chest.

"Because tonight," she murmurs, "I've got other plans."

She takes my hand, tugging it until I rise to my feet. Then she gives another insistent pull, this time toward the stairs. "Come on."

I don't need to be asked twice.

CHAPTER TWENTY-SIX

BLAIR

I'm perched on my favourite boulder on the pebble beach down from Lachlan's house, phone in hand, the afternoon sun warm on my shoulders. Finn and Gus are closer to the water and in the midst of a fierce but giggly tug-of-war battle with a long strand of seaweed.

Self-publishing. Why couldn't I do that?

Lachlan's words from last night have been rattling around in my head, so here I am, scrolling through author blogs and success stories, trying to wrap my head around it all.

Seven figures. One author earns that. Actual millionaire money, for writing books on her laptop in her PJs. Okay, I'm sure only a tiny minority reach those dizzy heights, but it seems plenty of others are earning six figures. Buying houses. Quitting day jobs. Supporting their families, all from stories they wrote themselves and published independently.

I wouldn't even need to earn that much. But if I could make enough to survive on, doing something I love, being my own boss . . . No more reporting to anyone. No more taking the fall for decisions I disagreed with. Full creative control over my work.

The idea sends a little thrill through me. I could actually do this.

Then a voice pipes up in the back of my head: *For every success story, there must be a hundred failures you're not reading about.*

I force the thought away, annoyed at myself. What's with the imposter syndrome? Why can't I believe I'm capable of this? Lachlan does. If *he* thinks I can do it, why don't I? I used to read submissions from debut authors all the time. I know what a good story looks like. So why can't I trust myself to write one?

"Blair!" Finn calls. He's standing by the shore now, scanning the waves like a pint-sized marine biologist. "See any otters yet?"

"Not yet, but keep looking, buddy. They're sneaky."

I'm just beginning to picture it—a life of writing in the mornings, walking this beach in the afternoons, answering to no one but myself—when my phone buzzes.

Clara Levinson.

I blink. Clara is a publicity associate at Everhart & Greene. I always liked her but I never thought I'd hear from her again. Not after my very public fall from grace.

Hey Blair,

Hope you're doing okay after . . . well, everything.

I was at a networking event last night and got chatting with Nora Cartwright from Cedar House. She asked after you, specifically whether you might be available for work.

I'm not sure what she has in mind, but thought you might be interested. Let me know if you want me to pass along your email.

I stare at the message, my heart doing a little skip. Cedar

House. A real player in children's publishing. I've always respected Nora Cartwright, their editorial director.

I assumed I'd burned every bridge. What could Nora possibly want with me? Maybe she needs freelance help—some remote editorial work?

Well, there's no harm in finding out more, right?

I tap out a quick reply.

Thanks, Clara. Yes, please do pass along my email. Appreciate you thinking of me.

I send it then just sit there staring at the screen, trying to process what this might mean. Maybe my career in children's publishing isn't dead in the water after all.

"Blair?" Finn's voice snaps me back to the present. "Do you think an otter and a boy could really be friends?"

I slip my phone into my pocket and give him my full attention. "It's not impossible. When I was looking up otters for our story, I found this documentary called *Billy & Molly*. It's set in Shetland."

"That's in Scotland," Finn says knowledgeably.

"It is. A man named Billy found a young otter who'd lost her mom. He fed her until she was strong again, and they became friends. But before winter, Billy stopped feeding her so she could learn to fend for herself. After that, she visited him less and less, until she stopped coming altogether."

Finn's shoulders slump. "Oh. Is that what happens in *our* story? The boy never sees the otter again?"

"Well, sometimes life surprises you. Molly did come back one day. And she was pregnant."

His face lights up. "She came back! Will your otter come back too?"

"You'll just have to wait and see."

◆ ◆ ◆

That evening I'm hanging out by myself in the granny flat. Well, correction, Gerald's here too.

These days I only come back to water him or to grab something I haven't moved into Lachlan's bedroom yet. I pretty much live in the main house now. But tonight I've got my weekly video call with my parents, and that's still a granny flat activity. They don't know about Lachlan and me, and honestly, I'm not sure what they'd think if they did.

I set my laptop on the little table by the window and call them. Within moments Mom and Dad's faces pop up on-screen, both grinning from their kitchen in Staten Island, coffee mugs in hand.

"There's our Scottish lass!" Dad beams. "You look well, Blair. Is that sea air working its magic?"

"Either that or all the walking. Finn's got more energy than a golden retriever—and I've been walking one of those too."

"Ah, Gus," Mom says warmly. "I feel like I know that dog from all your stories. Go on, tell us about your week."

We chat about the weather (gorgeous), the local food (I've just discovered tablet, which is basically Scottish fudge, and I'm obsessed already), and my adventures with Finn. I find myself editing carefully, talking about our trips to the library and the beach, but leaving out the parts that might make my parents ask awkward questions about my living arrangements.

"And how's everything else going?" Mom asks. "You seem so much more relaxed than when you first arrived."

If I were going to tell them about Lachlan, this would be my opening. The perfect moment to admit he's become more than just my employer. To tell them how he makes me laugh with his dry humour, how he looks at me like I'm something precious, how Finn has quietly claimed a corner of my heart.

But something stops me. The words won't come.

It's not that I don't trust my parents. We've always been close and I've never been one to keep secrets from them. But this feels different. It's like Lachlan, Finn, and I exist in this perfect little bubble here in Ardmara, and talking about it out loud with my mom and dad might pop it.

Or maybe I'm just not ready to put words to whatever this is yet. Especially when I've no idea where it's going.

"Everything's good," I say instead. "Really good."

Dad adjusts his glasses. "And you're still enjoying the nannying?" He quickly adds, "And that wasn't my way of asking about jobs back in New York! I know better than to ask about that."

I grin at his hasty backpedal. "Well, funnily enough, I heard from an old colleague today." I tell them about Clara's message and Nora Cartwright asking about me. Both their faces light up.

"That's encouraging," Mom says, leaning forward. "Maybe there's a chance for you to get back into children's publishing after all?"

"I don't have any details yet," I say, trying to temper their expectations. "All I can do is wait and see if Nora even gets in touch."

Briefly, I wonder why I'm telling my parents about Clara's message when I've already decided not to mention it to Lachlan, at least not until I've heard from Nora herself. Maybe because they're part of my New York life and Lachlan isn't? I'm not sure I'm ready for those worlds to meet.

"Still, it's exciting," Dad says. "We both miss you, you know."

"I know. I miss you guys too." And I do, I really do. But the thought of leaving here, leaving Lachlan, Finn, and Gus . . .

"Remind us, how much longer are you acting as a nanny for this boy?" Mom asks.

"He goes back to school on the fourteenth of August, which is . . ." I pause, doing the mental math.

"In a week," Mom supplies helpfully.

A week. How did that happen? When I first arrived, six weeks felt like forever. Now, with Lachlan's arms around me every night, and Finn chattering about otters and whatever else every day, time has slipped through my fingers.

What happens in a week? When Finn doesn't need me anymore? When *Lachlan* doesn't need me anymore? We've been so caught up in the spell of this summer that we haven't talked about . . . after.

Mom, Dad, and I chat for a few more minutes before saying our goodbyes. When I close the laptop, the granny flat feels too quiet, Gerald's leaves stirring in the sea breeze drifting through the open window.

One week.

I need to talk to Lachlan. Tonight. We can't keep pretending this summer will last forever.

CHAPTER TWENTY-SEVEN

LACHLAN

I'm tucking Finn into bed, and Christ, it feels good to be back in charge of the bedtime routine. Don't get me wrong, Blair's brilliant with him, and the lad adores her. But these quiet moments before he drifts off? They've always been ours.

"Da," Finn says sleepily, snuggling deeper into his pillow. "Are we going to the summer festival this weekend?"

I pause before answering, one hand still smoothing his duvet. The festival. Right. For one weekend every August, the town transforms into a bustling carnival of music, food stalls, and families everywhere you look. Last year I left Finn in Struan and Douglas's capable hands and stayed home with Gus, a book, and a dram. Crowds, noise, forced merriment? My idea of hell.

But this year . . .

Blair's in the granny flat right now, chatting with her parents. I know fine well she'd love the festival. The music, the community spirit, all of it.

"Aye," I hear myself saying. "Maybe we will."

Finn's face brightens, even through his sleepiness. "Really? With Blair too?"

"We'll see, lad."

He grins and closes his eyes, satisfied. Within minutes his breathing evens out, and I press a soft kiss to his forehead.

"Love you, Finn."

I'm heading downstairs when I hear the back door open and close. Blair's call must be finished. Perfect timing. I can pull her into my arms and keep her there a while. Doesn't matter that she's been in my bed every night for weeks. I still can't get enough of her.

I pad through to the kitchen, where she's at the sink, pouring a glass of water. I don't bother with words. Just slip in behind her, hands at her hips, mouth brushing her neck.

She tilts her head back with a soft smile, giving me better access. I take the invitation, trailing my mouth along the line of her throat. My hands slide up from her hips, across her stomach, then higher, fingers brushing over the swell of her tits.

Her breath catches, but instead of leaning into me, she covers my hands with her own, stilling them. "Lachlan," she murmurs, gentle but firm. "Wait. There's something we need to talk about." She turns in my arms so we're face to face, her hips brushing my crotch in the process. My cock had already been thickening, and this *really* doesn't help, but I shove the hunger down and make myself listen.

"Aye? What is it?"

"It's only a week until school starts back."

I let out a low breath. "The summer's flown by. Hard to believe."

She watches me, waiting. When I don't say more, she rests her palms lightly against my chest. "Which means it's not long until my job here ends."

233

"Aye." The word comes out rougher than I mean it to. I rub the back of my neck, stalling for time.

I've been avoiding this, pushing it to the back of my mind every time it tries to surface. What happens when Finn's back at school? When Blair's got no reason to stay?

The thought of losing her laugh in the kitchen, her daft voices at story time, her warmth in my bed . . . it's like contemplating losing a limb.

"You're wondering . . . what next?" I manage.

"Yes." Her voice is steady, though her hands press harder into my chest. "I don't mean to pressure you. I just . . . I need to know what's coming next. For me. For us."

Us. Such a small word, carrying so much weight.

"Aye. We do need to talk about it. But there's something I need to do first."

Her brow furrows, but she waits.

"You told me once that I should take Finn to Corraig. Show him where he spent his first few years. Where he, his mum, and I lived together." The words taste heavy. "You were right. I need to do that, and I think it's time. For him. And maybe for me too."

I drag in a breath. "I've kept that door shut a long time. Before I can think about what's next, I need to open it."

Understanding softens her expression. She doesn't push, doesn't ask for details I'm not ready to give. She just nods.

"You could come with me and Finn. Only if you'd like to, that is."

She bites her lip, and for a moment I think she's going to say no. That it's too much, too personal, too complicated. But then her hesitancy eases into a small, tender smile. "Of course I'll come with you."

A weight I hadn't realised I was carrying shifts off my shoulders. "Thanks, lass. How about this Saturday?" I clear my throat. "And on the Sunday we can take in the summer festival." If she's willing to come to Corraig, I can bloody well face the crowds.

She smiles again. "That sounds good."

"Then after Corraig, we'll figure things out. Aye?"

"Yes," she says, and there's something in her voice—trust, maybe, or hope—that squeezes my chest.

I cup her cheek, my thumb brushing over her warm skin, then lean down to kiss her. Her lips part without hesitation. And when I break the kiss to press my mouth to the curve of her neck, she sighs and melts against me.

CHAPTER TWENTY-EIGHT

BLAIR

The wind whips my hair across my face as I stand at the ferry's railing, watching Ardmara shrink behind us. Even from this distance I can see rows of little flags strung between streetlights along the waterfront, bright splashes of colour for the summer festival. It's already in full swing. Ellie assured me she's performing both days so I'll get to hear her on her fiddle tomorrow.

Out here on the water all the bustle feels far away. It's just sea, sky, and the steady hum of the engines under my feet.

"Look!" Finn shouts, jabbing a finger toward the bow. Beside him, Gus noses the railing, tail wagging, eager to see whatever Finn has spotted.

Sleek grey shapes arc through the water, surfacing and vanishing in quick, playful rhythms as they pace the ferry. Dolphins. Finn's grin goes incandescent.

"Amazing." I lean over for a better look. "They're probably racing us."

Finn nods and giggles, his cheeks flushed pink from the salt air and excitement. He's been bouncing on his toes since we boarded, thrilled to finally be a passenger on his father's ferry instead of just watching it from shore.

I turn my attention to Lachlan, standing a few feet away with one hand braced against the railing. He catches my eye and manages a smile, but I can see the tension in his shoulders, the way his jaw is set just a little too tight. He's putting on a brave face but this can't be easy for him. Riding the ferry to Corraig without being at the helm. Knowing that this time he'll actually have to set foot on the island.

"Careful," I say, nodding at his white-knuckled grip on the rail. "You'll strangle that thing."

"Keeps my hands busy."

"If you need a better anchor, I'm right here."

Something flickers across his face. Gratitude, maybe, or just relief that I get how hard this is for him. He glances at Finn, who's still scanning the waves, though the dolphins are gone now. "Fancy seeing the bridge?" he asks his son.

"Really? Can we?"

"Aye, of course."

So we follow Lachlan through the passenger areas toward the front of the ferry, Gus's tail swishing at the prospect of adventure. Lachlan gives the bridge door a quick rap before pushing it open and stepping inside.

The bridge is smaller than I expected but impressive in its efficiency, all clean lines and gleaming instruments, windows offering a panoramic view of the water ahead. At the wheel stands a man with weathered features and grey hair. When he sees Lachlan, his face splits into a big grin, the crow's feet at his eyes crinkling even deeper. "Well, well. Look what the tide washed in."

"Innes." Lachlan gives a short nod but there's warmth behind it. "Meet Blair and Finn. Blair, Finn, this is Innes MacLeod. He covers the sailings I don't do."

"Hi!" Finn chirps.

"Nice to meet you." I extend my hand and Innes shakes it with a firm grip.

"Innes has been very good to me," Lachlan says. "Switched his schedule so I could do the runs that fit around Finn's school."

"Just made sense," Innes says with a shrug. "Family comes first."

I can't help but smile at that. "That was really kind of you."

He dips his head then looks at me with a glint of curiosity. "So, Blair, if you don't mind me asking, how do you fit into this here crew?" He nods toward Lachlan, Finn, and Gus.

"Oh. I'm, uh, the nanny."

"Well . . ." Lachlan clears his throat, colour creeping up his neck. "She's a wee bit more than the nanny."

"They kiss," Finn announces matter-of-factly. Which, of course, sets us all off laughing.

"Out of the mouths of babes!" Innes says. Still chuckling, he crouches a little to meet Finn's eye. "Now, young man, how'd you fancy a turn at the wheel?"

Finn's mouth drops open. "Really?"

"Of course. You're up, captain." Innes nudges a wooden box into place by the wheel. "You might need this."

Finn scrambles onto the box and grabs the wheel, his grin stretching ear to ear. Lachlan steps in behind him, steadying him, his much larger hands closing gently over Finn's.

"Steady as she goes, lad," he says, his voice low.

My heart squeezes at the sight. Father and son, guiding this massive vessel like it's the most natural thing in the world.

♦ ♦ ♦

The ferry docks at Port Mairead, where whitewashed cottages huddle around the harbour as if bracing against the Atlantic wind. We file off with the other foot passengers—no car today. Stronaveagh, the village where Lachlan grew up, is a mile and a half along the coast, but he suggested we walk there. Said it'd let Gus have "a bit of a runabout". I figure it also buys Lachlan a little extra time to brace himself before facing the village he hasn't set foot in for four years.

We set off along a coastal path that hugs the shoreline, Gus's nose twitching at all the new scents. The narrow trail winds between patches of heather and gorse, bursting with purple and yellow. To our left the sea glitters, to our right green hills rise. Finn skips ahead with Gus, glancing back every so often to make sure we're still following.

As the path curves, a rocky islet comes into view just offshore, dotted with black-and-white birds waddling about. "Puffins!" Finn shouts, pointing.

My breath catches. I've seen them in documentaries and children's books before, but never in person. They're adorable. Flashes of bright orange beaks and feet, their little tuxedo bodies shuffling about like they're waiting to be seated at a black-tie dinner.

I glance at Lachlan, grinning, but his jaw has tightened again. I slip my hand into his and give it a squeeze, and for a moment at least it seems to draw him back to me.

Finn, oblivious to the tension radiating from his dad, chatters on about the puffins, then points excitedly when a seal's whiskered face breaks the surface of the water before dipping under again. A few steps later he's chasing a butterfly. His delight is infectious—for me, at least. Lachlan only seems to retreat further into himself the closer we get to his old home.

Soon we crest a small hill and a village comes into view below us: stone cottages with slate roofs clustered along the shoreline, more houses trailing up the slope behind. A small church with a square tower and what looks like a community hall sit near the centre. From up here it looks like something off a postcard or a period drama set—timeless, unchanged for decades, as if the outside world has forgotten it exists.

Lachlan halts. The wind tugs at his hair but he doesn't otherwise move. His shoulders have gone rigid, his jaw tight enough to crack.

"You okay?" I ask softly.

He gives a single nod but no words. Then, after a moment, he sets off again, each step heavier than the last. We make our way into the village and Lachlan leads us to a low cottage facing the small harbour, its bright blue door shouting louder than the muted greys and browns of the cottages around it.

He stops outside it, still saying nothing.

I glance at him uncertainly. "Is this the house you used to live in?"

Another wordless nod. The silence stretches so I turn to Finn. "Do you remember this place, buddy?"

Finn wrinkles his forehead, concentrating hard. "Aye, I think so." But he sounds doubtful, like he's trying to convince himself rather than actually remembering.

Before any of us can say more, the front door of the neighbouring cottage swings open and a man about Lachlan's age steps out. He's broad-shouldered and sun-browned, with dark hair that looks like it never fully obeys a comb. He stops dead when he sees us, eyes going wide, disbelief flashing across his face.

"Bloody hell," he breathes. And then he strides over and hauls Lachlan into a fierce hug. Lachlan is rigid in his grip, and for a moment I'm not sure he's going to react at all. But then he lifts a hand and hesitatingly pats the man's back.

When the man finally lets Lachlan go, he turns to Finn and beams at him. "Finlay! I don't believe it. Last time I saw you, you barely came up to my knee."

Finn blinks, uncertain, clearly not recognising him.

"I'm Torquil," the man says, crouching a little as he offers his hand. "But everyone calls me Torq. I grew up with your mum and da."

Finn shakes his hand, a shy smile forming. "Nice to meet you."

Gus, apparently deciding he should introduce himself next, trots over to Torq and plants himself in front of him, tongue lolling, awaiting his hug or handshake.

Torq ruffles Gus's ears with a laugh. "And who's this handsome lad?"

"That's Gus," Finn says.

Torq's gaze swings to me. "And you must be . . . ?"

"Blair," I say. "I'm the nanny."

I don't expect Lachlan to say what he said to Innes, that I'm "a wee bit" more than that. This is different. This man knew Leanne. Grew up with her.

"She's . . ." Lachlan begins. "Well, she's more than the nanny, actually."

For a beat, everything hangs on Torq's response. Then he chuckles. "Good for you, mate. I'm glad you've found someone. We've all been worried about you, you know."

Relief softens Lachlan, loosening his shoulders, easing the tightness around his eyes.

"Right then," Torq says. "Let me go round some folk up. Don't you dare disappear on me, Lachlan Munro." He strides off toward the next cottage along.

I lay a hand on Lachlan's shoulder, just meaning to steady him, but he glances away. When he looks back, his eyes are suspiciously bright and he's blinking hard.

Finn stares at him in horror. "Da? Are you crying?"

Red tinges Lachlan's cheeks. "Aye, lad. Even Da cries sometimes."

Without hesitation Finn grabs one of his father's hands and squeezes it tight. Then he shoots me a look and jerks his chin toward Lachlan's other hand, as if to say, *Well? What are you waiting for?*

I take it, weaving my fingers through Lachlan's and giving his hand a firm squeeze. A promise that he isn't facing this alone.

"Lachlan Munro, as I live and breathe!"

We all turn to see a woman with a hand pressed to her chest. A man follows her from her cottage, then three kids tumble out as well, wide-eyed and curious. Torq flashes us a grin and heads straight for the next house, knocking on its door too.

"Brace yourselves," Lachlan mutters under his breath. "A *lot* of introductions are coming."

CHAPTER TWENTY-NINE

BLAIR

Festival music drifts after us as we walk from the ferry terminal back to the house, a cheerful mix of fiddle, guitar, and accordion. I wonder if it's Ellie performing. Part of me wants to check it out, but honestly, we're all too beat to care about anything except getting home.

Finn conked out on Lachlan's shoulder somewhere between the ferry docking and the harbour road. One minute he was chattering about all the people he'd met today, the next his head was lolling against his dad's neck, his little arms hanging limp. Lachlan carries him like he weighs nothing, one big hand steady at his back, the other looped around his legs.

When we get back to the house, Lachlan tips his chin toward the stairs and murmurs, "I'll get him settled."

I watch him carry Finn up, noting how he takes the steps slowly, careful not to jostle his sleeping son. Then, kneeling, I slip off Gus's collar. He barely even lifts his head in acknowledgement. He's wiped too. After a quick drink from his bowl, he flops onto his bed with a small sigh.

When Lachlan comes back down, he sinks into one of the

kitchen chairs with a soft exhale. There's something different about him tonight. He's lighter somehow. Like something that's been wound tight for years is finally starting to uncoil.

"I was going to make myself a camomile tea," I say, already moving toward the kettle. "Fancy one?" But when I glance back at him, I can tell tea isn't what he needs. "Or something stronger?"

"I'll take a dram of whisky."

He starts to get up but I wave him back down. "Sit. You carried Finn all the way from the ferry. I've got this."

A few minutes later I set his glass down then settle across from him with my steaming mug.

"What a day, eh?" he says.

What a day indeed. The reunion with Torq, the parade of islanders who emerged from cottages and gardens to greet Lachlan. Finn being passed from hug to hug, surprised but delighted by all the attention. The stories people shared about Leanne, about Lachlan, about their years on that little island. The way Lachlan gradually thawed as the afternoon wore on, his smiles coming easier, his laughter more genuine.

"You doing okay?" I ask.

He takes a sip of Scotch, considering. "Aye. Better than I thought I'd be. A lot better, in fact." He stares into the amber liquid. "I should've done that a long time ago. Seeing the house . . . seeing them all again . . . It felt like breathing after holding it in too long."

"Thanks for letting me come with you."

"Thanks for being there." His gaze finds mine across the table. "I'd never have done it without you."

The weight of that admission settles between us. Part of me wants to ask what this means for us, what happens now that he's faced his past. He did say we'd figure things out after Corraig, and here we are, home again after visiting the island. But it doesn't feel like the moment to press. Not tonight.

So instead I say, "You still up for the festival tomorrow? I mean, you had a lot of people in your face today, and that's not really your thing. Think you can handle round two?"

"Aye, let's do it."

"Really?"

That half-smile I've grown so used to tugs at his mouth. "It'll be fun."

CHAPTER THIRTY

LACHLAN

The music carries to us on the breeze long before we reach the harbour: drums thundering in rhythm, pipes skirling over the top, bold enough to rattle windows. Finn's practically bouncing out of his trainers beside me, and even Gus is feeding off the energy, tail going like mad as he trots at my side.

Blair tilts her head, grinning. "Is that—oh my God, it *is* bagpipes! This is officially the most Scottish thing I've ever heard. Do you think the pipers will be in kilts?" She shoots me a sideways look, mischief dancing in her eyes. "And when am I going to see *you* in one?"

I grunt. "Not likely, lass."

"Shame." Her gaze lingers on my navy button-down, then drifts down to my chinos. "Though I've got to say, you look good today. Nice to see you in something smart other than your captain's uniform."

She's right. At the weekend I generally just put on whatever I find first in the drawer. But today? Aye, today I made an effort.

But forget me. That sundress—soft yellow catching the light, skimming her curves like it was made for her. Her hair is down and sleek, her fringe framing her bonny face. She thinks I look good? She should see herself.

"Da! Quit staring at Blair, you're slowing us down. I want to see the stalls!" Finn hops from foot to foot impatiently.

Christ. My own son, calling me out.

"Sorry, lad." I give him an apologetic wink. "C'mon, we're almost there."

The waterfront is packed with folk. Bunting stretches between lampposts, stalls line the street on both sides, and the air is thick with frying onions, sugar, and sea salt. Laughing kids dart through the crowd carrying candy floss bigger than their heads.

It's busy, all right. Last year I stayed home. Couldn't face it. But this year's different. *I'm* different. Walking into the crowd with Blair at my side, my son buzzing with excitement, and Gus trotting along like he owns the place . . . it feels less like bracing myself, more like belonging.

"Oh my God, Lachlan, look at this place!" Blair's eyes are wide, her voice full of wonder. She points out details I'd have walked right past—the hand-painted stall signs, the sweet smell of tablet, a juggler tossing bright clubs into the air. Seeing it all through her eyes, it's not just noise and crowds. It's something special, something worth showing off.

"Da! There's Flora!" Finn pipes up, pointing to her behind a bake stall.

Sure enough, there she is, arranging cakes with her good hand while her other—still braced but now out of the sling—rests at her side. She looks up as we approach and breaks into a bright smile.

"Great to see you all out together." She gives Blair and me a meaningful look. Blair's cheeks go rosy, but Flora just winks. "Don't worry, dear. Half the town's already guessed."

Christ. Is it that obvious?

"Empire biscuits!" Finn's delighted shout saves me from having to respond. "You're back to making them again!"

"Aye, and do you know what's even better? This one's on the house." She hands him one—two biscuits wedged together with jam, the top one iced and crowned with a jelly sweet. "For my favourite six-year-old."

While Finn demolishes it, Blair takes in the display. "Flora, these look amazing. Is that clootie dumpling?"

"Aye." Flora beams.

I nod at her wrist. "Shouldn't you have got someone else to run the stall this year?"

"Och, I can manage a cake stall, thank you very much."

Blair's already counting out coins. "I have to try it. My gran used to make clootie dumpling. I haven't had it since she passed."

She takes a bite, eyes closing, her face softening. "Oh . . . that's just like hers. Takes me right back to her kitchen in Toronto."

Flora glows at the praise. "Proper clootie dumpling is hard to come by these days. It's a dying art."

Just then, Logan and Rosie barrel through the crowd like twin hurricanes, Isla close behind. Their faces are painted with elaborate designs—Logan is a fierce tiger, Rosie a rainbow butterfly, and Isla a glittery unicorn.

"Look at our faces!" Logan yells, nearly bowling over an elderly woman with a walking stick.

"Logan Fraser, mind where you're going!" Douglas's voice carries over the bustle before he appears, looking as frazzled as ever. Struan saunters behind him, hands in his pockets, grinning like chaos is his idea of entertainment.

Finn stares at the kids' painted faces in awe then turns to me with pleading eyes. "Can I get mine done too?"

As if I've ever been able to say no to that look. "Aye, of course."

"I'll show you where they do it!" Logan crows, already shoving back through the crowd.

Blair calls a quick goodbye to Flora, and we follow the kids through the festival. At the face-painting table, Finn rocks on his heels, waiting his turn, jittering with more energy than his small body can hold. Whether it's sugar from Flora's biscuit or just the festival buzz, I can't tell. Probably both.

"Heard you were over on Corraig yesterday," Douglas says to me. "How was that?"

"Hard," I admit. Then, after a beat: "Good, though."

Blair slips her hand into mine, and I give it a squeeze. Yesterday we faced ghosts together, and today I'm still standing. Thanks to her.

A woman I don't know stops Blair for a quick chat about the weather and the festival. When she moves on, I ask, "Who was that?"

"Shona from the post office."

Struan smirks. "Four years here, Lachlan, and you still barely know anyone. Meanwhile Blair's been here one summer and already knows half the town."

He's not wrong.

"Aye, well. Time I did something about that, eh?"

Struan raises his brows. "That right?"

"Blair must be rubbing off on me."

Douglas claps my back. "Good man."

Finn reaches the front of the queue and soon he's proudly showing off a small otter on his cheek.

An otter. Of course.

"Oh, Finn!" Blair lays a hand on her chest. He grins back at her.

We drift through the festival together, the kids pulling us from stall to stall. Feels a bit like Gus isn't the only one tugging on a lead today. Logan wins a rubber duck from the hook-a-duck, while Rosie misses every coconut on the shy but laughs like she's won anyway. Isla spots a stall selling flower crowns, bats her eyelashes at Struan, and moments later has one on her head. Blair pauses now and then to admire the craft stalls. Hand-painted mugs, driftwood carvings, bright watercolours of the harbour. She looks at it all with the same delight she shows Finn's drawings, like every bit of it's worth her attention.

Before long, all four kids are clutching Irn-Bru slushies, tongues already turning orange. I know it's a bad idea—sugar on top of sugar—but it's one weekend a year, and I'm not about to be the killjoy.

Struan disappears for five minutes and comes back with plastic cups of lager for Douglas and me, a glass of wine for Blair, and a whisky for himself. Douglas takes a long pull of Golden Stag and, for the first time all day, actually looks relaxed.

The kids spot a bouncy castle and charge straight for it, kicking off trainers before I can say a word. "Not sure that's the best plan after those slushies," I mutter, but Struan just claps me on the shoulder.

"Quit worrying, mate. Drink."

So I do.

But after a few minutes of bouncing, I remember I didn't put any sun lotion on Finn today. "Finn, get down here a minute."

Predictably, he ignores me.

"Would you mind asking him?" I say to Blair. "He never says no to you."

She bumps her shoulder into mine. "Like father, like son, huh?"

Sure enough, a minute later she's got him standing still long enough to rub lotion on his face and arms before he clambers back onto the castle.

We linger a while longer, letting the kids bounce and shriek, then continue on to the storytelling tent. Inside, canvas walls filter daylight to a warm glow. Ellie sits in a low chair at the front, a picture book open in her lap, surrounded by a semicircle of wide-eyed bairns sitting cross-legged on cushions. Her voice is calm but animated, and every child is glued to her like she's some kind of story sorceress.

Our lot march right in and sit down, while me, Blair, and the guys hang back at the rear of the tent with the other parents and grandparents.

It's a Katie Morag tale, and it doesn't seem to matter that Finn and his pals missed the start—they hang on Ellie's every word anyway. As does Blair. Like she's six herself.

When Ellie shuts the book and everyone claps, Blair leans close to me and whispers, "I loved those stories as a kid. Made me think Scotland was full of adventures and mischief. And it turns out it is. I just didn't expect the mischief to come from a golden retriever and a grumpy ferry captain."

"Grumpy? Have I been grumpy today?"

"No, you've not. You've been charming all day. Maybe I should check you for a fever."

I grunt, trying for stern, but my lips twitch anyway.

"Right, that's me done for now," Ellie says, standing and smoothing down her long skirt. "But I'll be back in half an hour with more stories." Spotting us, she waves us over. The four kids swarm her first. "Look at these beautiful painted faces!"

Logan growls like he's the fiercest beast to ever stalk the Highlands. Rosie flaps her arms like a butterfly. Isla beams, glitter sparkling on her unicorn horn.

Ellie laughs, admiring them all, then her gaze turns to Finn. "Oh, that otter is wonderful!"

Finn puffs up with pride. "It's the otter from Blair's story. It's *really* good. You should be reading it!"

Ellie turns her attention to Blair. "And how is the story coming along?"

"Nearing the end now. But really, it's just something I've been working on for Finn."

"But Da says it should be a book. Like, a real one!"

"And I stand by that comment," I say.

"Wait, *Lachlan's* heard the story?" Logan puts his hands on his hips. "Blair, you said after Finn, we'd be the next to hear it. That's not fair!"

"Aye!" Rosie chimes in, never one to let her twin fight alone. "We want to hear about the otter too." She crosses her arms like a tiny lawyer.

Blair holds up her hands, laughing. "It's not even finished yet."

"You said that last time," Isla points out. "Just read it to us already."

Ellie chuckles. "Sounds like you'd better finish it soon, Blair. And maybe next year you can read it here, in the storytelling tent." The kids erupt in noisy agreement.

"Talking of performing," Struan says to Ellie, "you ready for tonight?"

"Yes! Though I'm not used to being the centre of attention this much. Normally it's just me in my wee library. But today I've been telling stories to the young ones and I'll be up on stage playing music tonight. That's more spotlight in one day than I usually get in a month."

"Ach, you'll be great," Struan assures her. "You always are."

Douglas smirks. "Aye, besides, everyone will be too busy watching Struan flick his curls around, eh?"

The group laughs, Isla hardest of all. "It's true, Daddy! You *do* flick them!"

Struan rolls his eyes then sighs and gives a dramatic toss of his hair, earning more laughter. Ellie laughs too, but more softly than the rest of us. She fidgets with her skirt. Must have jitters about tonight.

"Don't worry, Ellie," Blair cuts in, "we won't be so distracted by Struan's hair that we forget to cheer you on. Right, Douglas?"

"What? Oh, aye, right." He flashes Ellie a smile. "You'll be great."

◆ ◆ ◆

The sun's slipping lower now, painting the harbour in peach and gold. As if on cue, fairy lights strung between the lampposts blink on, turning the whole festival into something out of a storybook.

Struan ruffles Isla's hair. "Right then, princess, I'm off to make some music. You be good for Lachlan and Douglas, aye?"

"When am I not good?" she asks, perfectly serious, as if the idea *she* could misbehave is absurd.

He heads towards the temporary stage near the Fisherman's Memorial, the sea glittering behind it. A few minutes later he's up there with his guitar, joined by Ellie with her fiddle and Rab, a fifty-something fisherman, on accordion. The three of them look right at home together.

"Evening, Ardmara!" Struan's voice booms through the mic, all easy confidence. "Who's up for a wee bit of Highland music?"

The crowd cheers, and the band launches into a fast, rollicking reel that grabs everyone in its grip. Near the front, couples start swaying, then properly dancing, turning the whole thing into an impromptu ceilidh in the glow of the sinking sun.

Blair's already shifting with the music, eyes bright, caught up in the rhythm. She lifts her chin, hopeful. "Want to give it a shot?"

My gut tightens. I've been putting myself out there more today, but this? Dancing? In front of half the town?

"I'm not much of a dancer," I say.

Her smile falters, just for a second, but she recovers quickly. "No worries. I'll just . . . uh, dance with Gus when we get back to the house. If I can wake him up. Poor pup was exhausted when we dropped him off."

Christ, she's always so upbeat, trying to make a joke out of things even when I let her down.

The song comes to an end and Struan's voice booms out again. "Brilliant stuff! Good to see so many of you already dancing. But I couldn't help noticing there's a beautiful American among us who looks *desperate* for a dance." His gaze lands on Blair and his grin turns devilish. "And yet nobody's invited her up. Do I have any volunteers? Douglas, maybe? Go on, Douglas, ask her for a dance!"

Laughter ripples through the crowd and heads turn towards Blair. She gives a small, helpless laugh of her own, her cheeks going pink.

That does it. I'm not standing here like a bloody statue while Douglas—or anyone else, for that matter—dances with Blair. No chance.

"Actually," I say, taking her hand, "I can manage one dance."

She turns to me, her face lighting up brighter than the bulbs strung overhead. "Really?"

"Aye. Really."

I lead her to the makeshift dance floor as the band strikes up another tune. I can feel eyes on us—hell, I can hear the whispers—but the second Blair steps into my arms and we start to move, everything else fades away.

She's right there with me, following my lead even when my feet get it wrong, laughing when I spin her a bit too enthusiastically. Her dress swirls around her legs, her hair glowing in the last of the sunlight, and Christ, she's beautiful.

"See?" she says, grinning up at me. "You're not so bad at this."

"Don't speak too soon," I mutter, but I'm smiling too.

The music swells, Ellie's fiddle soaring over the top, and I find myself relaxing into it. Into this. Into her. Some of the cheers feel aimed at us specifically, but instead of making me self-conscious, they push me to hold Blair closer.

Off to the side, Finn claps along, beaming at us, until Isla grabs his hands and pulls him into their own little jig beside us. The crowd lets out a collective "aw" at the sight of them, and Blair laughs, her eyes sparkling with joy.

When the song finally ends, I don't let go. Not immediately. Not with the whole town applauding, not with Blair breathless in my arms, smiling up at me like she's exactly where she's meant to be.

CHAPTER THIRTY-ONE

BLAIR

Finn is curled on the couch beside me, still in his pyjamas, strawberry jam smudged at the corner of his mouth. Our breakfast plates are scattered across the coffee table, and cartoons flash on the screen. Lachlan would freak out if he knew we'd snuck food out of the kitchen, but what he doesn't know won't hurt him. And honestly? With only three days of summer vacation left, we deserve a little indulgence.

"Can we do a treasure hunt today?" Finn asks. "You hide stuff and I'll find it."

On-screen a cartoon pirate is waving a map and shouting about buried gold. Kids really are impressionable.

"Absolutely," I say, wrapping an arm around him for a squeeze. "But let me caffeinate first." I lift my mug and take another sip.

After a whirlwind of a weekend, he slept in later than usual this morning. When Lachlan kissed me goodbye before leaving for work, he told me to take advantage of it, so I rolled over and dozed for another hour—until Gus decided I needed company. Seventy pounds of golden retriever leapt onto the bed then sprawled beside me. Pretty sure Lachlan wouldn't have approved of that either. No doubt I shouldn't be encouraging Gus, but he was so warm and cuddly I couldn't bring myself to push him out.

Now Gus sits by the coffee table, tail sweeping lazily against the rug, eyes fixed on me with that unmistakable "When are we going for our walk?" look.

Not yet, Gus. Not yet.

I reach for my phone and check it while Finn giggles at something on the TV. A notification catches my attention. An email from Nora Cartwright.

My heart does a little skip. It's been a few days since Clara asked if she could pass on my email to Nora. I'd begun to wonder if maybe she wouldn't get in touch after all.

Dear Blair,

I hope this message finds you well. We haven't met in person, but I've followed your work with interest over the past few years.

I know the AI app project at Everhart & Greene was a difficult situation, and it was clear to me you were unfairly made the scapegoat. Please don't let that episode over-shadow what was, until then, an impressive body of editorial work.

One of my senior editors is leaving Cedar House, and as we begin the search for a replacement, your name was the first that came to mind. I'd love to speak with you about the role and think you'd be a terrific fit for our team.

If you're open to a conversation, please let me know your availability. We're hoping to move quickly with this hire.

Warmly,
Nora Cartwright
Editorial Director, Cedar House

I read it again. Then a third time. I have to blink a few times, make sure I'm not hallucinating.

A job offer. And not just any job offer, a senior position. A step up from what I had at Everhart & Greene. At Cedar House, a publisher I've always admired, with authors I've secretly fangirled over for years.

She knows about the AI scandal but she doesn't care. This is my career being handed back to me. My professional identity. My reputation. Everything I thought I'd lost forever.

I can hardly believe it. I'm grinning at my phone like an idiot.

Then Finn laughs at something on his cartoon, and I glance up at him. He's still got that smear of jam on his mouth, his hair sticking up in every direction, pyjamas half twisted around him. Gus, meanwhile, is still by the coffee table, tail swishing, wearing that "When's our walk?" expression.

A tight, fizzy knot forms just below my ribs.

What about them?

◆ ◆ ◆

The front door clicks, followed by Lachlan's heavy tread across the hallway. Normally, this is Gus's cue to launch himself at his master like a furry missile, and Finn's to come charging behind, both of them competing for who can greet him first. But today? Not so much. Gus is flopped on the living room rug, Finn is half draped across me on the couch, and I'm letting the TV do the heavy lifting.

Lachlan pokes his head around the doorframe and grins at the sight of us. "Lazy day?"

"Hey, we weren't total sloths!" I say. "We walked along the beach. Stopped by Flora's to see how she's doing. Even made it to the playground." What I don't add is that we somehow ended up right back here afterward, like this couch has its own gravitational pull.

He steps in, lips quirking. "Aye, sounds exhausting." He plants a kiss on my cheek, ruffles Finn's hair, and gives Gus a fond scratch. "You do all look knackered, though. Reckon you've earned a quiet day."

"Guess what?" Finn pipes up, grinning mischievously. "Blair and I had breakfast here today. On the sofa!"

Lachlan clutches his chest in mock outrage. "*What?* You mean to say you've been committing breakfast crimes under my roof?"

I give Finn a playful nudge with my elbow. "Thanks a lot, traitor. Last time I trust you with a secret."

Finn giggles, completely unrepentant, and stretches out even further across the couch until I'm practically pinned. Lachlan settles into the armchair across from us, watching us with a soft smile. I try to smile back but it feels forced, tight at the edges.

All day I've been composing messages to him. *Hey, got an interesting email today. Can we talk?* Delete. *So, hypothetically, what would you say if I told you I might have a job offer back in New York?* Delete. *Remember how we said we'd figure out our future after you faced your past? Well, MY past just came knocking.* Delete, delete, delete.

I decided it'd be better to tell him face to face. Except now that we actually are face to face, I'm no closer to blurting it out.

Not that I could drop this bomb in front of Finn anyway. Later. Once he's asleep.

"... what do you think?"

I blink, realising Lachlan's been talking and I've been lost in thought. "Sorry, what was that?"

Finn groans. "She's been doing that all day! Like she's not really here." He waves a hand in front of my face. "Earth to Blair!"

My cheeks go hot. "I'm sorry, I've got a bit of a headache. Not really feeling myself."

"Da was saying he got off the ferry at Corraig today," Finn supplies helpfully, and my attention snaps back to Lachlan.

"What? Oh, that's amazing!" The smile that spreads across my face is genuine this time. "I'm so proud of you."

But instead of sharing my enthusiasm, Lachlan pushes up from the armchair and crouches in front of me, frowning. "Forget about that. Are you coming down with something? You got a temperature?" He presses the back of his hand to my forehead.

"I'm fine. It was just a busy weekend, that's all. Maybe I took too much sun—something I never thought I'd say in Scotland." I tack on a laugh, but it comes out thin even to my ears. *Plus an email came in today that's rocked my world.* "But really, you got off the ferry? That's huge!"

His frown deepens. "Want me to get you something? Paracetamol?"

Tylenol, I translate automatically. "No. Honestly, I'm okay."

"Well, if you're sure." He squeezes my hand and the warmth of his touch sends a pang through my chest.

Maybe when we talk later, he'll make this easy for me. Maybe he'll say he loves me and that my place is here with him and Finn. Take the decision out of my hands. Because honestly? I'm not sure I'm capable of choosing between the life I thought I always wanted in New York and whatever this is we're building here.

"The festival was so much fun, wasn't it?" Finn says, all innocent. Then, unknowingly twisting the knife: "Do you think we'll all go again next year?"

Lachlan, straightening, chuckles and glances down at me. "Well, we'll just see, won't we?"

Actually, I'd like to know the answer to that myself. Will I still be here next year? Still tangled up in this messy, wonderful little life with Lachlan and Finn and Gus? With Ellie and Flora and the chaos of the Pit on Saturday afternoons? Or will I be back in New York, riding the Staten Island Ferry to work every day like none of this ever happened?

And what if I turn down the job offer and things don't work out here? If Lachlan decides I was just the woman who helped him out of a dark place, not the one he wants forever? What if my self-publishing dream fizzles out before it even starts? Then what? Then I'll have thrown away my one shot at getting back the career I spent my whole adult life building.

No wonder I feel like I'm unravelling.

"You three stay here," Lachlan says, heading for the door. "I'll change then sort dinner."

"Don't be silly!" I get to my feet. "You've been out at work all day. I'll—"

He steps back and gently pushes me down to the couch, his hands warm on my shoulders. "Stay. I've got this."

He smiles at me, steady and sure, and I force myself to smile back. But my fingers worry at one of my rings like it's the only thing holding me together.

CHAPTER THIRTY-TWO

LACHLAN

After Finn is finally out for the count—took three stories tonight, the wee negotiator—I pad through to my bedroom.

Blair is in the en suite, the door open. Fresh from the shower, a towel snug around her, she's brushing her damp hair. Beads of water chase one another down her arms and back. It shouldn't undo me, not after weeks of her living here, but it does. Every bloody time.

I move in behind her, sliding my arms around her waist, nuzzling into the curve of her neck. She smells of my soap mingled with the warm sweetness that's just her, the mix intoxicating. I press a kiss below her ear, and when she angles her head back, our mouths meet.

She turns fully, and I cup the back of her head with both hands, deepening the kiss. My cock hardens quickly, and soon it's trapped snug between our bodies.

With my tongue I tease the seam of her lips until she opens, but . . . she's tentative. Hesitating.

"Everything all right?" I pull back. "Is it the headache?"

"I'm fine," she says quickly, but her eyes tell a different story.

There's something in them I don't quite recognise. Uncertainty? Unease?

I brush my thumb across her cheek. "We could have an early night. Just sleep." God knows I'm aching for her, but her well-being trumps everything.

"No. I want you. I *need* you tonight." Her eyes drop to the bulge in my joggers, and a smile flickers across her lips. "And I think you need me too." She presses closer and kisses me again, and this time there's nothing tentative about it. She kisses me like she's drowning and I'm air, tongue lashing mine, nails biting into my shoulders. She grinds against my cock, frantic with need.

She's different tonight, driven by something I don't understand.

"Blair—"

"Please," she whispers against my mouth. "Just . . . please, Lachlan. Kiss me. Make love to me."

Like I could say no to that.

I claim her mouth with mine, one hand gripping her hip, pulling her even tighter against me, and the other trailing along her collarbone, following the water beading down her skin. The kiss grows hotter, deeper, until her hands are tugging at my clothes. I help her strip them off me—T-shirt, joggers, boxers— until I'm bare before her.

She gazes at me hungrily, then she brings her hands to my chest, rubbing them over my pecs and down my torso. One hand wraps around my cock and gives me a couple of rough pumps, and my knees nearly buckle. I tear her towel off her, and her small tits bounce free, nipples already tight. My gaze drags lower: pale skin smooth all the way down to the golden curls between her thighs, slick and begging for me.

"Christ, lass," I mutter.

I cup her tits, circling her nipples until she's moaning my name. Lowering my head, I take one into my mouth, sucking gently, teasing with my tongue. She arches against me, a gasp tearing from her throat. When it turns to a moan, I switch to her other tit, lavishing the same attention before letting go with a wet pop.

"Come here," she breathes, eyes burning with desire as she pulls me down with her to the cool tiles.

"Here? Not the bed?"

"Here," she confirms, lying back. She draws her knees up towards her chest, opening herself for me, her pink folds glistening.

I can't hold back. I drop between her legs and lean over her, my cock nudging at her pussy—not pushing in yet, just sliding through her wetness. The scent of her arousal hits me, sweet and heady. My hands roam her waist, her hips, down her thighs.

"Ready?"

Her eyes lock on mine, and she nods. "Yes."

That's all I need. I push forwards, sinking into her until I'm in as far as I can go. Her eyes squeeze shut, and a groan rips from my chest. Christ, she's so tight, gripping me all the way.

"Okay?" I manage, searching her face. It's deeper like this, with her knees tucked up.

She opens her eyes. "It's perfect."

I set a rhythm, driving into her hard and sure, braced on my knees against the cool tiles, her pussy hot as sin around me. Every flicker in her expression undoes me. The flutter of her lashes, the soft "oh" on her lips.

Gripping one of her bent knees, I spread her wider, and the new, tilted angle has her gasping.

264

"I'm so close!" she breathes, and then she's clenching around me, pulsing, coming apart on my cock.

"You'll be the death of me," I rasp, pounding even harder, and then I'm coming too, shooting deep inside her, every muscle taut until finally I collapse against her, spent.

Afterwards, I carry her through to my bed and lie down with her. She clings to me like she doesn't want to let go, arms locked round my shoulders, face buried into my neck. Her breathing, still uneven, is warm against my skin.

I rub slow circles between her shoulder blades. "You all right?" I murmur after a while. "You've been a bit off tonight."

Her fingers tense on me, then ease. "There's something I need to talk to you about."

"Aye?"

"I . . . got an email today." Her voice is muffled against my neck. "From Cedar House. A publisher in New York. They reached out about a senior editor position."

My hand stills on her back.

A job. In New York.

I'd been beginning to picture a future with Blair. Her silly voices whenever she reads to Finn. Her laughter echoing through the house. Her body beside mine each night. And now . . .

But this is what she's always wanted. The dream she thought had slipped through her fingers. This is her chance to get it all back.

How can I stand in the way of that?

I force my arms to stay steady around her. Force my voice level. "Blair, that's . . . incredible. What an opportunity."

She lifts her head, those pale blue eyes searching mine. There's something in them I can't pin down.

"It is, isn't it?" she asks.

"Aye. Of course." I sit up, helping her up with me, even as my chest feels like it's caving in. "I'm proud of you. Glad these people at—what was it, Cedar House?—glad they can see what a catch you are."

The words taste sour but they're true. She deserves this. Even if it guts me.

"And the timing works out perfectly," I add, trying for a smile. "Finn going back to school, your nanny job here wrapping up . . ."

She watches me for the longest time before nodding slowly. "Right."

I hug her again, though every part of me is screaming at the thought of this house without her. At having to explain to Finn that Blair is leaving. At things going back to how they were before.

But I hold her tight, like I'm solid, when inside I'm anything but.

"This headache," she says finally, drawing back. "Think I'll sleep in the granny flat tonight. Besides, I should probably break the habit of sleeping with my boss before I start a new job."

I let out a laugh but it comes out thin. "Aye. Right."

She dresses quietly then pauses at the door, hand on the frame. "Lachlan?"

"Aye?"

She doesn't turn. "I just . . ." She shakes her head. "Never mind."

And then she's gone.

For the first time in weeks, it's just me in the bed. And the sheets still smell like her.

Sleep doesn't come. My head's too full. My chest too empty.

CHAPTER THIRTY-THREE

BLAIR

I toy with the last forkful on my plate, appetite gone even though dinner was good. Normally I'd have finished everything—especially the mashed potatoes, or "mash" as Lachlan and Finn say—but tonight I can't. My stomach's been in knots for hours, bracing for this moment.

Finn scrapes his chair back from the kitchen table, his plate cleared. "Can I go play now?"

"Hold on, lad," Lachlan says. "Before you run off, there's something we need to talk about."

God. Here we go.

"Oh." Finn settles back into his chair and looks between his dad and me with curious eyes. "Okay. What?"

Lachlan turns to me. Looks like I'm the one who has to break the news. Fair enough. Makes sense, I suppose.

"Remember earlier, when you had quiet time in the living room because I had to do a video call?"

Finn nods, swinging his legs under the table.

"Well . . ." I take a breath, my hands twisting in my lap. "I was speaking with someone about a job back home in New York."

The call had been a formality, really. Nora made it clear the position was mine if I wanted it—senior editor, better salary than I've ever had, a chance to rebuild everything I lost. And after my conversation with Lachlan last night, with him congratulating me and telling me what excellent timing it was, I said yes.

"A job?" Finn's voice is small, uncertain.

"You're going back to school soon and you won't need a nanny anymore." I force myself to meet his gaze, even though it feels like my heart is cracking apart.

The light in his brown eyes dims. He glances at his dad, then back to me. "But . . . I thought . . ."

Lachlan reaches over and squeezes his son's shoulder. "We knew this was coming, lad."

Finn swallows, trying to hold it together, trying to be brave. "When?"

"Thursday," I say gently. "The same day you go back to school."

His eyes widen. "But this is Tuesday! You mean you're only here tomorrow and then you're gone?"

His voice cracks on the last word, and I feel like I've just kicked a puppy. Speaking of which, Gus chooses this moment to pad over from his bed in the corner, whining softly like he's picked up on the mood. He rests his golden head on Finn's lap, and Finn's small hand automatically strokes his fur.

The sight of them both looking so sad nearly undoes me. I glance at Lachlan, hoping for some support. His face stays steady for Finn's sake, but his jaw is tight, his eyes shadowed.

"You can hang out with Blair all day tomorrow, lad."

"But what about *The Otter and the Boy*?" Finn blurts. "You haven't finished it yet!"

"I'll . . . I'll email your dad the ending."

Finn's look says it all. Not good enough. Then, more softly, he says, "Will you come back to visit at least?"

My throat tightens. The question hangs in the air between us, and I don't know how to answer it. Because how can I promise something I'm not sure I can deliver? Leaving is going to hurt, and coming back would tear the wound wide open again. For me. For them.

◆ ◆ ◆

After dinner I slip back to the granny flat to collect Gerald. He's still on the windowsill, looking a bit neglected. Poor guy. I've barely been here the past few weeks—he's probably bored out of his mind. Well, time to fix that.

"Come on, buddy," I murmur, carefully lifting his pot. "Let's find you a new home."

Now that I've broken the news to Finn, I've got a bunch of other folk to tell. Might as well start with the closest: Flora.

I knock on her front door, Gerald balanced in my arms.

"Blair, dear!" Flora greets me with her usual warm smile. "What a lovely surprise. What can I do for you?"

"Hi, Flora." I shift Gerald to one arm. "I wanted to let you know that I'm heading back to New York. I got offered a job there and I've accepted it."

Her face falls. "Och, I'm sorry to hear that. That house will feel much emptier without you. When do you leave?"

"Thursday morning."

"Thursday? But that hardly gives me any time to organise a going-away party!"

I can't help but laugh. "Flora, I don't need a going-away party."

"Och, don't be daft." She waves her good hand. "Of course you're getting one."

"Really, I don't want you to put yourself out," I protest, still chuckling. "Especially with your wrist still healing—"

"My wrist is fine. This brace is just to humour the doctor. And you are absolutely having a party. You can't just slip away without a proper send-off. That wouldn't be right at all."

There's no winning this argument so I hold out Gerald instead. "I wanted to give you this as a parting gift. Although really, it's more of a favour for me. His name is Gerald. Do you think you could look after him?"

Flora takes the pot, lips quirking with amusement. "Why, hello there, Gerald," she says to the plant. Then to me, eyes twinkling, "I think I can manage that."

"Be good for Flora, Gerald," I tell him solemnly. "No drooping dramatically if she forgets to water you."

Flora chuckles. "I'll take excellent care of him, don't you worry."

"Thanks. Even though I was only here for a short while, I can safely say you're the best neighbour I've ever had, Flora."

She brushes off the compliment with characteristic modesty, though I catch the pleased flush in her cheeks. "Besides, this isn't goodbye. I'll be seeing you at your going-away party, you hear me?"

"I hear you," I say, smiling despite the tightness in my chest.

I leave and head into town, mentally running through the rest of my list. Ellie. Struan and Douglas, and their kids. The Lighthouse Café staff, though that'll have to wait until tomorrow, once they're open again. Shona from the post office . . .

It's going to be exhausting, all these conversations. All these explanations about opportunities and timing and how this is for the best.

At least my parents were excited when I told them earlier. That's something.

Besides, sometimes in life things *are* hard. Even though I'm leaving Scotland, I managed to bring some light into Lachlan's world. Helped him open up about Leanne. Encouraged him to face his past on Corraig. So I can go back to New York knowing I've done some good here, made his and Finn's lives a little brighter.

That's some comfort, though it doesn't stop the ache in my chest from deepening with every step.

CHAPTER THIRTY-FOUR

LACHLAN

My gut tightens as we approach the waterfront, the four of us—me, Blair, Finn, and Gus—walking together into town for the last time. Blair's packed and ready to go. Suitcase loaded in her hire car. Her flight leaves Glasgow in the morning, which means she'll be driving down tonight, straight after this party. In a few hours she'll be gone, and every step we take towards the harbour feels like a countdown.

I keep telling myself tonight should be a celebration. Smile, talk, eat, drink. Send Blair off with nothing but warmth and good wishes. But Christ, I'm not ready for goodbye.

I glance sideways at her and my chest does something complicated. She's always been beautiful, but just to really rub things in, tonight she's fucking devastating. Navy figure-hugging dress, her hair sleek and sophisticated in an elegant bun, a hint of colour on her lips that makes me want to taste her. She looks ready for New York. Ready for publishing events and important meetings and all the brilliant things she's going to achieve. And it just about kills me.

"Da, do I look smart enough?" Finn tugs at his collar. Shirt and trousers tonight, instead of the shorts and T-shirt that have been his summer uniform.

"You look very handsome, lad." I ruffle his hair. He's been unusually quiet all day but I can't blame him. We're both struggling with this.

Gus pads alongside us, tail lower than usual, like even he knows something's ending.

When we reach the open space by the Fisherman's Memorial, Blair gasps. "Oh my God!"

It's like the summer festival has been brought back for one more evening: bunting back up between lampposts, fairy lights glowing along the harbour rail. By the memorial, a couple of tables are laid out with traybakes, bottles chilling in tubs, and rows of glasses waiting to be filled.

And then there's the turnout, more than I expected. Not just the usual faces—Struan, Douglas, Ellie, the kids—but a proper crowd. Even Torq and some of the Corraig folk are here, though that doesn't surprise me. They knocked on the bridge door earlier to say hello, on the last ferry run of the day.

A chorus of fond greetings erupts—"Blair!", "There she is!", "Welcome, lass!"—and Blair presses a hand to her chest, cheeks flushing.

Flora bustles over, beaming. "Told you I'd manage a party. Before these decorations went back into storage, I convinced everyone we could get one more use out of them. What do you think?"

"It's amazing. But it's too much just for me."

"Don't be daft," Flora says. "We have to see you off properly. You matter to us, Blair. All of us. Now, what can I tempt you with?"

As Flora leads Blair away to get her a drink—"Something

soft, please. I'm driving tonight"—everyone gravitates towards her like she's the sun. Cue laughter, hugs, promises to keep in touch. Part of me is proud of how much she means to everyone. But mostly? I'm bloody envious. This is my last night with Blair and I'm having to share her with half the town.

Finn hugs my side, clinging like a barnacle on the ferry's hull.

"Look, lad, there's Logan, Rosie, and Isla. Why don't you go off and play?"

He shrugs. "Maybe later."

I get it. I'm hardly in the mood for a party either.

But no. I can't let myself wallow in this. Blair's given us a gift: shown us how to be happier, more open, more alive. I can't let our wee family slip back to how we were before she came. It's up to me now to keep that light burning, even when she's gone.

I force myself to straighten and summon up a smile. "Actually, you know what? How about we play a game of tig? I can be it. Well, me and Gus can."

Finn's face lights up for the first time all day. "Really? You'll play with us?"

"Really. Come on, Gus." I give his lead a gentle tug. "Let's show these kids what we're made of."

Soon I'm chasing all four around, trying to tig them, while they laugh, whoop, and shriek with delight. It's daft, it's noisy, and for a few minutes it almost works. The heaviness lifts, just a little. Gus enjoys the game as much as we humans do, if not more.

Tomorrow the kids will be back in school uniforms, sitting in classrooms. Tonight, though, they're wild things, and I'm running wild with them. After a while I catch Blair watching us from the crowd, a smile curving her mouth. I grin back at her.

We go on playing until Ellie taps a microphone, checking it's working. By this point I'm breathless and the bairns are all rosy-cheeked. Seems like it's speech time, and apparently I'm the only grown-up without a drink. I'm about to sort that when Struan waltzes over, a bottle of lager in each hand.

"You've earned this, mate." He passes me one of the beers.

"Right, everyone!" Ellie says. She's standing by the memorial, smoothing her skirt with her free hand, a nervous smile tugging at her lips. "If I could have your attention for just a few moments."

The crowd gradually quiets, conversations dying down as everyone turns towards her.

"Normally when I do public speaking," she begins, "it's to a group of children, and the words have already been written down and printed in a book. This is . . . different. But maybe I can be inspired by Blair and step out of my comfort zone. After all, she came to this place where she didn't know anyone, so I should be able to manage a short speech."

She takes a breath, finding her rhythm. "I don't want to let Blair go without saying a proper goodbye to such a wonderful friend. In such a short time, you've become so important to me—to all of us. You're going to be missed terribly."

Something lodges in my throat as Ellie goes on about Blair's kindness, her way with Finn and the other kids, how she brings light wherever she goes. Every word rings true. Every word makes this harder.

"You know, mate," Struan mutters, leaning close, "you're a bloody idiot if you let her get on that plane without telling her how you feel."

Christ. He picks his moments.

I glance at Blair, embarrassment written clear on her face as Ellie piles on the praise.

"It's her dream job," I murmur back. "I'm not going to stand in her way. She's twenty-seven. She's got plenty of time to find love after she's settled in her career. And maybe . . . maybe I'll find it again too. Before Blair, I never thought I would. Now I know it's possible." But even as the words leave my mouth, they ring untrue. I'm not convinced there will be anyone else. Not quite like Blair.

"Putting her needs above yours?" Struan says. "That's sweet. Also? Bollocks. You need to tell her how you feel. Let her decide what she wants. Don't make that call for her."

Shit. Is Struan right?

I look across at Blair again, lit up under the fairy lights, radiant and gorgeous. Soon she'll be gone. Back to her real life, her career, her future. Everything she's worked so hard for.

But what if . . . ?

Before I can talk myself out of it, I down my beer, shove Gus's lead at Struan, then stride over to Ellie.

"Sorry," I say, hand outstretched for the microphone. "Can I . . . ?"

Ellie blinks, puzzled, but passes it over. And now all eyes are on me. My hand shakes slightly as I bring the mic to my lips.

Fuck. What am I doing?

Finn's wide eyes lock on me, and for a moment my throat closes up. Everyone's watching. Waiting.

Then I find Blair in the crowd, and suddenly everything else fades away.

"I'm proud of you," I say. "For landing this amazing publishing job. I know you're going to be brilliant in New York. But . . . the thing is . . ." I swallow hard, my heart hammering so loud I'm sure the microphone must be picking it up. "Before you go, there's something I need to say. I love you."

A collective intake of breath ripples through the crowd. Blair presses a hand to her mouth, staring at me, stunned.

"I was lost at sea for a long time," I continue, the words coming easier now. "But Blair, you've given me back more than I thought I'd ever have. You've given me hope. You've shown me how to live again, not just survive."

My voice cracks but I push on. "I don't want to clip your wings. If you want to go back to New York, you should. Of course you should. I'd never stand in your way. But if you want to try your hand at your own stories, I know you'll make a success of that too. And I'd be glad to support you until you're on your feet."

I take a shaky breath. "I just want you to know you've got choices, Blair. And one of them is here. With me. With Finn. With Gus."

Silence. Total silence except for the gentle lap of waves against the harbour wall.

Every eye turns from me to Blair. She stands rooted, breath caught, as if she can't quite believe what I've just said. I wait for her to speak, to let me down gently, to explain why this is impossible.

Instead, she moves, parting the crowd, slow, steady steps until she's in front of me. Tears are gathering in her eyes. She clears her throat like she's about to speak but nothing comes. Her lips part but there's no sound.

She just stands there, eyes wet, mouth trembling, and I brace for the rejection I know is coming.

Then she rises on her toes and kisses me.

It's soft at first, tentative, like she's testing if I'm real. Just her lips against mine, her breath, and the world falling away. No ferries, no career in New York, no ticking clock. Just us. Just this.

Everything else disappears.

When she pulls back, I don't know what's coming next. Was that her goodbye, wrapped up in a kiss? Is she about to thank me for a wonderful summer but tell me she really must go?

The whole harbour holds its breath with me. Then, finally, she speaks—so softly it's like it's just for me, yet the hush is so complete everyone hears it.

"I'll stay."

For a heartbeat, nothing. No one moves, no one speaks. It's as if her words have frozen us all. Did she really just say that?

And then the noise hits. A roar of cheers, clapping, whistles, laughter.

I think I'm the last one to catch on. But then it finally sinks in and my hands find her waist, hauling her against me, and I kiss her again.

The cheers only get louder. "About bloody time!" Douglas shouts from somewhere in the crowd.

Blair's lips part from mine then brush my ear as she whispers, just for me, "I love you too."

Those four words slam through me harder than all the celebration exploding around us.

Finn barrels into us, his arms wrapping around both our waists in a fierce hug. Gus, apparently having pulled free from Struan, bounds over too, lead dangling behind him, and suddenly we're a tangle of arms and paws and laughter.

And then we're surrounded, people pressing close, patting our backs, calling out their congratulations.

Struan finds me and, grinning, says, "When I told you to tell Blair how you feel, I was thinking more of a private conversation after Ellie's speech. But what you did worked too!"

I clap Struan on the shoulder then my eyes are on Blair again. On the woman who just chose me, chose us, chose Ardmara.

Turns out tonight isn't an ending after all. It's the start of something new. Something bloody brilliant.

EPILOGUE
BLAIR

A year later

"And so the boy whispered, 'Don't worry, I'll come back tomorrow.' And the otter answered with a little chirp, as if he understood."

I close my copy of *The Otter and the Boy* to the sound of eager applause echoing through the storytelling tent. A sea of kids sit cross-legged before me, Finn front and centre, Isla, Logan, and Rosie squashed in beside him. All four beam up at me like I've just performed magic.

At the back of the tent, clapping along, are the children's parents. And among them are *my* parents, fresh off a flight from New York, their faces lit with pride.

And beside them? Lachlan. Standing tall, the warmth in his green eyes hitting harder than the applause, than anything else in this tent.

"Wasn't that wonderful?" Ellie, seated to my right, flashes her emcee smile as she addresses the crowd. "Let's give Blair another big hand for sharing *The Otter and the Boy* with us."

The clapping erupts again, even louder this time, and I blink hard, willing myself not to cry in front of a bunch of kids. A year ago I was hiding in the granny flat, scribbling story notes and wondering if I'd ever find my way back to the career I'd lost. Now here I am, a published author—self-published, sure, but published nonetheless—reading to a tentful of children.

"Does anyone have any questions for Blair?" Ellie asks, and immediately a forest of little hands shoots up.

Ellie points to a girl near the front. "Yes?"

"Do the boy and the otter get to live happily ever after, like in fairy tales?" Her high voice is adorably serious.

I can't help smiling, thinking of Finn last year, worried the otter might forget the boy after he was healed and had found a mate.

"Well," I say, "the best advice I can give is to read the story and find out the ending for yourself. But let's just say I've got a good feeling about that."

We go through some more questions but there's no chance to get to every raised hand before our time is up. People start filtering out of the tent, chatting and laughing, some first taking a moment to come over and congratulate me.

"Great reading, Blair," Douglas says warmly. "You had them hooked."

"It was really good!" Rosie agrees.

Logan nods. "But now . . . bouncy castle time! Bye, Blair!" The twins shoot off like rockets.

"Well, that's my cue to go," Douglas says. "Later!" He follows after them with a weary grin, but he's not alone—Ellie threads her hand through his, flashing me a quick smile. I wave her off, warmth bubbling in my chest. It's so good to see them together at last.

And they're not the only ones. Next Struan comes over with Isla, and with them is Ainsley, the hairdresser who moved to town last year, and her little girl, Lily. Lily's younger than Finn and the others, but she more than makes up for it with sheer determination.

"I liked your story, Blair!" Lily announces, her small hand tucked trustingly into Isla's, their bond already that of sisters.

"Thanks, Lily."

"But now I want my face painted." With her free hand, she gives her mom's sleeve a bossy little tug.

Ainsley laughs, rolling her eyes, while Struan throws me a grin. "You did great, Blair. But we'd better get this one to the face-painting stall before she stages a protest."

Together they head out, Isla patiently steering Lily while Struan slips an arm around Ainsley's waist.

Soon it's just me, Finn, Lachlan, and my mom and dad in the tent. Oh, and Gus, of course. After watching other people come over to hug me or pat me on the back, he decides he'd better give me a nuzzle too.

"Gus is every bit the charmer you said he was," Dad says, scratching behind the dog's ears like they're old pals. "Though I have to say, he's got some serious competition from this young man here." He ruffles Finn's hair affectionately.

"Not sure where that leaves me," Lachlan says drily.

I grin at him. "Jury's still out, it seems."

"Oh, not at all!" Mom slips her hand through Lachlan's arm. "We love this man, and it's so nice to finally see him in person after all those video calls. Honestly, Lachlan, I thought you looked handsome on screen, but in person . . ." She squeezes his biceps appreciatively. "Michael, you never had arms like these."

"Oh my God, Mom. Seriously?" I groan.

Lachlan just chuckles, clearly not minding the attention one bit.

"Did you like Blair's story?" Finn wants to know.

"We loved it," Mom says. "Your granny would be so proud of you, Blair. Telling your own stories, building a life in this beautiful place where she grew up. It's exactly what she would have wanted for you."

My throat tightens. "Thanks, Mom."

"But don't think settling here gets you out of coming home to visit us." Dad pulls Finn in against his side. "What do you think about Christmas in New York, buddy? Just like in *Home Alone 2*."

Finn's eyes go wide. "Really?"

"Maybe not *exactly* like *Home Alone 2*," I say. "Toy stores, Christmas trees, ice skating? Yes. Burglars and flying paint cans? Hard pass."

Mom laughs and, finally releasing Lachlan's arm, squeezes Finn's shoulder. "Well, you can tell us all about what you want to see in New York while we go find you a treat. You mentioned a biscuit earlier, didn't you?"

"An Empire biscuit!" Finn crows. "The best kind!"

"That's the one." Mom beams at him. "Come on, you and Gus can help us track some down." Then, to Lachlan: "Assuming it's okay with you that we take the boys for a few minutes?"

"Er, aye, of course. We'll catch up with you later."

And with that, Mom, Dad, and Finn head off, Gus trotting happily at their side. For the first time today, it's just me and Lachlan.

He steps in close and takes my hand, our fingers slotting together like it's the most natural thing in the world. "I'm so proud of you," he says. "You had them spellbound from the first word to the last. Christ, Blair. You're incredible."

I reach up and cup his cheek, my thumb brushing the soft prickle of his beard. He isn't the guarded man I met last summer. There's an ease in him now, a steadiness. The worry lines are still there but they're softer now, balanced by laugh lines that crinkle when he smiles.

"You know what's incredible? How happy you look these days. How happy we both are."

He tucks a strand of hair behind my ear, fingers lingering at my neck. "Hard to believe it's been a year since you decided to stay."

"Hard to believe I almost didn't. I only ever imagined being here for a few months. Now I can't imagine leaving."

"Good," he murmurs, leaning closer, his breath warm against my skin. "Because I'm not letting you go anywhere."

And when his lips claim mine—sure and tender—I know just how lucky I am to have found my anchor in this messy, beautiful life.

A NOTE FROM THE AUTHORS

Can't get enough of Lachlan and Blair? Subscribers to our free email newsletter can download a bonus epilogue in which they visit New York.

Up next in the *Scottish Single Dads* series: *Built for Love*, Struan and Ainsley's story.

Find out more at amymcgavin.com.

Bonus Epilogue

Next Book